THE MOTHERS

Rod Jones' first novel, *Julia Paradise*, won the fiction award at the 1988 Adelaide Festival, was shortlisted for the Miles Franklin Award and was runner-up for the Prix Femina Étranger. It has been translated into ten languages. His four other novels, *Prince of the Lilies*, *Billy Sunday*, *Nightpictures* and *Swan Bay*, have all either won or been shortlisted for major literary awards. Rod Jones lives near Melbourne.

Rod
Jones
The
Mothers

TEXT PUBLISHING
MELBOURNE AUSTRALIA

textpublishing.com.au

The Text Publishing Company
Swann House
22 William Street
Melbourne Victoria 3000
Australia

First published by The Text Publishing Company 2015

Cover and page design by Text
Typeset by J & M Typesetting

Printed in Australia by Griffin Press, an Accredited ISO AS/NZS 14001:2004 Environmental Management System printer

National Library of Australia Cataloguing-in-Publication entry

Creator: Jones, Rod, 1953- author.
Title: The mothers / by Rod Jones.
ISBN: 9781922147226 (paperback)
            9781921961649 (ebook)
Subjects: Mothers—Fiction.
            Motherhood—Fiction.
            Family secrets—Fiction.
Dewey Number: A823.3

This book is printed on paper certified against the Forest Stewardship Council® Standards. Griffin Press holds FSC chain-of-custody certification SGS-COC-005088. FSC promotes environmentally responsible, socially beneficial and economically viable management of the world's forests.

This project has been assisted by the Commonwealth Government through the Australia Council, its arts funding and advisory body.

Contents

To Maria

What makes you read the contours of your body
like lines on the palm of a hand
so that I cannot see them otherwise than Fate?
RAINER MARIA RILKE

Part One

Alma

FOOTSCRAY, 1917

AT FIRST SHE thought it was a boy watching her. He stood, hands in pockets, hat pushed back on his head, bicycle propped against a tree. Had he stopped out of curiosity, or was he calculating some advantage to be gained? He was not tall— hence her impression that he was a boy—but he looked strong, with shirtsleeves rolled up over meaty arms, coatless on this winter afternoon. Although it was Saturday, there was no one else around. She was not afraid of him, but nor was she able to forget he was there.

Alma had been sitting on the bench with her valise, in the new Footscray Park, for the greater part of the afternoon, watching her children run around the garden beds and play hide-and-seek among the trees. How long exactly? She couldn't tell. Her husband, Frederick Fairweather, owned a timepiece;

Alma did not. Already the trees cast long shadows across the lawns. Still the man watched.

Her children, Edward, seven years old, and Olive, six, were hungry: with all the uproar at home, they had missed their midday meal. They were too young to comprehend the significance of what had taken place but they must have realised that this Saturday in May was different from any other day they had known.

Alma had gone to her mother's house for help. The wind was cold and the streets empty. She carried the valise, Teddy and Olive beside her, her plush hat pulled down over her blonde hair, her mouth grim. She was wearing a blue woollen coat, thick stockings, boots. Teddy and Olive both had their father's black hair and dark eyes. Her mother wouldn't even let them in the door. 'You've made your bed,' she told Alma, 'now go and lie in it.'

When Alma had married in 1909, a month after her sixteenth birthday, she was already pregnant. Frederick Fairweather was a great admirer of the playboy Edward VII, and she thought Frederick had even modelled himself on the former Prince of Wales, with his girth and his beard, his cigars and his whores. The King had produced bastard children, but Alma was determined that their child would be born in wedlock. Her son was born the following year and Frederick had insisted on naming him after the King. A few months later, on the 6th of May 1910, the King had died of heart disease.

Her husband had been engaged in several occupations, none of which had lasted very long. He worked for Stan Hollibone, the undertaker, and Alma thought Frederick cut a dashing figure in his tail coat and striped trousers. But he had quarrelled with Hollibone over money. Then Frederick had an interest in one of the tourist launches operating on the Maribyrnong River; then he had been the manager of a dance orchestra, then a proxy for a publican who was wanted by police and had to make himself scarce for a while. Alma's marriage had not been happy. Now this had happened. Her husband had turfed her out.

Eventually the man in the park wheeled his bicycle over. 'Why are you crying?' he asked Alma. She noticed he was wearing a black armband. He had a mouth like a beak; his grey-blue eyes never left her.

'Who are you?' she asked. Alma was unsure whether she should speak to him at all.

'I'm Alfred,' he said.

She told him why she was crying.

'My mother will know what to do,' he told her.

Alfred hoisted the little girl onto his shoulders, insisted on carrying the valise as well as wheeling his bicycle, and the four of them set off like that down Ballarat Road. Before long Alma relieved him of the valise: she was afraid little Olive was going to fall. Alfred could wheel the bicycle with one hand and secure Olive's legs with the other.

They passed a horse and dray outside a house, loaded with somebody's possessions. A man emerged from the front door carrying two wooden chairs and added them to the pile. People in Footscray were always moving in or moving out. Evictions were frequent. A stack of someone's furniture in the street was a common sight, but this one finally focused Alma's mind. Before nightfall, she would have to find somewhere for herself and the children to stay.

It was nearly dark when they arrived at the house in Empire

Street. Alma knew this part of Footscray: her father had worked in the nearby quarry.

'Now, Alfred,' Mrs Lovett said when she looked up from her kitchen table and saw them at the back door. 'What is it you've gone and done this time? Who are these people?'

'I decided to nick off early from the drill hall. I rode down to Footscray Park and that's where I found them. They have nowhere to go.'

Alfred herded Alma and the children into the kitchen and introduced them to his mother. Mrs Lovett was a big woman with pink puffy hands. She smiled at Alma. 'Bring the children over here beside the stove. They must be freezing.'

Alma looked around. There was a high loaf on the bread-board, a tin of plum jam, a brown china teapot. On the stove, some potatoes were bubbling in an enamel pot. And there was a photograph on the mantelpiece, a soldier in uniform, a badge on the collar, wearing his cap. He looked so young.

Teddy was eyeing the tin of jam. 'Sit down and have a bite with us,' Mrs Lovett told them.

Teddy and Olive devoured the thick slices of bread and jam, then waited to be offered more.

Mrs Lovett held her teacup with her little finger extended and Alma had to frown at the children to stop them laughing. Alma could hardly talk, she felt so nervous.

'Did something happen at the drill hall?' Mrs Lovett asked her son. 'Did you rattle the sergeant's nerves again?'

'Jesus Christ! I have to work on Saturday mornings and I don't see why I should have to give up my afternoon to march up and down inside that cold hall with those damned Citizen Forces, following orders in case the bloody empire needs me.'

'Now, Alfred,' his mother chided him. 'No need for that kind of language.'

Alma decided to speak up. She turned to Mrs Lovett and said, 'You are very kind to have us in.'

'It's what our Pastor Goble preaches: charity begins at home.'

'I've heard of him—Goble of Footscray.'

Neither Alma's father nor her mother had been church-going people, and she was largely indifferent to religion.

'Mr Goble was a great comfort after the loss of my son,' Mrs Lovett said.

Alfred explained that his little brother, Archie, had enlisted in E Company of the 7th Battalion, the 'Footscray Company' it was called, its colours tan and red, the 'Mud and Bloods'. 'Archie finished his training at Broadmeadows and was due to leave for France last year, but he was struck by a car as he stepped off the running board of a tram in Mount Alexander Road. Killed instantly,' said Alfred bitterly.

'Only eighteen years old,' added Mrs Lovett.

As Alma discovered during tea that evening, Mrs Lovett was worried because Alfred had begun hanging around with one of the Footscray pushes—the Dingoes, they called themselves. He had already been in several fights with soldiers.

'Well, I can tell you right here and now that I have no intention of joining up! Not E Company. Not the 7th Battalion. Not any of their other bloody companies or battalions,' said Alfred. 'Give me the company of the Dingoes, any day.'

The Lovetts had moved from Tasmania three years earlier. The Huon Valley was all Alfred had ever known, but his mum didn't want her boys working in the Mountain River sawmill that had claimed her husband. At present, Alfred worked for Mr Ward, a maker of harnesses and horse collars in Footscray, though he had also worked at an iron foundry in Seddon.

After their meal, Alfred took a cigar from his pocket and put it in his beak of a mouth. The match flared and the tip of the cigar began to glow and the kitchen filled with the rich, sickly smoke. Alma discovered that night that she and Alfred were nearly the same age: she would be turning twenty-four in July, while his birthday was later, in November.

The children were finding it hard to stay awake. Olive kept nodding off and waking every few minutes, and Teddy was rubbing his eyes.

'How long have you been married to this husband of yours?' Mrs Lovett asked.

'Seven years,' Alma said.

'And he just kicks you out? No, my girl, there's got to be a reason for a man to behave like that.'

'He didn't come home last night. Then he just turned up at eleven o'clock this morning, drunk, with a woman.'

'With a woman? You mean a woman from the street?'

Alma hesitated at this. She really didn't know. All she knew was the way the woman smiled with embarrassment, her lips covering her teeth, and that she had worn a green hat, and Frederick had introduced her as Mrs Leicester. This is Mrs Leicester. She lost her husband in France, he'd said. Alma felt that Mrs Lovett didn't really believe her.

There was a sleep-out in the corner of the back verandah, with timber walls and louvre windows, where Mrs Lovett said they could stay for a few days, until things at home were put to rights. 'A man has a duty to support his wife and children,' she pointed out. She said she would mention their situation to Pastor Goble in the morning after church.

Alma put the children down on stretcher beds. She covered Teddy with a rough grey blanket. He lay on his back, eyes staring up at her for a moment, before he closed them and kept them closed. His breathing was regular but Alma could not tell if he was asleep.

Alma hugged Olive, making soothing sounds, no words, just the cooing that reassured the child when she was upset. A series of long sobs shuddered through the girl's body, then she grew heavy in Alma's arms and in another minute she was asleep. Alma lowered her onto the stretcher, pulled the blanket over her, and she was surprised to notice several individual drops fall on the sleeping girl's face. It was as if someone else were crying. Alma rose impassively and moved away, wiping her tears with her sleeve.

The single bulb was dim but she could make out her own face in the hexagonal mirror set into the door of the cedar wardrobe. Her hair had escaped from its pins and wisps clung to her broad forehead. Her tired blue eyes stared back at her. 'What's wrong with me?' she thought. 'I can't even keep my husband.'

When she opened the wardrobe door, there were some trousers and shirts hanging inside: she guessed that Mrs Lovett hadn't been able to bring herself to give them away. The sleep-out must have been Archie's room.

In spite of her exhaustion, Alma could not get to sleep. The day would not die. She kept thinking of the things Frederick had said to her, and how her own mother had turned her away. She dreaded the days to come. One of the children would

9

break something. Or she would inadvertently cause offence. The soft heart of Mrs Lovett would grow hard and she and the children would be back on the street.

She rolled onto her side and heard the canvas of the stretcher creak in the dark. She missed her own bed. The woman in the green hat was probably warm in that big, comfortable bed, which had been Alma's wedding bed, where she had given birth to her two babies and slept every night for seven years. Now she had no bed to call her own.

A door opened, then quietly closed. A cautious footstep on the bare boards beside the sleep-out. Someone was standing there, listening in the dark. Then she heard the crunching of boots on the cinder path down to the outhouse by the back fence. She knew, without knowing, that it was Alfred.

Alma's father had been a powder monkey in Mr Eldridge's quarry. He drilled a hole in the cliff face, planted the charge and rolled out the fuse wire. Some of the men were missing fingers but Papa kept all his. When Papa came home, he used to sit in a wide green armchair in the parlour, with a smoker's stand, and Alma on his knee. She liked to bury her face in his vest and shirt where she could smell the curiously comforting traces of gunpowder.

Her father had died not from gunpowder or dynamite, but simply from walking up the cart track to get his midday dinner—the horses reared and broke their harness and the powder wagon had run him over. Even so, whenever she heard a charge go off at the quarry, her heart skipped a beat.

This part of Footscray was known as 'The Settlement'. At

one end of Empire Street was the Colonial Ammunition factory, at the other Kinnears Ropes. Behind Eldridge Street there was a lane—grassy and muddy in winter, covered in daisies in springtime—which ran along the edge of the cliff. Sometimes mobs of sheep were driven down the lane on their way to Angliss's Meatworks. From the lane there was the sudden drop down to the quarry.

Since March the quarrymen had been on strike for an increase to the minimum wage. Now Mr Eldridge had paid them off, and there were four hundred and fifty men out of work.

The next morning after breakfast, Alma and the children accompanied Mrs Lovett to the Baptist church. Alfred refused to go. He said he had some jobs to do, but, as Mrs Lovett told her on the way, Alfred hadn't been inside a church since the day of Archie's funeral.

It was a long walk to Paisley Street. All Alma's feelings of panic from the previous afternoon returned. 'What am I going to say to a minister?' she thought, as she walked along Gordon Street with Mrs Lovett. 'How do I know that he will believe me?' Her head spun as the future unfolded in her mind.

She called, 'Teddy! Olive! You go on ahead!' Then to Teddy alone: 'You hold your sister's hand, mind!' When they were out of earshot she told Mrs Lovett what was tormenting her. 'The minister will tell me to go back to my husband,' Alma said. 'He will tell me to get down on my knees and to beg him to take me back!'

'I can't believe what I'm hearing. Mr Goble would never say

a thing like that. Never! Everyone is equal in his eyes. I'm sure he will do everything that might be done to bring comfort to an abandoned wife and her children.'

'What's so awful is that Frederick was able to change everything so suddenly, as if on a whim! He just tore everything down and threw it away in a moment, everything that up until yesterday had been sacred—our family, our home. How can I ever love him after what happened yesterday? Now I feel nothing but hatred for him.'

'Oh, hatred,' said Mrs Lovett disapprovingly. She looked ahead to make sure the children could not hear this kind of talk.

'We scarcely know each other, since we met only yesterday through your kindness, for which I shall remain eternally grateful. But let me tell you a little thing about me, which might be right or might be wrong—I cannot be other than I am. Once I turn against someone, if someone does me a wrong, then it is impossible for me to have anything to do with them again. Yes, it is true, I am a great hater.'

'My dear child, it is a sin to hate.'

'Actually I have been thinking ill of him for some time, ever since he made the acquaintance of—that woman.'

'Wait a minute. I thought he had just met her. Now you tell me he has known her for some time.'

'Yes, yes, I think he knows her. They seemed like chums.'

'Like chums?' Mrs Lovett repeated. She looked at Alma with a new scepticism, as though she would have to reconsider everything she had been told. 'Of course, I realise how awful your situation is, I really do, but if you knew for some time that the two of them had a relation…'

'Oh!' Alma said. 'But that is just it. I do not know. Perhaps

Frederick has been cosy with her for some time, but I really do not know.'

'Can the love between husband and wife die in a single day?'

'You think I am suffering from pride by not going back to him on bended knee.'

'What you are saying sounds very much like pride.'

'When he brought her to the house yesterday, that's when I said, enough.'

'So he did not actually kick you out of the house?'

'Well, he told me I could like it or lump it, so it amounts to the same thing. I will not be his doormat!' Alma said.

'Can't you find it in your heart to forgive him?'

'Don't you see? Once faith is torn, the cloth remains torn forever.' Then Alma relented. 'I'm very confused. My feelings are pulling me in opposite directions. I can't judge which is the right way.'

'Let us wait and see what Mr Goble has to say.'

Teddy and Olive had stopped on the corner to wait for them. Together they turned into Barkly Street and walked the rest of the way to Paisley Street in silence.

As they entered the imposing brick church, Mrs Lovett whispered, 'Let's sit up the front. The pews fill quickly.'

The four of them sat in the sixth row. 'It's a good thing we came early,' added Mrs Lovett, looking around as the congregation filed into the church. 'Mr Goble has been the minister here for twenty years. Sometimes hundreds of people come to listen to him preach.'

From time to time she checked on her children. Teddy and Olive were on their best behaviour, looking around at all the unfamiliar faces, the bare-headed men with their reddened, newly washed necks and their starched collars. The air was loud with conversation as people chattered with their neighbours.

A lonely-sounding bell began to ring in the steeple. It went on for several minutes, then subsided just as suddenly with a few careless clangs, and an expectant hush descended over the congregation.

Mr Goble was a man of about fifty. From where they were sitting, Alma had to crane her neck to see him. He stood six feet four inches: so tall that, according to Mrs Lovett, he needed a specially reinforced bicycle. His wife had died from typhoid fever in the 1890s and Mr Goble had never remarried, though he had been known to dance a lively mazurka at social functions.

A shock of greying wavy hair swept back from his high forehead. Although shadowed with exhaustion, his eyes were lit with hope. A tired, compassionate smile persisted under his moustache. He was wearing an old suit and Alma noticed, along with the sagging shoulders and curling lapels, that one of the buttons on his waistcoat was missing. But he had attached a clean white collar to his shirt, and he gave, above all, an impression of great dignity.

Mr Goble called on his congregation to understand Christ's 'personal socialism'. He talked about his time as a worker and a trade unionist before he became a pastor. When he was fifteen years old, staying at the Bethel of the Victorian Seamen's Union in Port Melbourne, he had felt the Lord's Grace descend upon him. He preached solidarity between workers, the brotherhood of man, the example of the Good Samaritan. Before the war, Mrs Lovett whispered, Goble had preached against the arms industry and compulsory military training. He was known to eat little, accept the minimum stipend for his work, and spend his days out on his bicycle, helping the poor.

A crowd milled around him on the steps after the service. At his residence next door, there were others who also wanted to speak to Pastor Goble.

Alma waited with the other supplicants in the parlour. There were a few hard chairs, but they were already taken, so she and Mrs Lovett and the children stood together against the wall. The door of Mr Goble's study opened and closed. Mr Goble lumbered in and out of the room, seeing this one, asking a question of another, fetching documents from his portmanteau. He was so tall that he had to stoop under the lintel of the doorway.

Despite Mrs Lovett's moral support, Alma felt alone in that crowded room. This was the class of humanity to which she now belonged. Waiting with the charity cases, Alma felt she had made a mess of her life.

Finally it was her turn. Mrs Lovett said she would come in with her.

'Now you two wait out here,' Alma told the children. 'We'll only be a minute.'

Mr Goble sat on the other side of the desk in his threadbare black suit. His eyes blazed as if with the light of another, better world. After the introductions, Mrs Lovett went back to wait with the children.

'I have helped many women who have got themselves into trouble,' Mr Goble told Alma. She knew he must have mistaken her for one of the women she had seen plying their trade outside the Plough Hotel.

'I did not get *myself* into trouble,' Alma told him. 'It was my husband who caused the trouble.'

'I do not judge you,' he said calmly. 'Whatever misfortune has befallen you, I shall try to be of assistance. If you need money, for example, I can help you.'

He was still smiling at her, full of good will. Yet Alma felt that he *was* judging her, waiting for her to share some shameful secret.

'Do I give the impression that I am of bad character?' Alma had a needle of temper, which she usually tried to keep in check, but she was sensitive to any slight to her honour, and especially any aspersion on her fitness as a mother. 'Anyway, why should I be judged? Just because the bugger kicked us out onto the street?' Straightaway, she regretted her outburst. 'I'm sorry. I think it's just that the events of the last few days have begun to catch up with me.'

'It's quite all right.'

'I didn't mean to use such language.'

'I have heard worse. I used to work on the wharves. You've never heard swearing until you've heard a wharfie.'

But at the moment he was telling her it was quite all right, another voice inside Alma was telling her it was not true. It *was* really all her own fault. Where had these doubts come from?

'Mrs Lovett seems like a kind of angel, allowing me and the children into her home in my hour of need.' Alma drew in a deep breath to keep her feelings under control. 'If it had not been for Mrs Lovett, God knows what would have become of us!'

Mr Goble continued to look at her with his pale, intelligent eyes. 'I have seen many times how some small act of kindness can transform a life,' he said. 'We cannot predict the consequences of caring for another, how it might save that person from despair, or how it might help her achieve a completely new understanding of her life.'

His voice was quiet, almost a whisper, yet she felt it soak deep inside her, warming her heart. Now, being in his presence was like bathing in sunshine.

'The act of kindness might be something apparently insignificant, something tiny,' Mr Goble went on. 'But that selfless impulse to help another is the most powerful magic. I think Mrs Lovett understands that. It is God's love working through us, transforming men's and women's lives. Bringing about change so that the poor can live full, happy lives—that is the true work of Christ, and those of us who call ourselves His followers.'

'I don't know why I'm crying,' laughed Alma, brushing away her tears. 'I'm not usually one to turn on the waterworks. Your words have affected me, that's all.'

In the end, Mr Goble suggested that Alma write to her husband requesting he send money to support the children. He could send it care of Mrs Lovett, or, if they preferred, she could ask her husband to send money directly to Mr Goble, and he would pass it on. Everyone in Footscray knew where to find him.

'Very well. I shall write to him. But I won't hold my breath waiting for a reply.'

Alma felt that Mr Goble didn't really understand how precarious was her position; no one but she knew just how loathsome it had become to continue living with her husband. People would judge her simply on the fact that it was she who had packed her case and taken the children and left the family

17

home; no one would be interested in the list of complaints against her husband that she could recite chapter and verse.

'How do you find our preacher?' Mrs Lovett asked, on the way home.

'It isn't really what he says,' said Alma. 'It's the way he says it.'

'Yes, that's very true.' Mrs Lovett gave her an appreciative look.

'I felt something quite strange while I was in his presence. I don't really understand it.'

'Mr Goble's charismatic gift does have an unusual effect on people,' said Mrs Lovett. 'I wouldn't be surprised if he has taken a shine to you. And,' she added slyly, 'he has been a widower for many years.'

Alma quickened her pace to catch up with the children.

'Well, he's a remarkable man, our Mr Goble,' said Mrs Lovett from behind her. And, to her surprise, Alma felt herself blushing.

'My dear, how glad I am that Alfred brought you home to us yesterday. I am pleased that you and the children will stay in our house for a while. You must pray and continue to believe that things will soon get better for you. Yes. I can feel it in my bones. Soon things will be ever so much better!'

OFF THE KITCHEN was the washhouse with the copper. On Monday mornings, before he left for work, Alfred lit the fire under the copper and soon the house filled with the smell of soap and ash. There were Teddy's and Olive's clothes to wash, as well as the sheets and towels Mrs Lovett had let her use. Alma stirred the washing in the copper with the wooden stick.

Mrs Thomas from next door didn't have a copper, and Mrs Lovett let her use theirs when they had finished their wash. When Mrs Thomas arrived as usual that Monday morning, with her washing basket of woven cane, Mrs Lovett introduced Alma as her niece, visiting from the country with her children. It was clear Mrs Thomas didn't believe a word of it.

'How'd you get down to town? On the train, I suppose,' asked Mrs Thomas.

'Yes, that's right.' Alma turned back to her work.

'On the train with the little ones, eh? Was it a long ride?'

'Long enough.'

'Where did you leave from?'

'A little place, you wouldn't have heard of it.'

'I might have,' Mrs Thomas said.

'Up near Bendigo.'

'Ah, up Bendigo way,' Mrs Thomas said, sounding disappointed. 'Your husband has a farm up there, does he?'

Mrs Thomas's eyes narrowed, the ghost of a smile appeared on her lips, and Alma saw that the woman was one of those naturally suspicious beings who, simply through believing nothing, make themselves seem shrewd.

'That's right.'

'What kind of farm?'

'Wheat,' Alma said with a sudden decisiveness. 'And sheep. We run a mob of sheep, too.'

Mrs Lovett had begun the lie, so Alma felt she had no choice but to stick with it. Still, she didn't like pretending to be someone she wasn't. Listen here, you old sow, she felt like saying to Mrs Thomas, it was my husband who kicked *me* out, not the other way round, so why should I be made to feel ashamed of anything? But even as these words replayed through her mind, the dreadful feeling of doubt returned, eating away at her version of events, and her tale of being kicked out by her husband had begun to sound, even to her own ears, as hollow and concocted as her story of the farm.

When she had finished, Mrs Thomas carried her basket of wet washing home to peg on the line out the back of her house. Each of the houses in Empire Street sat on its quarter acre

20

block, gardens at the front, big backyards, and paling or corrugated iron fences. Most of the houses had a vegetable plot and some people, like the Lovetts, kept a few chickens.

Mrs Lovett had told Alma she supplemented Alfred's wages by giving piano lessons on Saturdays. The children would arrive with their shillings tied in a knot in the corner of their handkerchiefs, she said. Now, while their own wash was flapping in the sunshine in the backyard, Mrs Lovett was practising in the parlour, thumping out a hymn. She sang along loudly.

When other helpers fail and comforts flee
Help of the helpless, O abide with me.

When she was finished, she remained seated, her face flushed with the joy of it.

'I would give anything to learn to play the piano as well as you,' Alma said.

'Do you mean to say that you cannot play at all?'

'My mother didn't have the money to spare.'

'Well,' said Mrs Lovett, 'it is never too late to learn.'

Alma sat on the seat beside Mrs Lovett, staring at the ivory keys grooved like fingernails, separated by the thinner, rounded black keys. Each note seemed to contain a feeling of its own, which lived on a moment in the air, before it died. The blinds were drawn nearly all the way down. The room smelled sour and airless. In the evenings the family usually sat in the kitchen, where it was warm from the stove.

Mrs Lovett showed Alma how to practise simple scales, told her what a crotchet was, and a quaver, and explained to her the key of C. 'Don't worry. If you practise every day, you'll soon improve,' Mrs Lovett encouraged her. 'Practice makes perfect.'

At the front of the house there was a verandah, and a neat

front garden where Teddy and Olive played on the grass. Boot came to play with them, too. He lived down the street, a red-headed boy who wore a brown boot with a steel stirrup. He had been struck down with polio. His mother, Peggy, sometimes called in for a cup of tea.

At the bottom of the backyard was the henhouse, where the children collected eggs. The lavatory against the fence smelled of wood and newspaper. Mr Lyon down the street kept pigeons. Each afternoon he released them from the coop. Alma could hear their wings flapping, freed of the day, wheeling overhead; she watched them ascend, a scatter of torn paper, then regroup, and soar off together in another direction. Now, that was freedom.

Alma spent her days in the kitchen, looking after the children and doing whatever chores she could find. She clung to the safety of Mrs Lovett's home, lest the world unleash some further humiliation on her. Teddy and Olive should have gone back to school, but she let them stay home, day after day. She didn't want their classmates or anyone else she knew to find out what had happened. But Alma lived in fear of Mr Mabbitt, the truancy officer. Lists of local parents who had been fined for their children missing school were published in the *Advertiser*. The fine for truancy was two shillings— some families had been fined eight shillings for repeated offences. If the worst happened, where would Alma find the money to pay?

Finally, it was Mrs Lovett who raised the matter. 'Your children should be at school, Alma. We don't want Mr Mabbitt knocking on our door.'

After two weeks living at Empire Street, Alma took Teddy

and Olive back to the state school in Geelong Road, explaining to the headmaster that there had been illness in the house.

Alma walked her children to school along Gordon Street. Sometimes before picking them up in the afternoons she walked up Droop Street into Footscray to buy tea and flour and meat and, as a treat, if there was something left over from the money Mrs Lovett gave her, half a pound of broken biscuits.

The streets were full of returned soldiers, some of them crippled and useless, others unemployed, embittered, looking for trouble. Groups of them, still in uniform, blocked the footpath. Alma had to push past them, carrying her string bag of shopping. She heard the rattle of rotten lungs of those who had been gassed. There were those who were blind, or deaf, those with faces liked minced beef. She saw more than one with the arm of his shirt pinned where the arm ought to be; some were on crutches, or with bandages wound around their heads. These men weren't able to find work, especially with all the strikes this year. Some of them were drunk, what people had come to call 'the soldier problem'. The war had made the men like that. They blocked her way, or said things about her as she passed. 'Now there's a nice piece, isn't it, Reg?'

'I'll say! Come over here, love, I've got something for you.'

'I've got something bigger!' the first man said.

'Oh, have a heart! Don't you know how to treat a lady?'

They turned and stared at her rudely as she passed.

She stopped to read the faded and torn posters glued to walls and lampposts. Some dated back to Empire Day in May, advertising talks against the war by Adela Pankhurst and Vida

Goldstein. On other posters there were lists of the fallen. She read that of the two hundred and fifty men of E Company who had landed at Gallipoli, two hundred and twenty had been wounded or were dead. It was not just Gallipoli and the Anzacs. The Western Front. The Middle East. Most of Footscray had voted against conscription in Mr Hughes's referendum last year.

Walking the children home from school, Alma heard the first factory whistle of the afternoon, and already she felt nerves knotting in her belly. Soon Alfred would be locking up the harness shop and getting on his bicycle to come home. Her nerves had nothing to do with Alfred—why should they? It was, she told herself, just part of the excitement of being in a stranger's home, finding out where everything was kept, learning the rhythms of another household.

At home, the children waited at the front gate to greet him. Alfred rang the bell on his bicycle as he swept around the corner, taking one hand off the handlebars to lift his hat to them. He had taught Teddy how to shake hands with him like a grown-up. Alma went to greet him too, though she was more reserved. Still, Alfred's return from work in the afternoons had become a compass point in her day.

Alfred played with the children in the backyard while Alma went to the kitchen. She peeled the potatoes and put them in a pot of salted water to boil. There was no meat until payday. As she reached for a sheet of newspaper to wrap the potato peelings, her eye happened to catch an article reporting a speech by the Prime Minister, Billy Hughes. The paper was a couple of weeks old.

This is Empire Day, and we, in whose veins leaps the blood of our race, are glad and rejoice in being privileged to call ourselves British citizens under the banner of the Empire.

Alma finished reading. 'What a lot of nonsense,' she thought, then wrapped the potato peel in a neat parcel and dropped it in the rubbish tin.

They ate at six o'clock. The children enjoyed mealtimes with Alfred. He told them stories, made jokes and pulled frightening faces. Their mouths stretched into smiles and the trouble left their eyes when they were with Alfred.

He told them the story of the sleeping princess. Mrs Lovett was out the back at the time, and the three of them had Alfred all to themselves.

'Was she a real princess?' Teddy asked.

'Oh yes, a real princess. Now there are ugly princesses, of course, but this was a pretty sort of princess—in fact, she was almost as pretty as your mother.'

Alma got up from the table, went to the sink and began to wash the dishes. With her back turned, she listened.

'Now this princess lived in France, which is probably a place you've never heard of, but it is far across the ocean, so far away that they even speak another language. Soldiers from all over the world have gone there to fight Kaiser Bill.'

'Have you ever been to France, Alfred?' Teddy asked.

'Of course I have, my boy,' Alfred told him. 'I sailed the seven seas when I was with the pirates.'

'You were a pirate?' Teddy asked.

Alma bit her tongue: she felt that it wasn't quite fair of him to tease the boy like that. Later, Alfred sat showing them his collection of cigarette cards, which he had pasted into scrapbooks. He had the complete set of cricketers from Murray's tobacco, but he also had stage stars and circus performers, as well as a set from Ogden's cigarettes called 'How to Hold Pets'. Alfred said that some cards had been sent to him by relatives, others he had collected from his own tins of cigarettes.

Alma wondered—but did not ask—whether Alfred had a sweetheart. He sometimes mentioned this or that shopgirl in conversation about his working day, but casually, without self-consciousness, so Alma thought he was probably not interested in those girls.

Having married young, Alma never had a job, but now she realised she would have to look for work. All the locals knew that since the war began there were more than two thousand people working at the Colonial Ammunition Company at the end of Empire Street. If the war went on much longer, they would need even more workers. She could see the high brick wall of the factory from Mrs Lovett's front gate. Many of the workers were girls or widowed or deserted wives. Alma had seen and heard them filing out the turnstile at the factory gates at knock-off time, excited by the moment of freedom, walking in groups of two or three, arms joined, chattering at the tops of their voices.

After work, men from the factory went to drink at the pub on the corner of Ballarat Road and Gordon Street. She could hear the roar of voices in there as she walked past. Groups of men stood in the open windows with pots of beer and called out to her. At least there was six o'clock closing now, brought in last year, after a campaign by the temperance movement. But after the pubs closed, the footpaths were still crowded with drunken men.

Alfred was not like those men. He came home straight after work and, anyway, his mother was a member of the Women's

Christian Temperance Union. True, on Saturday nights he did go into Footscray with his mates, and he told Alma that they bought beer from a sly-grog shop, after the pubs had closed. Alma read an article in the newspaper about the Dingoes getting into fights with other larrikins outside the Trocadero Theatre. She hoped Alfred was not involved in that.

There was something about the set of Alfred's mouth that Alma liked, the furrow of determination in his upper lip. When he was splitting logs, his sleeves rolled above his elbows, he studied the place where the axe would hit. Mrs Lovett noticed her watching him split the wood. 'There are not too many boys who have Alfred's willpower,' Mrs Lovett said. 'Alfred's a good egg.'

When she had arrived at Empire Street that Saturday, Alma had only two pennies in her purse. Now Alfred had begun calling her 'Tuppence'. Perhaps he meant no harm, but she felt there was something aggressive about the nickname. It made her even more acutely aware that she was a burden.

As well as the children's expenses, their clothes and food, there was the shame of living on Mrs Lovett's charity, especially since she knew that Mrs Lovett was hardly in a financial position to support them. She had not received a reply to the letter she wrote to her husband with Mrs Lovett's help, requesting that he send money to support his children. She didn't know what else she could do. Alma imagined him opening the post after his morning glass of brandy, reading the letter with a contemptuous smile and setting it on fire with the tip of his cigar. One day, when anger at her situation made her suddenly decisive, she put on her coat and walked to her old home to have it out with him.

It felt strange, walking up the path to the house like that. She knocked loudly, determined to fight for her rights. The fact that she had dithered for so long made it all the more urgent that she bring her husband to justice now.

The door was opened by a stranger. He was an Irishman, to judge by his accent. 'Fairweather, you say? Never heard of him.' The man seemed puzzled. 'You're his *wife*?' He seemed not to understand what she was asking. No, he told her conclusively. He knew nothing about Frederick Fairweather—or Mrs Leicester either, for that matter.

On Saturday afternoons, as he now refused to attend the drill hall, Alfred organised a game of tip-and-run on the road in front of the house. All the boys in the street came to play. Teddy joined in the games, happy for the company, while Olive sat with her mother. Alfred would drive the leather ball hard with the homemade bat. The lad retrieved the ball from wherever Alfred hit it—over the neighbours' fences, even as far as the next street. After playing each stroke, Alfred held his heroic pose for a few moments with the bat above his head, his body angled. Alfred taught Teddy how to bowl, let the little fellow take his turn with the bat and praised him with a 'Well played, sir!' or 'Nicely struck!' Teddy broke into a smile that lit up his whole face.

Alma sat on the verandah with her little girl, watching the game and listening to the piano inside. Winter sunshine sucked the sour smell of damp timber from the house and, for a few minutes, Alma felt almost peaceful.

On Sunday mornings the children now went to Sunday

school and Alma sat next to Mrs Lovett in church. This terrible war in Europe, Pastor Goble told his congregation, was only for the benefit of profiteers. He preached of the need for solidarity among workers against the war-mongering capitalist class.

Alma liked listening to Mr Goble. But the way some of the women at church looked at her made Alma feel that she was being judged. Even people she did not know must have heard something about her, the way they gawked. A part of Alma was still back in the park with the valise, ashamed, nowhere to go. The following Sunday, she let Mrs Lovett take the children by herself.

Those first weeks when she was learning to play the piano, it was as if there were some intelligence hidden in the music that knew more about Alma than she did. As she held her hands poised above the keys, she was filled with anticipation, as though something extraordinary were about to happen.

Alma's mother had kept her home from the age of twelve like a servant, a domestic drudge. Alma had not been allowed to play with other children because there were always more chores. If Alma complained, her mother slapped her, and even kicked her. Other girls in her street had stayed on at school and taken music classes and learned to sing. Alma used to stop what she was doing at the trough and, hands still in the soapy water, she would listen to the sound of a piano or a girl's lovely voice drifting to her on the evening air. When Mrs Lovett offered to teach her to play, it was the memory of her unhappy child-hood that drove Alma to grasp the opportunity. She spent every free moment during the day practising in the gloomy parlour.

Before long she could play 'Abide with Me' well enough—or so she thought. One afternoon, however, when she went outside for a breath of air after she had been playing the piano and singing the hymn, she spied Mrs Thomas's ruddy face peering at her over the side fence. 'Was someone skinning a cat in there?' Mrs Thomas asked.

'I've only been at it for a few weeks. Does it really distress you so very much?'

'Well, that kind of noise can grate. I admit I do have sensitive nerves.'

But, Alma reasoned, Mrs Thomas must have had to listen to far worse, with all those students coming here for lessons. Why does she pick on my playing in particular?

Alma said, 'I am sorry that my *noise* disturbs you. I hope that soon you might be telling me how nice my playing sounds.'

'Don't they have pianos up where you come from? Up at—where was it—near *Bendigo*?' Mrs Thomas looked at Alma mischievously.

Alma went straight back inside and sat at the piano. Her fingers struck the keys with confidence; idea became sound. And when the piano was finally silent, the music—a feeling she could not put a name to—lived on inside her. *There*, she said silently to Mrs Thomas. *Put that in your pipe and smoke it!*

Life felt safe with the Lovett family, but it was as if Alma's old life had been stolen. She knew it was unreasonable to feel this way. The Lovett family had stolen nothing and given her everything.

In the evenings, after she had put the children to bed, Alma sat up by the wood stove in the kitchen while Alfred flicked through his albums of cards. His collection had once occupied all his free time, but he seemed bored now. Mrs Lovett sat with her knitting, but soon enough found herself nodding off, and went to bed.

With his mother out of the way, Alfred came to life. He told Alma stories from the harness shop. Everything about Alfred was quick and excited as he spoke. He was a good mimic, imitating his customers' mannerisms and their voices. Alma felt that she could see right into his character. Alfred needed to make himself look important to people. The hours he spent working in the great world, his expertise with horses, his popularity among his customers—without these, he might have felt that he was nothing.

One afternoon when the baker's cart had stopped in front of the house and housewives were coming out to buy their bread, Alma watched Alfred go instinctively over to the old draught horse and stroke his nose and talk to him.

Charlie Cotton at the end of Empire Street owned a new Chevrolet motorcar that Alfred said cost £250. Alma noticed more and more cars in the streets of Footscray. She told Alfred that she thought the age of the horse and buggy was over.

'Can you give a car an apple when you feel like it?' Alfred asked her. 'Can you slap a car's mudguard and feel her warm flesh quivering? Can you brush a car and make her coat gleam in the sunlight?' He waited for an answer. And when she said nothing, he cried, 'Well? Of course you can't!'

Now, sitting by the wood stove late one night in bitter July, Alma suddenly asked him, 'You don't suppose your mother is getting sick of us staying here?'

Alfred leaned forward in his chair, reached across and placed his forefinger against her lips. 'Hush,' he said. Alma was shocked. How dare he touch her in such a familiar way? And especially such an intimate part of her person—her mouth!

She pinched his coat sleeve and gently removed the offending hand. Had she been guilty of anything in word or deed that might have encouraged him to assume such familiarity? Did he not believe she was a respectable woman? Did he privately think of her as a different kind of woman?

Alma sighed deeply. She herself had come to feel that in a way she deserved what had happened to her. She might have tried harder in her marriage to Frederick. Perhaps if she had turned a blind eye to his failings, she would still have a husband to support her.

'I wish your husband was dead,' Alfred said.

'Why?'

'So I could marry you.'

She turned and slapped him full across his cheek. His hand instinctively leaped to the spot. 'Jesus Christ! What did you do that for?'

'It serves you right, too. Next time I'll knock your block off.'

But Alma felt afraid. She had known the moment she slapped him that it was a mistake. The physical contact would only provoke him. In fact, she couldn't have done a more sexual thing.

He had said he wanted to marry her in a light-hearted way. She knew he was teasing her. But she also knew that such talk, and such feelings, were dangerous.

'I'm sorry,' she said now.

'No worries. She'll be right,' Alfred said, still rubbing his cheek.

'Why do you sit up so late, after your mother goes to bed?'

'Oh, have a heart! What are you having a go at me for now? I like to sit up and keep you company for a bit, that's all.'

'You make it sound like I am a patient sick in hospital.'

'I know you have trouble sleeping.'

'So you know, do you? How do you know?'

'I just know.' Alfred looked away: she knew he had been spying on her. 'I love talking to you,' he went on. 'Just imagine, we could get married one day and we could be chums and live in the same house and I would never be bored.'

'I am sure your mother wouldn't like to hear you talk like that.'

'I am not talking to my mother.'

And when she said nothing in reply, he asked, 'Well, shall I stay talking to you or shall I wake my mother and talk to her?'

'Stay,' she said. He made a lunge for her in her chair, but she neatly evaded him. Of course, she realised, this was just a game; if he tried, he would easily overpower her.

He went over to Mrs Lovett's single shelf of books and selected Palgrave's *Golden Treasury*. 'Will you read to me?' he asked.

'You can read perfectly well yourself,' she laughed at him.

'I only got to the eighth grade.'

'And I only got to grade six! Anyway, you can read—I've seen you.'

'I'd like to hear *your* voice reading.'

'Do you have a favourite?'

'I don't mind. You choose.'

He dragged his chair in close to her, as though it were poetry he wanted. Alma chose a poem by Alfred, Lord Tennyson:

Theirs not to reason why,
Theirs but to do and die...

As she read to him, she felt his upper arm pressing against hers. How close he was sitting! Now his hand was touching hers, under the guise of helping her turn the page. Alfred listened to the poem gravely, ready to snatch back his trespassing hand.

Lying on the stretcher that night, waiting for sleep, her eyes staring up at the unpainted boards of the ceiling, the silence of the house was like a question.

On Saturday nights, Alfred came home late. He told his mother that he was 'going to the Troc'.

One afternoon after work, Alma questioned him about the fights.

'Sometimes there's a blue with the Eagles,' Alfred told her. 'They own the footpath outside the Trocadero on Saturday nights and we reckon it's our job to take it away from them. But the blokes we really hate are the Ranch. They put one of our mates into hospital, a few months back. They use bike chains, broken bottles, razors. I wouldn't put anything past those Yarraville buggers.' He stopped himself. She could see that he hadn't meant to swear in front of her. He recovered, then went on. 'There's the Checkers in Yarraville, too. They own everything on the other side of Charles Street. The locals hate us. They say we give the place a bad name. The councillors, or at least some of them, call us larrikins and say the best thing that could happen would be to put us in uniform and send us off to France to fight for King and country. We might be larrikins, but we're onto that kind of bulldust. The only purpose of the war is to make the rich richer. Look at the toffs filling their pockets with the profits from selling armaments!' He glared at Alma, daring her to contradict him.

On Sunday morning as soon as the others had left for church, she heard a knock at the door of the sleep-out. She had been half expecting him to try something like this, but now the moment was here, she was frozen to the spot. All she knew was a screeching in her ears, the premonition of danger.

'Go away, Alfred,' she called. She kept thinking that Mrs Lovett would arrive home early. Or that Mrs Thomas next door might hear them.

Finally, Alma opened the door. He put his arms around her shoulders and buried his face in her hair. 'You must know I'm sweet on you,' he breathed.

EVERY SUNDAY MORNING in July, while the others went to church, he came to the sleep-out. As soon as they were alone, they undressed and lay together on the creaking stretcher. All the time she was with him, she heard phantom doors opening and closing, as though part of Mrs Lovett had stayed home, on patrol, and this voiceless ghost of conscience had recourse to her through the slamming of doors—until she reasoned that those sounds must have been coming from the Thomas house.

She did not love Alfred. Yet she was allowing him to believe that she might. It was he who loved her. That much was clear. So what? she reasoned. A young man believes he loves every pretty woman who smiles at him.

'I shall never do it with him again,' she promised herself

after the first time, 'or even allow myself to think about it.' But it was too late. Her resolutions were useless. She was the Alma she wished to be, from day to day, and she was the other creature she knew herself also to be when she was alone with Alfred. She knew they would keep coming back to each other now, meeting secretly. She hadn't realised how much she had needed warmth and touch, how much she missed being wanted. But she had lost herself, and she had lost her peace. She was already two people by now.

Week after week, it went on. They undressed, took their pleasure together; then, overcome by panic and guilt, they dressed again quickly and separated.

Alma went to sit in the parlour, the room where she had sat so often at the piano, rehearsing in her mind what she would say to Mrs Lovett when she arrived home with Teddy and Olive, how she had passed the morning, the chores that had occupied her. The blinds were usually drawn to protect the rug from fading; she opened them and the emerald and ruby stained-glass panes poured their radiance into the room. She heard the sound of the gate opening and closing. She supposed Alfred was going off on his bicycle, hoping perhaps that the whoosh of speed and wind might cleanse his guilty feelings.

Alma knew she had to keep their sexual life a secret. She blamed herself, not Alfred, for what had happened. Although they were nearly the same age, he was still a boy in many ways. She sat on the hard black oilcloth couch; a fox was draped along the back, head and all. The beady glass eyes and fixed smile gave it a slightly exasperated look. The longer she sat in the room with the exalted light coming in through the stained glass, as in a church, her sitting there itself came to seem like a trespass. She might have been living on the Lovetts' charity, but now, in a sense, she was earning it.

On weekday afternoons when he came home from the harness shop now, instead of playing with the children, Alfred sat with her, taking turns to read from Palgrave's *Golden Treasury*. Once he bought her flowers. Alma kept them in a vase on top of the piano, where Mrs Lovett couldn't help but notice them, though she said nothing. When the flowers died, and the curled dead petals littered the top of the piano, Alma collected them in a paper bag, too precious to be thrown away.

One Saturday afternoon in August she was sitting on the front verandah, preoccupied, the children playing in the street, waiting for the piano lesson to finish so they could all go inside, when Alfred came and sat next to her. He seemed not to notice that something was wrong.

SHE LAY ON the stretcher in the sleep-out and listened to Mrs Lovett chiding her son in the kitchen. 'What was in your head, Alfred? Cabbage?'

'It wasn't my fault,' he said, without conviction.

'Ah!' his mother exclaimed. 'I suppose you are going to try and put all the blame on *her* out there!'

A claw of panic raked through Alma's belly. It made her shudder to hear herself being referred to like that. She was glad that Teddy and Olive were down the street, playing with their friends.

'Oh yes! Blame it on our charming guest! See, she came to live with us on purpose just to get you into trouble. Butter wouldn't melt in your mouth!'

Alma began to shiver uncontrollably.

'It is a pretty mess you've got us in. A very pretty mess indeed!' Mrs Lovett went on.

'But I never thought this was going to happen.'

'Oh, I dare say. You never thought! It serves you right.'

'I didn't do it on purpose!'

'Of course you didn't, you idiot! As if she hasn't already got enough on her plate. A woman in her situation, married to another man, a deserted wife, and now in the family way—'

All Alma could do was lie there, even though she wanted to run away and hide—anywhere but here in this house in Empire Street at this moment. Mrs Lovett's words, spoken coldly and objectively like that, sounded so cruel, so heartless, they could have been talking about someone else. But they weren't. They were talking about her, Alma.

'So you went knocking on her door, pestering her?'

Alfred tried to say something. His voice was dispirited, scarcely audible.

'Imagine how delighted your dear father would be, were he still with us, to hear this news, or even your brother Archie.'

The mention of his little brother was too much. Alma heard Alfred break down, sobbing. 'Why am I always the one to get the short end of the stick?' he blubbered. 'I should have taken Archie's place and gone to France to fight. If only I'd been fired off in a gun, all this would never have happened.'

'Stop feeling sorry for yourself.'

'All the fine lives that have been lost in Flanders, I could have been one of them...'

'I told you. Stop whining.'

'Do you know what I'm going to do? I am going to sign up first thing in the morning.'

'What good will that do? How is that going to change anyone's situation? Maybe you will be smarter some day.'

'Mother—do you feel ill? You look very pale.'

'Of course I feel ill. How would any mother feel, hearing this news when she comes home from the shops expecting no more than a pleasant evening by the fire. This is a dreadful business! We must be sure no one finds out. It won't take much to set the neighbours' tongues a-wagging. How am I ever going to be able to hold up my head in church?'

Alma knew she was the cause of this tide of woe that had begun to spread through the Lovett household. She had betrayed Mrs Lovett's kindness. Alma must have seemed to her like a thief who had crept into their home and robbed Mrs Lovett of her son.

Teddy and Olive returned from their play, faces flushed from the cold air and innocent fun. Alma emerged from the sleep-out and hugged them. She followed the children into the kitchen to see the others. Mrs Lovett put on a pretence of normality; Alfred was withdrawn. Teddy gave his mother an inquiring look. With a slight shake of her head, she pretended nothing was wrong and tried to reassure him with her eyes: Alfred will be back to his old self soon.

That evening after they had finished eating and the children had been put to bed, they sat around the kitchen table. Mrs Lovett bore the heavy look of one who is struggling with many contradictory thoughts at once.

'You put your own appetites ahead of your children's happiness?' Mrs Lovett asked her at length.

Alma felt like she had been slapped. 'Why do you have to put it like that? It makes me sound like I am greedy, that I eat all the food while they have none.'

Mrs Lovett drew straight in her chair. This gesture made Alma feel that she really was selfish.

'Alfred has a responsibility. But he cannot be expected to support another man's children,' Mrs Lovett said. She had meant to say it kindly, Alma knew, but it had come out sounding mean.

Alma stared at the tabletop, the oilcloth with its drab pattern. She felt at a strange remove, as though this were all taking place somewhere far away, and what they were discussing had little to do with her.

'Will I have to go to court, Mother?' Alfred asked. He couldn't disguise the panic in his voice.

'It would serve you right if you did,' his mother told him.

Alma had never felt so alone. She knew how people would think of her. Alfred had picked her up in a park, a public place. She had moved into Empire Street, dependent on the charity of Alfred and his mother. There was already stigma in that. Now this.

Alfred had made no move to comfort her. He looked too guilty even to meet her eyes. Mrs Lovett propped her elbows on the table. 'I thought that if Alfred gave you a ring, it might make things easier.'

Easier? Easier for *her*? For *Alfred*? For *me*?

Alma held up her left hand. 'I am already wearing a ring. It is the ring my husband gave me.'

'I meant, if Alfred gave you a ring, it would be like a promise to marry you. It might be more acceptable to people.'

'I don't see how that would change one single thing,' Alma replied. 'Anyway. Divorces take years, don't they?'

Mrs Lovett rested her puffy hand on the table next to her empty teacup. The kettle was on the boil, filling the kitchen with steam, but none of them got up to take it off. 'Well, people are fools, and there's nothing more certain than that,' Mrs Lovett told her. 'Doubtless some tongues will be wagging, but with a bit of luck they'll get tired and stop.' Then she added, 'It's just that—it might be better if you kept out of sight.'

'Out of sight?' Alma asked. 'But I have children to walk to school, and clothes to hang on the line. Do you really think you can hide me away?'

'Then at least be discreet. I would not like to have the neighbours think you shameless.' Mrs Lovett spoke in a severe tone Alma had never heard her take before.

'Shameless? I can assure you, I feel very much ashamed.'

'You cannot imagine how much it would pain me to see our family's disgrace on public display.'

She thought she knew Mrs Lovett. Now, suddenly, Mrs Lovett was like another person.

A divorce would free her to marry Alfred, but where was she going to find one of those? Alma's greatest fear was that Welfare would take away her children. The decree nisi and decree absolute would be invoked, the grounds of adultery or cruelty or desertion—the things she read about in the *Argus*. All those questions—Whose desertion? Whose adultery? Whose cruelty?—would have to be answered in public, and decided by a judge who had to be called Your Worship, and barristers, she had heard, cost fifty pounds. The mysterious way in which an ordinary woman became a 'co-respondent'—

that's why Alma could not offer Alfred the respectability he craved. What kept her awake that night was the prospect of having to go to court and all their names appearing in the newspapers. Everyone would know the truth about her.

Even if she did somehow manage to get a divorce, Alfred would not be one step closer to marrying her. Any day now, she felt, Mrs Lovett would sit her down and ask her to leave the house. Alma and the children would be alone again, penniless, back in the park where Alfred had found them. Good Lord, where would she go? How long would it be before she ended up with the whores in front of the Plough Hotel, and the government taking the children?

To make matters worse, little Teddy fell ill. For three days he lay feverish and moaning. All through the night she sat on the wooden chair beside his pillow, which was soaked with perspiration. She was frightened it might turn out to be diphtheria. The Waters baby had been taken by it. Alma kept the candle burning until it had wasted away to a stump, then guttered out. At dawn, she stretched herself out on her bed and immediately slipped into sleep. It was nine o'clock when she woke, and sunshine was sliding in through the gaps at the edges of the blind. Teddy's eyes were open. She rushed to his side, stroking his face and kissing him. His cheeks were cooler. She said a silent prayer of thanks. Her child was going to live.

Alfred came home from work one morning not long after he had set out. Alma and Mrs Lovett looked up as he came through the kitchen door. 'Alfred!' Mrs Lovett cried. 'What are *you* doing home? Are you sick?'

He flopped in a chair, his face pale. Mr Ward had sent him home, saying there was not enough business coming in to pay his wages.

Alma had been following news of the Great Strike. It had begun with the railway and tramway men in New South Wales and soon spread to other states. Wharfies, coal lumpers, coalminers, seamen, firemen, gas workers, slaughter men, butchers and draymen were all on strike. Alma knew from her own experience that flour, bread, meat and milk were in short supply in the shops. The streets were dark at night: a shortage of coal had led to electricity restrictions.

That afternoon Alfred went to the foundry in Seddon to try to get his old job back, but the men there were on strike too.

Alma found an advertisement in the paper and showed it to Alfred, looking over his shoulder and reading aloud: 'The principal classes of work for which men may be required are coaling, loading, discharging, despatching, working ships, handling wheat, flour, foodstuffs, &c.' The advertisement called for men to register at the Athenaeum Theatre in Collins Street.

He looked horrified. 'Don't you see that they're calling for strikebreakers? You don't expect me to scab, do you?'

'Is that what it means?'

'I'll tell you something. I'd rather go hungry than be a dirty scab.'

As the weeks of the strike passed, Alfred's mood did not improve. Being out of work hurt his pride. In the yard he passed her silently. If she tried to speak to him, he pretended

45

not to hear. At the table he would not meet her gaze.

There was no money coming into the house, and Alfred's mother had to rely on her meagre savings. Alfred was no longer the same young man who had rescued Alma. No wages, shortages of food in the shops because of the strike, bad news from the war on the Western Front—it all seemed to weigh on him. Although he had never been one to go to the pub, one afternoon he brought home bottles of ale and sat on the back porch, bundled up in his greatcoat, drinking.

'I have failed in my efforts to reform you,' Mrs Lovett told him.

'Nothing to reform.' Alfred added that the Christian Women's Temperance Union had only succeeded in giving her a weapon with which to irritate him.

From her bed in the sleep-out, Alma listened to them arguing.

'I can see that you are unhappy, my boy. And, it's true, the world has given us troubles, lately. But you won't find answers at the bottom of a bottle. You are behaving like an ungrateful child.'

'What have I got to be grateful for?'

'You should be grateful for all God's gifts.'

'What?' he asked. 'You mean all this?'

Alfred sawed a piece from the loaf and spread it with dripping. He sipped his hot tea, and opened the newspaper. 'Strike's still going at Angliss's,' he said, to no one in particular. He opened his mouth and took a bite of his bread.

Alma had heard that the bosses had been bringing in black-

46

legs to the meat works—returned soldiers, some of them.

'Four hundred blokes from Millers Ropes in Yarraville are out. Bert Davies says Kinnears will be next.'

Kinnears was closer to home. 'Why have the rope workers gone on strike?' Alma asked.

'The blokes at Millers went out because the bosses wanted them to take delivery of some New Zealand hemp.'

'Is there something wrong with New Zealand hemp?'

'No!' Alfred let out a snort. 'You see, the hemp was moved from the port and brought to the factory gate by scabs.'

Alma carried the children's boiled eggs to the table in the pot and placed one in each of the wooden eggcups in front of them. She was mortified to have been made to sound foolish. She resolved to learn all she could about the strike from now on. She sawed off the tops of the eggs and Teddy and Olive dipped in their crusts. Alfred had turned back to his newspaper.

'I see there was another brawl outside the Troc on Saturday night.' He caught Alma's eye and smirked.

'What's the Troc?' Teddy asked, eating his egg.

'It's the pictures,' Alfred said. 'Haven't you ever been to the pictures?' Teddy shook his head. Alfred said to Alma, 'We should take them to a matinee one Saturday.' He turned to Teddy. 'Would you like to go and see Tom Mix?'

Teddy looked imploringly at his mother. '*Can* we go?' he begged her. Teddy had seen pictures of Tom Mix in his cowboy hat in magazines.

'One day,' she said. Alma didn't have the threepence admission to the stalls and, now that he was out of work, Alfred could not spare the money either.

Alfred told Teddy how the Dingoes got into fights with

47

other pushes. Sometimes they fought with razors. Teddy looked on in fear and fascination as Alfred took his straight razor from his jacket pocket, opened it, and ran his thumb over the honed blade.

'What nonsense are you talking about now?' his mother demanded.

Mrs Lovett disliked newspapers. Everybody in Footscray read the *Advertiser* to hear the latest news of the strikes, but she didn't. 'Man's quickest interest is in the misfortune of others, and that's what newspapers are for,' she said. 'Apart from that, you should not be telling such things to the boy,' she added.

'If they try anything on me, I'll be ready,' Alfred said, closing the razor and putting it back in his pocket.

Alma understood that Alfred was boiling on the inside. He was angry with her, angry to be out of work, angry with the world. There was a part of him that wanted to get into a fight.

'Oh, look what's on at the pictures,' Alfred said. '*The Millionaire's Double* with Lionel Barrymore. I wouldn't mind being a millionaire's double for a day or two!' His face broke into a broad smile. It was the first time Alma had seen him smile since she had told him her news.

One afternoon, on her way to the henhouse, she passed Alfred, sitting by himself on the back step with a bottle of ale. He refilled his glass and drank it straight down. There were streaks on the inside of the glass from drinking too fast. With every drink, the devil showed more clearly in his eyes.

When she came back, he was standing on the step, barring her way.

'You know, Tuppence, I've been thinking. It's a fact that you're a married woman.' His mouth was smiling, but his eyes

48

were not. 'And since you're a married woman, there's not much I can do about it.'

Whenever a man began by saying 'it's a fact', it meant that this indisputable fact put her at a disadvantage. Alfred loved facts; he couldn't abide anything that couldn't be proven in black and white. Still, he did love horses, she had to admit that, and a horse was something more than just a fact.

She saw the furrow in his upper lip, the groove of stubbornness. Not so long ago, she had liked the shape of his mouth. She had admired his determination. Now it made him look as though he had set himself as an enemy against her.

'When you first came to my room,' she asked, 'was it just a visit?'

'It wasn't just a visit.'

'That's what I thought, too.'

She waited for him to say the words of love that wouldn't come. She'd felt all along that, because she was a married woman, he thought she should have known better.

Alfred said, miserably, 'I didn't mean to get you into trouble.'

'I know you didn't mean it.'

'But there are ways of fixing trouble.' Alfred crossed his arms and leaned against the doorway.

'What do you mean?' Alma felt suddenly afraid. She had sometimes heard whispered stories of women who knew how to do things with wire coathangers. Occasionally, there were accounts in the newspaper when things had gone wrong in seedy boarding houses in the slums of Fitzroy and Collingwood.

'I heard there's a doctor in Williamstown who might be able to help.'

'Is that what *you* want?'

He took a cigar from his jacket and clamped it in his mouth. He held the match in his hand, but did not light it. He seemed to change his mind, or perhaps he lost his courage. 'This is a waste of time,' he said, and stepped aside to let her through.

Alma took in a deep breath. 'Very well,' she said. 'I'll go. But you'll have to come with me.'

They set out for Williamstown the next morning. The strike was at its height. In Ballarat Road they saw a group of strikers yelling abuse at a truck that had just pulled into the loading bay of a factory. There were two men in the cabin—'volunteers', presumably.

'You fucking scab,' she heard a man call out.

'What did you say?' the driver challenged him.

'I said you're a fucking scab.'

The driver revved the engine, but could not move as the door of the loading dock was closed. One of the other strikers jumped on the step up to the lorry door and yelled, 'You little cunt. I'll get you!' He punched the driver, knocking him out of his seat. The other strikers swarmed onto the truck and pulled the two volunteers onto the ground. The last Alma and Alfred saw of them was the strikers taking the men to the vacant lot overgrown with thistles beside the factory.

When they got to the station there was a handwritten sign: there were no trains running that day. They could try to get a bus all the way to Williamstown, but the buses were running infrequently because of the strike. They spent the day instead walking along the streets near the river, looking at the deserted wharves, the ships with their cargo still waiting to be unloaded. At three o'clock they headed home to Empire Street.

On their way home, they saw a meeting of unionists in the street outside Kinnears. They stood on the corner of Ballarat Road to watch. There were hundreds of men from Millers and Kinnears. Wives stood at the side of the roadway, some of them with children in their arms. There was pride in their faces.

Alfred told Alma that a meeting of the Sugar Workers' Union on the 19th of August voted not to unload the *Kadina*. Five days later, there were a hundred and fifty men outside the gates waiting for those who had been at work that day. Members of the Artificial Manure Trades Union had walked out at the Mount Lyell Company in Yarraville rather than handle a 'black' cargo of superphosphate.

As they left Kinnears and walked home down the street, Alma heard people singing:

Solidarity forever,
For the union makes us strong.

I could do with a bit of solidarity, she thought. Still, seeing those people made her realise that she was not alone in facing hardships that winter.

Neither she nor Alfred mentioned Williamstown again.

A notice on a lamppost while she was out shopping caught Alma's attention. A demonstration against rising food prices was to take place on the banks of the Yarra river. 'I want to go,' she told Alfred, when she got home.

'What for? You haven't got a job and you're not a member of any union.'

'The price of tinned meat and kerosene has doubled since the war began. Bacon, butter, flour, tinned fish, oatmeal and cheese have all gone up by half.'

'What do you expect? The capitalist class is running this stupid war.'

'Will you mind the children? Or I could ask your mother.'

Alfred looked suspicious, as if she were trying to put something over him. 'You've never shown any interest in protest meetings before.'

'But you approve of people standing up for their rights, don't you?'

'I'll ask Mother to look after the children. I'll come with you.'

The trains were running that day. They travelled from Footscray Station to Flinders Street, crossed the Yarra at Princes Bridge and from there they could already see a great crowd gathered on the flat ground near the boat sheds. Women in the crowd were hooting and swearing at scab tram drivers going past. Two women were standing in a car with a banner reading 'Workers of the World Unite'. One of them was giving a speech through a megaphone.

'That's Vida Goldstein,' Alfred told her.

A public nuisance, she was called in the newspapers. A monster of her sex. Still, Alma thought, I wish I were confident enough to stand on a car and give speeches. Now, more than ever, she felt timid and insecure. The sound of those shrill, angry voices both thrilled her and made her afraid. Alma had already noticed the squads of uniformed policemen assembled under the trees, watching.

From Yarra Bank they marched to the commonwealth parliament in Spring Street. Just as Alma and Alfred passed the

Flinders Street clocks, half a dozen mounted policemen tried to disperse the crowd. All around them, people joined arms and held firm. The police horses withdrew. Alma felt proud to be part of this great company of people united in their cause. Alfred said he reckoned there must have been twenty or thirty thousand people marching with them up Collins Street.

On the 9th of September, the general strike collapsed, though some unionists held out. Some of the strikers were not re-employed. In Footscray there were band recitals and vaudeville nights to raise money for unemployed strikers. Needy children were billeted out with families still in work.

Finally, the rope workers went back on the 20th of September, and the failure of the strike was complete. The night of broken glass, the newspaper called it: Adela Pankhurst and Jennie Baines led thousands of women from Richmond, Port Melbourne and South Melbourne in a rampage through streets darkened by the continuing shortage of coal. Butcher shops in Swan Street, the posh emporiums of Collins Street and the Dunlop factory in Montague all had their windows smashed.

Alma wished she had been in their number. She understood the anger of those women. As well as her morning sickness, the usual nausea and vomiting she had suffered with the other two children, she often felt a rising urge to scream. A part of her wanted to descend into that kind of violence, marching with the women through the dark, throwing bricks, smashing windows, screeching out her hatred and frustration.

Alma's newfound political feelings were further inflamed when she read that Merv Flanagan, a striker in New South

Wales, had been shot and killed by Reginald Wearne, a strike-breaker and brother of a conservative New South Wales parliamentarian. When the ruling class started shooting workers, Alma imagined that revolution might not be very far away.

She read of the dramatic events in Russia. The Bolsheviks had seized power in St Petersburg. Lenin proclaimed, 'Today has begun a new era in the history of mankind.'

Something marvellous was happening. A new chapter in the history of the world, and she was part of it! The news from Russia unleashed a delirium of longing in her, like love. It was the way she used to feel as a girl, stuck in her drab existence, scrubbing pots for her mother, when a phrase of music reached her through the open window and lifted her heart.

The future stretched ahead, full of possibilities. People would cast off their narrow attitudes. Women would no longer be judged on whether or not they were married. Men and women would live together as equals, united in the dignity of their work. The new society was like a promise to Alma's unborn child.

She was thrilled when, in December, the second conscription plebiscite was defeated. Billy Hughes's jingoism had split the Labor Party, and now militants rose to leadership in the unions, the Wobblies, the Syndicalists, the One Big Union. In a few short months, the Melbourne Trades Hall was flying the Red Flag.

But this fever of happiness did not last. Alma was still pregnant, still married to another man, still dependent on the kindness—and the decisions—of others.

◆◆◆

'Brighten up, Tuppence,' Alfred told her. 'I'll be starting work at the iron foundry next Monday. It'll feel good to have a few bob in my pocket again. We might even have enough for you to have your baby like a lady in the hospital.'

Alma felt the ghost of the future move over her, a premonition of great privation and suffering ahead, the line of fate she had felt that first day, back in Footscray Park. She had been forced to get married because she was pregnant with Teddy. Now she was with child again, and this time it would be worse because she wouldn't have a husband. But what choice did she have? Yes, she blamed Alfred. She had to blame somebody. She compared him with an impossible ideal and found him wanting. She dwelled on his faults and not his qualities. Little things about him irritated her. The way he failed to pronounce the aspirate in the word 'hospital', for example. Alfred always watched the reaction of the other person before he took the next step; it was uncertainty which, every now and then, tipped over into bravado and sudden anger. He was sensitive about his height, too. All that was why he got into fights.

As she grew bigger, Alma spent most of her days indoors. The Lovetts still wanted to keep her a secret from the world. 'There is nothing that perks up the spirits of the neighbours like the news of a pregnant girl,' Mrs Lovett told her.

Mrs Thomas no longer came in on Mondays to use their copper, but she still poked her head over the fence. Alma overheard her asking Mrs Lovett slyly, 'That niece of yours still staying with you?'

Oh, she knew, all right. Everyone in Empire Street must have known. They would have seen Mrs Lovett walking the children to school. When Alfred left the house for work at the iron foundry, there was something furtive and ashamed in the way he cycled off quickly, looking neither left nor right.

Mrs Lovett's unspoken rebuke—to Alma, to Alfred, to herself—hung over them. She told Alma that she forgave her. But Alma knew that sometimes forgiveness came hard.

She felt troubled in her spirit. It was this feeling of apprehension that kept her imprisoned inside the house in Empire Street. She became a creature of the shadows, hiding in the sleep-out during the day, or spending hours alone in the parlour, practising the piano, so she would not have to face Mrs Lovett. Some days she was too scared even to go down the back to use the lavatory for fear that Mrs Thomas would stick her head over the fence and speak to her.

Alma had thought her guilty feeling would have faded with time, but she knew in her heart that was not the way these things worked. An official document, a wedding ring, would have changed everything. And yet, in another way, Alma knew it would have changed nothing.

The war on the Western Front ground on. In March, a new German offensive began, when they got to within thirty-five miles of Paris. On the evening of the 9th of April, while she was boiling some bacon bones to make soup, Alma's waters broke and Mrs Lovett prepared her own bed in the front room for the lying-in.

The children were sent to stay for two nights with Mrs Edmondson, who helped Pastor Goble in circumstances such as these. For short periods, she took in the children of deserted wives, the unemployed and the homeless.

Teddy and Olive had been curious, of course, about the baby. Olive in particular often asked, 'When is the baby going to come?' Teddy was more reticent. He still adored Alfred: it could have been out of loyalty to him, sensing something shameful, that Teddy was quiet about the baby.

During the night the pains began, but they were infrequent, and Alma knew the hard part was just beginning. She had forgotten the pain with her other two children, every part of it completely wiped from her memory. Now it all came back to her, and she reached above her head and gripped the cold bars of the bedstead, bracing herself.

Mrs Lovett sat beside Alma in a low rattan chair. When the pains became severe, she soaked the corner of a towel in hospital brandy and let Alma suck on it. She had folded the blankets, stored them away and fitted a rubber sheet over the kapok mattress. Next to the bed on a small table she had piled some old towels. A white enamel jug, chipped in places, stood next to the basin on the washstand. In the kitchen, the kettle had been on the boil all night. There was to be no doctor, no midwife. Mrs Lovett had delivered babies before. If there should be complications, she would send Alfred on his bicycle to fetch Doctor Greaves in Ballarat Road. In the meantime, Alfred was to keep away.

The contractions came, and the screams.

Alma pictured Alfred on the back step in the dark with his cigar, miserable and useless, blaming Alma for their situation. All her screams now would seem to his masculine mind like some brutal natural justice of the beasts. He'd be terrified.

She heard Mrs Lovett say, 'You need something to occupy yourself, Alfred. Why don't you go out and chop some wood?

We'll need to keep the stove burning.'

Alma, too, was glad Alfred had a task. She could hear the distant sound of chopping, the back door opening and closing, the thump of another armful of wood in the kitchen. He would like the reassurance of feeling the rough logs against his arms, so different from the distressing sounds of the female world in the front room.

After a while, the sounds of chopping and stacking ceased. He would have dragged a kitchen chair in front of the fire now, even though the April night was mild. She heard Mrs Lovett say, 'Why don't you try to get some sleep, Alfred? I'll wake you if anything happens.'

'How can I sleep? Just as things get bearable, that dreadful screaming starts again.'

'Go down to the henhouse. That always helps, when you're troubled.'

'You hear that? Another scream. Unpredictable, they are— that's the worst thing about it. Every time I hear her, it's like something inside myself being ripped apart.'

Alma heard him stomp out and slam the back door. She imagined him down at the henhouse, next to the fence, squatting on his heels, curled up, even trying to sleep for a few minutes in the midst of the familiar smells and sounds. He was part of the world of the chooks, not what was happening inside the house, and he would find comfort in the stench, the darkness. The fowls wouldn't mind his presence there.

All night Alma was in labour. Now, in the hour before dawn, the spasms were more frequent. She was sure all of Empire Street could hear her screams. To keep herself from thinking of the pain, she sang a nursery rhyme to herself, over and over: *Miss Molly had a dolly who was sick, sick, sick. So she called for the doctor to come quick, quick, quick.*

Early the next morning, the 10th of April, Alma gave birth to a daughter. She named the baby Molly. Since there was no doctor, no midwife, the birth of her little girl was never registered.

THE FOLLOWING WEEK Mr Goble arrived at the house in Empire Street on his reinforced bicycle.

'Look who's come to see you,' Mrs Lovett said to Alma, ushering him into the kitchen. Alma, sitting with the baby, detected the false cheerfulness in Mrs Lovett's voice, and guessed that this wasn't just a casual visit.

Mr Goble announced that he was the bearer of good news. He had managed to find a cottage in Seddon for Alma and the children. Alma guessed that Mrs Lovett had asked him for help to find her a place, so she could be rid of Alma. It was more than a mile from Empire Street, out of the way, in Pilgrim Street, where people wouldn't know what had happened to her. Teddy and Olive would go to a new school, the state school in Hyde Street, which was closer to Pilgrim Street than their old school in Geelong Road. Alfred had agreed to pay for their rent and housekeeping. It would be a new start, Mr Goble concluded with a smile.

When she heard the house was in Seddon, Alma's heart began to race. The foundry where Alfred worked was nearby; he might call in to see her after work. Of course, he would want to visit Molly.

Their house was in a row of worker's cottages, three rooms off the hallway, a fireplace with broken tiles. There was cold running water in the stone trough in the kitchen and the pan in the outhouse had not been emptied. From the backyard Alma could see the chimneystacks of the factories on the other side of Whitehall Street, and when the wind came from that direction, she could smell the tannery near the river. The corrugated iron roofs and fences in these streets had red and brown patches of rust, as though something inside them was bleeding.

She spent two days with a tin bucket and scrubbing brush, scouring the floorboards, washing down the walls. She kept the kettle on the boil, refilling the bucket with vinegar and hot water. She cleaned the mouse droppings out of the cupboards, and washed all the windows. There were some ragged curtains, which had to be washed, pegged out in the sun to dry and sewn up where the seams had split. She paid particular attention to the front step. It was a slab of bluestone, on top of which was a flat brass rail, and she wanted that brass shining so that the neighbours, when they passed, might form a good opinion of her.

Her days were busy. While Teddy and Olive were at school, she kept the house clean, made sure there was food to eat, tended to little Molly. She arranged to have coal delivered for the stove and the account sent to Alfred in Empire Street. On Saturdays, Alma heated a big pot of water and filled the tin hip bath she had placed on the kitchen floor. The baby was bathed first, then the other two children, then finally Alma herself.

Although Mrs Lovett hadn't said so in as many words, Alma felt that they would not be welcome to visit the house in Empire Street. The move to Seddon was to be a decisive break. The thing Alma missed most was playing the piano. Music gave her the feeling that she was on the threshold of discovering the key to her life. Her fingers striking the first chords of a song were like an intimation of happiness. But here in Seddon, there was no piano, no music, no joy, Worse, every possible future she imagined for herself and her children looked just as dull.

Mrs Lovett had been clear about Alfred facing up to his responsibilities. He had bought a few pieces of secondhand furniture and found a baby carriage that was being given away. He paid their rent at the real estate agent's office in Footscray.

He visited on Sundays. If the weather was fine, they went for a walk. To passers-by they might have been just another family taking the air or returning from church. For an hour or two each week, Alma had the appearance of respectability she craved. Her back straightened and she stood taller; a feeling of lightness and optimism lifted her spirits and her thoughts turned to the future. Perhaps she and Alfred might be able to live together and be happy, after all? At the very least, there was hope.

But then she had to put the thought out of her mind. She had been deluding herself. It was quite out of the question for Alfred to come and live with them. She knew nothing had really changed for him: living in Empire Street with his mother; riding his bicycle to work at the iron foundry; at knock-off time still showing off to the girls from the ammunition works.

Alfred gave Alma extra money when he could spare it. Two bob. Five bob. 'There you go, Tuppence,' he'd say, tossing her a few shining coins.

'You know I hate that name.'

'Where's your sense of humour?'

'I lost it a long time ago.'

The groove in his upper lip was deeper these days. Alma could sense Alfred's feelings shifting away from her. He might have still loved her—or told himself he still loved her—as the mother of little Molly. But the Alma who had instigated such a sudden, violent change in his life—to that Alma, he was less sympathetic. She blamed herself for his unhappiness. The young man had entrusted his soul to her. And what had she done with it?

If Alma had received undivided love from him, perhaps she might have been able to love him in return. She was grown-up enough at twenty-five to know that life rarely granted long periods of uninterrupted happiness. Even if she could obtain a divorce, even if they then did get married, she knew she would never be happy with Alfred, and that he would always be disappointed with her.

She made friends with Moira, the woman next door, who was twenty-eight. Her husband worked at the bottle factory in Spotswood. Moira, who had five children, was often worn out. The first time Alma invited her in for a cup of tea, she instinctively decided to trust Moira. Anyway, she knew that a lie would not explain Alfred's visits on Sundays.

'I didn't like to ask, but I thought it must have been

something like that,' Moira said. For once, Alma felt that she was not being judged. They became firm friends. Alma could rely on Moira when her spirits were low, and Teddy and Olive often went next door to play.

Times were tough. If Alma had only a few pennies in her purse, she bought half a pound of oats or some flour. Eggs were a luxury. So was meat. She stood before the window of the butcher's, staring at the meat she could not afford. What she wouldn't do for a nice lamb forequarter roast! The trays of meat were displayed on gleaming white tiles—purple rump and flank and skirt steak, crimson chops with their bands of thick white fat, strings of sausages, glossy ox liver, shallow cups of lamb's brains, flaps and folds of honeycomb tripe. The prices were written in shillings and pence on white cards. The butcher wore a blood-smeared white coat and a striped blue apron, a scabbard of knives bumping against his thigh. On the chopping block, one quick slap of the cleaver and he could cut clean through the bone. Mr Heritage was friendly, in the manner of butchers. Once he saw her standing there for ages and called her inside and gave her an ox-tail to make soup.

One ordinary Monday in November, in the middle of the morning, Alma was startled by the sound of factory whistles. It was not just one—every factory in Melbourne seemed to be blasting its whistle. She picked up the baby and went out the front, wondering what could be wrong. Already, women from neighbouring houses were standing at their front gates, looking up and down the street. Church bells began to ring. Cars and trucks driving along Whitehall Street were sounding their horns.

Moira, too, had come out of her front door. 'What's all this racket?' she asked over the low fence. 'I've never heard so many whistles.'

'There must have been an accident at a factory,' Alma said.

'The war's over!' cried Mrs Birtles from two doors down. 'Kaiser Bill has abdicated! Germany has signed an armistice!'

An armistice? It took a minute for Alma to understand. Then she felt herself grinning, and tears filled her eyes. She laughed at herself and quickly brushed away her tears.

'Things will get better now,' Moira said.

'Yes,' Alma sighed, but she could not feel the same elation. After this past hard year, blow upon blow, she felt numb. Things would get better? Alma didn't really believe it. The factory whistles went on for hours. Molly was exactly seven months old.

When Teddy and Olive came home from school, they too had caught the hysteria. Olive was hopping from one leg to the other, screaming, 'We won the war!' and 'The war is won!', just as she must have heard other children say at school. Teddy was solemn with emotion, overcome perhaps by being part of this great moment. Alfred turned up on his bicycle, unwashed, in his shirtsleeves and vest, straight from work at the foundry. Like everyone else that day, he had just downed tools. 'Have you heard the news?' he asked. 'Tomorrow's been declared a public holiday!' He promised to take Alma and the children into town to watch the celebrations.

He arrived at nine o'clock the next morning, wearing a suit and hat. Alma had put on her only coat and a hat with a wide brim. It was a clear-blue spring day in Melbourne and it was hard to find a seat in the train carriage, there were so many people going into the city, all in their best clothes.

As they descended the steps of Flinders Street Station, Alma could see the crowd stretched all the way up Swanston Street. Two huge Union Jacks billowed from either side of the clock tower of the Town Hall. The noise of the crowd was so loud, they couldn't hear each other speak. People were singing 'God Save the King'; as soon as they had finished, another section of the crowd took it up all over again.

Alfred edged his way through the crowd, the baby in his arms, Alma and the other two following. She held their hands so that they wouldn't get lost. Alfred held Molly aloft to see the brass band and the dignitaries on the balcony making their speeches and calling for three cheers. There were more jubilant crowds in front of Parliament House in Spring Street.

Later, at the Hopetoun Tea Rooms in the Block Arcade in Collins Street, the waitress brought them a triple-tiered plate with chicken sandwiches and cup cakes with their tops sliced, scalloped into butterfly wings, filled with cream and dusted with icing sugar—it was the last of these that Teddy found irresistible. He wolfed down his first, then sat looking imploringly, waiting for Alma to offer him another.

The noise of the crowds in the streets carried into the tea rooms. Baby Molly had fallen asleep in her pram.

'One of these?' Alma smiled, indicating the butterfly cakes. His desire for the cake was so urgent he was speechless; all he could do was nod vigorously. 'Are you quite certain you wouldn't like one of these lovely sandwiches instead?' she asked. Then, to put the boy out of his misery, she snatched up the last cake and placed it on Teddy's plate.

'Mind you don't make him sick, now,' Alfred warned. Teddy worshipped Alfred, but Alma noticed that lately the boy was more reserved. He still watched Alfred, waiting for some spark of enthusiasm to fly between them, as in the old days when they'd played cricket in the street. Now, as often as not, there was something frightened in the boy's expression, as though he expected to be disappointed. Alma hated to see such wariness in her child.

Not wanting to spoil the mood of the day, she deliberately avoided raising a subject which she knew always made Alfred uncomfortable. But while they were sitting there with their tea and cakes, for all the world like a happy family, she found herself speaking anyway, against all her own earnest resolutions. 'Now there's a contented young man,' she began, nodding towards Teddy, whose cheeks were still engorged with cake and cream. 'It will be easier for us all to take our happiness, now the war is over.'

Alfred half closed his eyes and a vague smile appeared.

'If only your dear mother,' Alma went on, 'would assent to you living with your child—your children—your—' she hesitated to say the words *your wife*. 'We all belong to you now, you know. We could have such a happy life together, if only—'

Alma broke off. Alfred's expression had changed. Second by second, all his enthusiasm for the day drained away and, although the shape of his smile remained, there was nothing of it left in his eyes. Was it dread of crossing his mother? Or some secret of his own he was nursing in his heart?

'I reckon things are all right as they stand,' he said, after a while. Then: 'Do you want more money—is that it?'

'No! Why, oh why is it so hard for you to get it into your head? Are you really such an idiot, not to be able to see what is missing here?'

Her strident tone made the children squirm in their chairs. Soon, Molly would wake and start crying, she knew, and they would have to leave the tea rooms, the afternoon spoiled, their special treat wasted, and all her own fault for not being able to accept her fate, for not knowing better than trying to change another human being. What she was asking, Alma realised, really was something he could *not* give—not to her, perhaps not to anyone.

'I don't see what more a bloke can do,' Alfred went on. 'I mean, fair crack of the whip. I give you extra money even when there's nothing left for myself. When I call in to visit, you always carry on like a two-bob watch.'

Alma wanted to scream. It was only by dint of great self-control that she smiled instead, and began to gather her things to leave. She was aware of people looking at them.

'Why do you always have to go and spoil everything?' Alfred said. With the change in mood, Teddy and Olive looked miserable. Alma tried to give them a reassuring smile.

They trudged to the station, then passed through the loading yards and sidings of Spencer Street and North Melbourne before continuing back to Footscray. Alfred escorted them as far as the front gate at Pilgrim Street, then made his escape.

In the weeks before Christmas, Alfred dropped in more often on his way home after work. Alma had tried to protect herself from the deceptions of hope. But the sight of him with his shirtsleeves rolled up, splashing water over his face and arms at the trough, reawakened in her body the memory of their love-making. When he had finished washing, she poured his tea and

68

stood behind him waiting, arms folded over her apron. She wanted him, but if anything were to happen, it would have to come from him.

Although Alfred was supporting them, and although he gave her something extra when the children needed new shoes, there were weeks when they had to survive on potatoes and porridge. There came a day when Alma was able to say to herself, I would rather live my life and raise my children however I might, without having to depend on any man. More and more, she was stung by the fact that she was dependent on Alfred.

She wanted him to go away. She wanted him to stay. A dull feeling of futility crept into every aspect of her life.

Alma and her children sweated through the heat of January but there was no school in February. The commencement of the new school year had been postponed. The Spanish influenza was rapidly spreading and Victoria was declared an 'infected area'. All places of public entertainment were closed. The Emergency Influenza Hospital was set up at Footscray Technical School in Ballarat Road, under direction of the school principal, Mr Hoadley.

'The state is in the grip of a deadly plague,' Alma read in the *Advertiser*. They stayed away from places where there were likely to be lots of people. Alma still went to the grocer and the butcher but she tried not to breathe the same air as the other customers. On one of his visits, Alfred reported that several people were down with the flu at the iron foundry. Mr McCracken, a foreman, had been admitted to hospital and there were grave fears for him. On Sunday morning, they walked past a service being conducted in the open air in front of a church. Many in the congregation were wearing masks against infection.

'You must wash your hands when you come inside,' Alma told her children, 'and gargle. I've bought a bottle of permanganate of potash and I'll keep it next to the sink. I've made some camphor bags and I want all of us to wear one around our necks.' She showed them the small woollen pouches with white tapes to tie around their necks, into each of which she had inserted a camphor lozenge. 'I'll put a few drops of eucalyptus oil on your handkerchiefs, and I want you to inhale often. There's nothing better than inhalation.'

On Wednesday the 5th of March, eight inches of rain fell in a single day. The cloudburst came in the afternoon. The day went dull, then dark. When the first raindrops arrived, the sound was like a handful of nails against the corrugated roof. The rain grew louder, and soon it was all Alma could hear. Gutters overflowed and rivulets of water leaked down the walls. For two hours, the deluge continued. How would the children get home from school?

Leaving Molly in the bedroom, Alma put on her rubber coat and made her way to the street corner. The force of the rain stung her face and the back of her neck. There was no traffic. People were inside their houses, or taking shelter wherever they could. Whitehall Street had become a river. She saw a motorcar sail calmly past.

She could go no further. She had to trust that the teachers would keep the children at school until it was safe to dismiss them.

At six o'clock, Teddy and Olive turned up, full of excitement.

The drains leading down to the Maribyrnong River had failed, Teddy told her, and a raging torrent was roaring down Gordon Street. The children were drenched; Alma quickly got them into dry clothes.

'The ammunition works is closed because of the flood,' Moira told her. 'Mrs Paton says her husband won't be going back to work until next Monday at the earliest. The shops and businesses in Barkly Street and Nicholson Street are flooded.'

It wasn't until Friday that Alma realised the extent of the damage. When she carried her shopping basket to Nicholson Street, she found many shops still closed. Furniture was piled up on the footpaths outside offices and people were still sweeping water and mud through their doorways.

Alfred came to the afternoon tea she prepared to celebrate Molly's first birthday on the 10th of April. Alma used her last three eggs to make the cake. There were no gifts. Alfred made the excuse that the child was too young for presents. He promised to save up and buy her a doll next year. 'There might be something for this young fellow, too,' he added. She watched him slurp his tea and wink at Teddy.

Molly took her first few tottering steps that day. Alfred picked her up and swung her through the air. 'Aren't you clever?' he kept saying. Alma could see how much Alfred loved Molly. But his pride in his daughter was short-lived: he could forget his shame only for a moment; stung anew by the returning realisation of his humiliation, he set the child down, saying, 'Well, I'd best be off.' He tucked the cuffs of his trousers into his socks, climbed on his bicycle and sailed off into the evening without looking back.

Alma knew that Moira must have followed these comings and goings, which might have been comical had they not left her feeling so desolate. Once or twice Alma was on the point of pouring out her feelings to her friend, but thought better of it. She didn't want to face up to those feelings, her secret hopes and fears, let alone talk about them.

One gloomy May afternoon, Alfred stayed later than usual. He made a show of warming his hands by the stove. She thought he must have wanted to talk about money. She feared he would tell her she had to wait until next payday.

The children had finished their mashed potatoes and gravy. It was already dusk; the wind was bitter and the darkening sky shrill with flitting birds, but she sent the children outside to play, anyway. Olive carried Molly in her arms. Alma heard the neighbouring children calling to Teddy to join their game.

She was full of nerves, and, she realised, desire. Usually, Alma wouldn't let Alfred kiss her, or even touch her hand, fearing what it might lead to. Each of them hoarded a stubborn resentment that had grown stronger than their needs. Now, suddenly alone together, Alfred looked uneasy. He wanted to talk; he couldn't talk. She recognised that imploring look men get.

He slid his braces from his shoulders.

'Don't,' she said.

'You're shivering.'

'It's cold.' She tried to laugh.

'Do you need a warm up?'

'I need to feel safe.'

'We'll be careful,' he promised.

But it wasn't easy to be careful. The Women's Christian Temperance Union had been campaigning to prevent the manufacture of prophylactics at Barnet Glass's rubber factory. She let him push her to the bed and pull up her skirt. He was rough with her, more confident. She suspected he had been with other women. Prostitutes, perhaps. Or some woman laid off from the ammunition works now the war was over. Alma was afraid of venereal disease which, the newspapers claimed, had been brought back by soldiers returning from Europe.

Ten minutes, they went at it. No words. Just the creaking bed, insistent, rhythmic, like the sound of someone sweeping a path.

He pulled out and finished over her with his hand. He got up and dressed, not even turning to look at her. When he left, Alma was able to breathe more freely.

A week passed and she did not see him. Did he feel guilty perhaps, or was he afraid of what their relapse might have signified to her? When he did turn up again to give her the five shillings, seeing how much he resented it, she asked, 'Do you remember that day you found us in the park?'

'Of course I do.'

'Do you wish you'd left me there?'

'No use crying over spilt milk,' he said.

Alfred had spoken without thinking, but it hurt her nevertheless. Is that what her life was? Spilt milk? A matter of regret? An accident?

'Don't you think I want a real life?' she cried at him. She wanted to strike him. 'A husband, a home for my children?'

'You always bring out the sob story,' Alfred said. 'Look. We met through my doing you a good deed.'

'Yes! And then you did me another good deed.'

So it went, on and on, every time Alfred came around. Since talking was a waste of time, they decided instead to save it. One day, a few weeks later, Alma heard that he was sweet on the Winch girl, who worked behind the counter at Griffiths Coffee Palace.

It was a miserable winter in Melbourne. The war might have been over, but in May seamen all over Australia went on strike; it lasted until August. Coal and food were in short supply. The foundry had to close through lack of orders and Alfred again joined the ranks of the unemployed. He had no money to give them. 'You'll have to go and line up at the Town Hall,' he told her.

Every day at the Town Hall, the Footscray Distress Committee distributed coupons for food and rent. When Alma arrived, there was already a long queue; everyone looked drawn and exhausted. She saw that Mr Goble was in charge. He was the same as ever, cheerful and resolute in a crisis. 'This must be Molly. My, how you've grown, young lady!'

Alma felt Mr Goble watching her, trying perhaps to gauge how she was coping with life. She was grateful for his kindness to her in the past, but equally she had never forgotten the first time they had met, when he said she had got herself into trouble.

The coupons allowed her to get through the next weeks, although Mr Gilbertson's butcher shop closed and Moran & Cato's rationed butter and eggs. Moira mentioned they had run out of coal and could not keep warm at night. Alma had enough to last a few weeks, so Moira's eldest, Paul, came in with their coal-scuttle. There was no side gate and he had to carry the coal from the shed back through Alma's house.

Alma was looking forward to the new year. A new decade. Some good luck, for a change. But 1920 passed, then another year. Children's birthdays came and went. She realised one day that they had been living in the house for three years. They hardly saw Alfred now.

One spring morning in 1921, there was a knock on the door. Molly ran down the hallway to answer it. Alma heard a man's voice and rose from her chair.

It was Mr Shepherd, the real estate agent. 'The rent is two weeks late,' he complained.

'But Mr Lovett pays our rent.'

'Well, I've seen neither hide nor hair of him this past month. I don't care who's at fault. If the arrears aren't paid without delay, you'll have to pack your things.'

Alma's stomach lurched. Pack your things. Homeless. The Plough. All her worst fears were coming to pass.

'I'll go and find out what's happened. The rent will be paid. I promise.'

'One week, not a day longer,' Mr Shepherd said. He looked at her warily. Alma knew she was just one of many tenants who got behind.

When she walked all the way to Empire Street, the house was locked up. The grass in the front was overgrown. Mrs Thomas next door had come out to the front fence to see who was standing there. She looked at Alma with surprising friendliness. 'Well, look who it is,' she said. 'The niece from Bendigo. Or thereabouts.'

75

Alma felt the same loathing she had felt when Mrs Thomas had mocked her piano playing. She frowned and asked when the Lovetts might be home.

'They moved away,' Mrs Thomas said. That was all. She wasn't going to give away any more than she had to.

'How can they just move away? Has the house been sold?'

Mrs Thomas let out a mirthless laugh. 'You'd have to ask their landlord.'

'But I thought—'

'You thought they owned the place? You poor thing. So many things you didn't know. That Alfred—he's quite a lad! He has an eye for the girls. But I suppose you already knew that.'

Mrs Thomas said she didn't have their forwarding address. 'I think they went back to Tasmania,' she added, unhelpfully.

Alma was facing eviction. She went to see the real estate agent in his office. 'So the bugger just disappeared?' Mr Shepherd asked. 'You should apply to the courts to make him support his child.'

But Molly had been born in secret. According to the law, she did not exist.

Moira showed Alma a piece she had cut out of the *Argus*. The Lincoln Knitting and Spinning Mills in Gaffney's Road in Coburg was expanding their operations and looking for women. Since opening in 1919, they had already employed more than eight hundred workers.

Once again Alma had to ask for Mr Goble's help. He arranged a grant of five guineas and helped her find a house in Eastwood

Street, near Kensington railway station, that cost £1-3/- a week. There was no way to pay Mr Shepherd the arrears. They left Pilgrim Street one Saturday morning, their few pieces of furniture piled in the back of an open lorry. They had to rush, as the driver charged by the hour, and there wasn't time even to say goodbye properly to Moira.

Teddy and Olive were enrolled at the Kensington State School, and Alma travelled with Molly by train early each morning to Batman Station. At the Lincoln Mills, Alma worked in the knitting department. There was a team of women who folded the garments as they came off the machines and piled them on long tables. She earned £2-4/- per week, a portion of which went to the Lincoln Mills crèche.

The men had the more important jobs, the machine supervisors and dyers and drivers. It was the women and girls who worked as sorters, inspectors, folders, finishers and menders. There were also the transfer girls and the loopers. The transfer girls brought the stocking tops to the knitting machines, where the loopers sewed together the foot of the stocking.

Alma had to stand all day with the deafening roar of the looms and other machinery. When she emerged into the sunshine at lunchtime, her ears rang from the noise of the machines. She was exhausted by afternoon. Her feet ached. The passengers on the train home often fell asleep. It was infectious: Alma felt her chin sinking into her chest, and she leaned against the shoulder of her neighbour as the carriage swayed. When the train braked coming into a station, all the bodies sat up and came awake for a second, seeing if it was their station; if it was not, they closed their eyes and immediately resumed their former position.

Alma made two friends at work, Lillian and Val, but she held back from men—she had learned in life that men cannot be relied on, that what they say is almost never what they mean; in every friendly remark from a man she got the whiff of Alfred.

In the lunch room she sat at the same table with Val and Lillian; if the weather was fine, the three of them took their sandwiches and found a sunny spot in the yard. Lillian lived in East Brunswick with her parents. Val was married and lived in Kensington. Neither had children. Alma told them her husband had died. She never mentioned a word about what had happened with Alfred. She had managed to bury her past and she had no intention of digging it up again.

The struggle to provide for her children, the privations her family had to endure, made Alma bitter. She had her hair cut short, the way women wore their hair since the end of the war. As her old skirts and blouses wore out, she bought a dress once in a blue moon, loose at the bust, with a lower waistline, the hem reaching to just below her knees. She did not wear make-up or jewellery, and felt like just another drab-looking worker on the train. She tried to eradicate any sign of gentleness lest it be seen by others as weakness.

When he turned fourteen, Teddy left school and went to work in the great network of sewers being constructed by the Melbourne and Metropolitan Board of Works. He earned twenty-five shillings a week. He came home from work a bit earlier than Alma, and when she got home she usually found him sitting in the kitchen in his filthy overalls, smoking a cigar.

The smell reminded her of Alfred, and she shooed him out to the washhouse.

Molly had started school at Kensington State School the previous year. She had to depend on her big sister for everything. Olive was the one who helped her get ready in the mornings, who walked her to school and came looking for her in the corner of the asphalt playground at lunchtime to make sure she was all right. In the afternoons, Olive minded Molly until Alma got home from work.

In his absence, Alfred became a monster in Alma's mind. She hoped Molly would forget all about him. It would be better that way: Molly had the surname Fairweather, like her brother and sister, so there was no cause for people to suspect she had a different father. She told Teddy and Olive that Alfred's name was never again to be mentioned, and that they were not to tell Molly that she had a different father from them.

Alma had fought for her children, and that was the story written into her face. The rod of iron will that had kept her alive in these difficult years now took the form of a private thought, a quietly burning determination that continued to fortify her—*Alfred will never see his daughter again.*

One night in July 1925, there was a great fire at the Lincoln Mills. The smoking ruins covered three and a half acres. The knitting department was completely destroyed. More than three hundred workers, mostly women, were put out of work. Alma was one of them.

It would take many months for the knitting mills to be rebuilt. Alma went without wages and once again they were behind with the rent. She looked for other work, to no avail. She couldn't feed and clothe her children. Olive had just turned fourteen and left school to look for a job. But there were so many people looking for work; if there was a job going, it usually went to a man. The only money coming in was Teddy's wages from the sewers.

Alma sought out her friend Val in the ladies' lounge of the pub in Macaulay Road, where she knew Val drank while her husband was in the public bar. The two women sat with their glasses of shandy. Alma had sixpence in her purse.

'When my friend Milly's husband died,' Val told her, 'there was an orphanage in Brighton where she sent her children to be looked after for a while.'

'I'm not sending Molly to any orphanage,' Alma said.

'It isn't only for orphans. They can take a child in for a few weeks or a few months if the mother is ill, or if the family has come into some other misfortune. Milly said they looked after her two little ones very well.'

On the 6th of October, Alma posted a letter to Mr J. C. Butler, the superintendent of the orphanage, requesting an appointment. She felt uneasy about the whole thing. The place was called the Melbourne Orphan Asylum. Wasn't an *asylum* meant for mad people?

A few days later she received his reply and took the train from Kensington, changing at Flinders Street for Middle Brighton. She walked the short distance through orderly streets that smelled of the sea. It was a calm October evening; the light lingered in the air. It wouldn't be so bad, she told herself. It's only for a little while; as soon as I start back at work, I'll come and get her.

The superintendent was a kindly man, used to dealing with people in difficult circumstances. A large mahogany desk almost filled his study. He kept his books in a glass cabinet. His manner was gentle yet decisive.

'Mrs Fairweather, I cannot promise anything, because the matter will have to be considered by the board, but I can tell you that I shall be recommending that Molly be taken into care. I consider hers a deserving case.'

Alma wept, at first out of gratitude, then out of sadness. She couldn't think how she would explain it to Molly.

Mr Butler helped Alma fill in the application:

Applicant: Mrs Alma Fairweather
Child proposed to be taken into care: Molly Fairweather, age
7 years, born Footscray. Church of England, baptised.
(Alma had invented this.)
Present Address: 61 Eastwood Street, Kensington
Date of Birth: 3 July 1893
Date of Marriage: 11 August 1909
Occupation: Folder
Employer's Name and Address: Lincoln Mills, Gaffney
Street, Coburg.
Usual income: £2-4/-
Present Situation: Unemployed.

Mr Butler screwed the cap back on his fountain pen and placed it on the desk. He then took up a pencil and wrote in the space on the admission form under FATHER:

Father of above child not married to mother. Mother not receiving
any assistance from him, and in the child's interest desires to sever all

connection with the father, so that the child may grow up quite ignorant of her illegitimacy.

On the 11th of November, 1925, the board passed the application for admission. The approval was signed by Messrs Berry and Peacock on behalf of the committee, and by Mr J. C. Butler himself. On Monday the 16th of November, Molly was admitted to the orphanage.

Molly

BRIGHTON, 1925

THE DAY MUM packed her suitcase and took her on the train to the Melbourne Orphan Asylum, she told Molly not to be frightened, that she had already met both Mr Butler, the Superintendent, and the Matron, Miss Thompson, and that they were both very nice.

Mum had not called it the Melbourne Orphan Asylum. She had told Molly that she was going to stay at 'the Children's Home', a happy place where lots of children all lived together. She was going to stay there 'just for a spell'.

'I'll come and see you every Sunday,' Mum promised.

'You won't forget?'

'How could I forget my little lamb? I love my lamb and one day very soon you'll come home again and everything will be just like it used to be, good as gold.'

As they walked along Dendy Street, Mum carrying the suitcase, Molly felt excited, as though something good was going to happen, but her stomach felt the way it did when something bad was going to happen.

The houses in Brighton were bigger than in Kensington. The curious trees lowered their heads and peered at her. Molly pressed in close against Mum.

'You'll be all right here,' Mr Butler told her. 'It's really just like being on holidays, except you'll be going to school.'

'What if I want to go home?'

Mr Butler smiled at her in his friendly way. 'I'm quite certain that you'll like living here with us.' He was a tall man in a three-piece suit with a watch chain across his vest. He had kind, blue eyes and a white moustache, though he didn't look old. But still Molly didn't want Mum to go home without her.

The floor of Mr Butler's office had black and white squares, which Molly tried to count in an effort to calm herself. Mr Butler asked her to sit down next to him. He asked Molly questions about herself. Which grade she was in at school. The names of her brother and sister. What her favourite colour was.

Mr Butler showed Molly and Mum to her new Cottage Home. The smell inside was different from any house she had been in. Was it lamb stew mixed with the smell of wet paint? No, not wet paint; it was floor polish. Mrs Field, the Cottage Home Mother, had just finished using an electric polishing machine on the linoleum.

The first thing Molly noticed about Mrs Field was that she had very broad hips. She was dressed in a brown skirt and a neat white blouse, but on her feet she wore a pair of old bedroom slippers with splits at the sides through which a couple of swollen toes poked out. She was red-faced and her eyes watered.

Mrs Field was admiring her floor when they came in. 'There you are,' she said to Molly. 'Do you like it here? I suppose you don't know yet, do you? I can promise you the food is decent. You get exactly the same as Mr Field and me. Come with me and I'll show you where I keep the treacle tin.'

Molly looked at Mum, who pressed her lips together and nodded.

Mrs Field took her upstairs to show her the dormitories, each with a row of six beds. She showed Molly which bed was hers. 'I'll be here every day to help you, Molly. I can already see that you are a very good girl, and I'm quite certain that you'll be happy, living here with us.'

Molly was quiet. What troubled her was the thought of not having Olive in her room. If Molly woke from a bad dream in the night, she would be in a room of strangers.

The orphanage had six main buildings. The administration building was the biggest, with its tower. It was where Mr Butler lived with his wife and also had his office. There were four other two-storey Cottage Homes where the children lived, as well as the hospital block. Every cottage had a married couple who were Cottage Mothers and Fathers.

In the dining room in Molly's cottage, there were lots of tables, each set for six children, pretty crockery, instead of the old enamel plates and mugs they had at home, and each girl had her own serviette, and a wooden serviette ring with a carving of a different animal. There was a serving hatch to the kitchen and beside it was the cupboard where Mrs Field showed her, as promised, the big five-pound tin of treacle.

'We have twelve acres of farmland and gardens here,' Mrs Field told her. 'We have a dairy herd so we get our own fresh milk. You can join in the milking, if you like! We grow our own vegetables. There are two gardeners, Mr Burrows and Mr Williams. When your mother comes to visit you on Sundays, you can have picnics in the garden.' Molly was already anxious about remembering all the new names.

When she came downstairs again, Mum and Mr Butler were gone.

When Molly turned to ask where Mum was, Mrs Field said, 'Your mother must have been called away.' She smiled down at Molly. But her mouth was wrong, her clothes were wrong, and those old slippers were wrong. Mrs Field was not her mother and everything felt new and wrong. Molly began to sob.

'What's this?' Mrs Field asked, and for the first time Molly detected a hint of tiredness and irritation in her voice.

'Nothing.'

'Little girls don't cry for no reason. You can tell me,' Mrs Field patted Molly's hair. 'You can talk to me about anything.'

But Molly could not tell Mrs Field why she was crying because she herself didn't really understand it. An immense feeling of grief and dread began welling up inside her. The hard part about being sent here was that there seemed no end in sight. No one had told her when she would be going home. Even the word 'home' hurt her now, because Molly no longer knew where her home was supposed to be.

The first night in her new home, Molly learned the golden rule: 'No talking after lights out!'

She lay awake for a long time in her new bed. It felt strangely quiet. At home in Kensington, the last thing she heard before she fell asleep and the first thing she heard in the morning was the clatter of the trains going past.

The moon cast half-shadows across the room. She looked around at the girls in their beds. Doris was asleep. Vera stirred and said something Molly couldn't understand. Perhaps in her sleep she was still on the other side of the world, in England, where the King lived.

The edges of the curtain fluttered in the breeze. Molly climbed out of bed and walked over to the window. She stood there and shared in the secret business of the night. She stared up at the sky: the stars didn't seem to have any interest in her. The children in the other Cottage Homes were probably all asleep in their beds.

She could see across the garden to where a lone light bulb glowed in one of the windows. She could not see anyone awake in the room, or anything inside the room.

A voice from behind startled her. 'What are you doing?'

It was Cheryl, her big bossy body sitting up in bed, looking at her, demanding an answer.

'I think someone is awake in the cottage over there.'

'That's the hospital block. That's where they put you when you're going to die.'

Molly said nothing.

'And another thing. You must lie very still in bed and pretend you are asleep, even if you are not. Matron makes calls in here during the night to see if any children are awake, because only wicked children can't go to sleep, she says. When you don't go to sleep or if you wake up in the night, Matron takes you to a room all by yourself and you have to sleep in a box with a lid on top.'

'I would scream for help,' Molly said. 'Mr Butler would come and rescue me.'

Molly thought she would be so frightened in that dark box that she wouldn't be able to stop screaming.

'If you scream, two men come and they hammer on the lid with lots of nails so that even if you do scream, no one can hear you.'

Cheryl was whispering, but Molly recognised a kind of delight in her voice, as she watched the effect of her words in Molly's face in the half-light.

'Bessie Tobias was taken to the hospital block last week,' Cheryl said.

'Did she wake up in the night?'

'No. She was sick.'

'Maybe they keep the light on all night to keep her awake, so she won't die.'

One of the girls behind them groaned in her sleep.

Molly tried to learn the names of the other children—not all of them, of course, because there were more than a hundred children living in the orphanage—but the names of the girls in her Cottage Home. She got to know the Sisson kids, whose mum had died. There was Charlotte, Frances and Violet. Doris and Elizabeth Connell were nice to her. Doris was a year older than Molly, Elizabeth a year younger. There was Dianne, who wore the same mustard-coloured pinafore every day. And there was Vera Wood, an English girl, who talked with an accent.

Molly tried to keep out of Cheryl's way.

On Sunday mornings, the children were collected and taken to different churches. Molly attended St Peter's Sunday school because Mum had told Mr Butler she had been baptised in the Church of England. The lady there gave her a postcard with a picture of God in the sky.

When Molly got back, Mum was waiting for her on the seats outside the administration building. She was wearing her old woollen overcoat, and it was the familiarity of her coat, more than seeing Mum herself, that made Molly burst into tears. Mum was so happy to see her. She wrapped her arms around Molly, squeezing her, and taking in deep breaths. Molly knew she was trying not to cry, too.

'Where's Teddy and Olive?'

'They're at home,' Mum said.

'Didn't they want to come?'

'They wanted very much to come and see you.'

'So why didn't you let them?'

Mum took the handkerchief from her pocket, dabbed at her eyes, then laughed at herself. 'Look at me. Aren't I a silly old thing?'

'You're not silly.'

'Yes, I am. I didn't want Teddy and Olive to come. I feel ashamed I had to send you here. I wish I was back at the knitting mills. Then I'd have enough money for you to come home.'

'I want to come home, too.'

'Are you very homesick, love?'

'What's homesick?' Visions of being alone in the hospital block suddenly rose in Molly's mind.

Mum just laughed, and gave her a cuddle. 'Come on. Let's have our lunch.'

She had brought egg sandwiches, some oranges and a brown paper bag of Milk Arrowroot biscuits. They had their picnic in the orphanage garden.

The garden was laid out in a formal design: a circular lawn with a round pond in the middle, and a fountain. On four sides of the lawn, curving paths cut in and formed their own circles, with hedges on their periphery and garden beds in the centre, so that the whole design was like a circle with intersecting rings. On the edges of the garden there were more paths leading to stands of fruit trees. Between the garden and the administration building stood three huge cypress trees.

Other groups of children and visitors were seated here and there on rugs. Mum kept asking questions—what school was like, whether her teacher was strict, what dinners they had at the Cottage Home. Molly could see that Mum was talking so much to hide the fact that she felt sad.

After lunch, Mum took her for a walk to the beach. The wind was cold. It was the first time Molly had seen the ocean, the shimmering light on the surface of all that endless blue water. The lines of waves rode in and broke on the sand. Mum called them white horses, though they were not horses at all.

When Mum was leaving she told Molly she would be back to see her next Sunday. Seven whole days! The week stretched ahead, the long days to be got through before she saw Mum again.

Teddy and Olive usually came with Mum on Sundays after that.

❖❖❖

Molly attended Brighton Beach State School No. 2048, which was situated within the grounds of the orphanage. Her classroom, with its rostrum, blackboard with the alphabet written across the top, the lines of wooden desks, looked just like her old one in Kensington. Outside children mixed with the orphanage kids. All the children wore the same uniforms and boots, so it was difficult to tell them apart, except that at twelve o'clock the orphanage kids went back to their Cottage Homes to have their dinner.

Her teacher was Mr Hammer, who wore brightly coloured waistcoats—the only item of his dress that changed from day to day. Sometimes there were fights between the boys, but not often. If Mr Hammer caught them fighting, he pulled the culprits away by their ears and took them to get the strap. Mr Hammer marked the roll, wrote on the blackboard in a very neat hand, and spent hours doing splendid drawings in coloured chalks. As long as the children were quiet, he took little interest in their progress. He walked slowly down the aisles of desks, his hands in his pockets, glancing over their shoulders to inspect their penmanship, pausing from time to time to smack a boy across the back of the head. This didn't count as punishment to Mr Hammer; he said it was just to wake them up.

Mr Hammer was watchful, even when you thought he wasn't. When he was writing on the blackboard, without turning his head, he could name any boy or girl who dared to talk. His talent for this was uncanny. In the dead of afternoon, when a band of sunshine stretched into their room, Mr Hammer would fold his hands behind his head and sway back on the rear legs of his chair, and at that moment he had on his face the look of a lizard sunning himself.

Sometimes, groups of boys stood along the painted white line that marked the limit of their section of the yard. They called out things to the girls, but not even the bravest boy dared step into the girls' yard. If the girls told on them, the boys would get the strap.

One Saturday morning, Molly felt sick. Mrs Field said she could lie on her bed until she felt better. She heard the noise of the other children playing outside, the whoops and cries of the boys playing their ball games, the repetitive singsong voices of the girls skipping rope and playing hopscotch.

Shortly before midday, she heard the girls coming in.

'Did you see the new girl?' asked Vera, who had come up the stairs with Doris and Elizabeth Connell.

'She looks strange, doesn't she?' said one of the others. 'Do you believe she really used to be in the circus?'

'No, she's a little fibber,' replied Vera.

'Well, I heard her say that in the yard. She said her whole family used to be in the circus.'

There were children leaving the orphanage and others arriving all the time. Usually they left when they turned fourteen and were old enough for Mr Butler to find them employment somewhere. There were also those whose family circumstances had changed and one or both parents were able to keep them now. Often the arrivals were all from one family—three, four or five brothers and sisters whose father or mother had died.

That night, the new girl sat at Molly's table. Her name was Bonnie Marconi. Molly had never met an Italian before. She had a dark complexion and her black hair fell naturally into tight crinkle curls.

'Did you used to be in the circus?' Molly asked.

'The circus? No! I just told the others that to keep them off my back. They were teasing me and saying that I look funny.'

Bonnie had three little brothers and one older sister. They had been sent here after their father died. Their father had worked on the railways, she said.

'How did he die?' Molly asked.

'He just got sick.' Bonnie missed her mother terribly. 'I am just waiting for the day when we can all go home again,' she told Molly.

'Mum says that *this* is home for the time being.'

Molly heard Bonnie crying during the night. 'Stop crying. You'll make yourself sick,' she whispered. She felt sorry for Bonnie.

Molly and Bonnie were soon best friends. When it was Molly's turn to be breakfast monitor, it was natural that Bonnie should help. They warmed themselves by the kitchen radiator while Mrs Field was in front of the stove. Steam rose from the big pot of porridge and misted the windows. It was warm and comfortable, waiting in the kitchen. Both girls were quiet. Bonnie had a dreamy look in her eyes, her mouth relaxed, her lips protruding. Molly knew that Bonnie was thinking of home.

Her own memories of her mother and sister and brother had to be kept safe at the bottom of her heart so that she would not always be thinking of them and feeling the hurt of being away from them. But sometimes one of those hoarded memories escaped and Molly felt it burning her throat and stinging her eyes.

She tried to pretend everything was all right, but as she got through her days, she felt self-conscious and foolish and above all she wondered if she had been tricked: as if somewhere—up in the sky, in heaven?—an unseen audience was silently laughing at her. Molly felt that she must be sillier than other girls to allow this calamity to happen to her.

But the companionship of Bonnie gave her strength. If I have a friend, Molly thought, then I mustn't be completely silly and useless. 'Bonnie?' she asked one day. 'Do you think we have been sent here because we did something wrong?'

Bonnie looked thoughtful. 'We might have,' she said. 'Do you mean like the sins they teach us about at Sunday school?

Molly had never been to Sunday school before coming to the orphanage. This was just one more way in which she felt inadequate; one more secret she had to keep, even from her friend.

'What sin did you commit?' Bonnie asked, when Molly hadn't answered.

The heat of injustice rose to Molly's face. 'That's just it,' she said. 'I don't know. If only I knew, I might be able to understand.'

'I didn't come here because of a sin,' Bonnie told her. She had already turned eight, and knew life better than Molly. 'The only reason we had to come here was because our daddy died.'

Molly put her arms around the other girl and held her tightly, and they became even better friends after that.

Molly soon got used to life at the orphanage. There was a chook shed where Mr Butler let the girls and boys collect the eggs as long as they promised to be careful and not break any. The chook shed smelled like things that had gone bad. Some of the eggs were brown, some speckled, and some had streaks of broken yolk and tiny downy feathers on the outside. At the front of the chook shed there were windows made with wire. When she was inside, the wind came through the wire, and just under the corrugated roof there was a gap with blue sky. Molly was always frightened she would break an egg or disappoint Mr Butler.

All the children loved Mr Butler. He told them at assembly that it was his duty to set out to win the children's love and confidence.

One of the older girls told Molly that Mr Butler had taken up his post three years earlier and that, thanks to him, many changes and improvements had been made. The boys now wore pyjamas instead of the cotton nightshirts they used to have to wear; and they had normal haircuts, not the shaven heads that used to make the orphanage boys stand out at school. On Sundays now, the girls were allowed to wear shoes instead of boots. Mr Butler had mirrors put in all the bathrooms and dressing rooms so they could see how they looked. And there was Miss Armitage, who came one afternoon a week to teach the girls needlework.

The first thing Molly made was an apron with plain stitching. She learned how to tack up the hem, then to finish the job with small neat stitches. She wore a thimble so as not to prick her fingers. Molly often made mistakes and had to unpick her work. She went on to make a nightgown, another apron, a plain pinafore of navy blue cotton, and also learned how to darn and mend, and, later, how to embroider and how to do fancy work.

One afternoon, Molly and Bonnie found themselves alone

inside the Cottage Home. Mrs Field was on an errand, and the other girls were playing in the garden. Idly, the girls began going through the cupboards to see what they could find.

Under the patterns in Mrs Field's sewing cupboard, Molly found a typed sheet of paper. 'Bonnie! Look at this!' she cried.

> *Prices for Children's Funerals*
> *Coffin and Conveyance to Brighton Cemetery*
> *Children under 4 years £2-0-0*
> *Children under 7 years £2-10-0*
> *Children under 10 years £3-0-0*
> *Over 10 years, rates to be arranged*

'If I die, Mum will have to pay two pounds ten shillings,' Molly said.

'No. She will have to pay three pounds,' Bonnie told her. 'Only children under seven cost two pounds ten.'

'So Mum could have saved ten shillings if I had died last year.'

'Don't talk about dying.'

'Why not?'

'It might come true.'

Molly folded the piece of paper, replaced it under the patterns, and the girls went outside. She felt guilty that she had seen that list. But why should she feel guilty? She tried to forget about it, but late that night, as she lay sleepless in her bed, she wondered how many children had died at the orphanage. She was certain that Mum and Teddy and Olive would cry at her funeral. Still, she felt bad because Mum would have to pay for her even when she had died.

When Molly had arrived, the hall was still being built. Now it was finished, it also served as their gymnasium. There were games organised there after school. She liked the smell of the rubber mats that were placed on the other side of the vaulting horse. The Roman rings hanging from the ceiling were tied to the wall when the hall was used for an assembly. The super-intendent's cottage was finished too, and Mr and Mrs Butler moved from their old quarters in the administration building.

Mr Butler bought a washing machine, so the older girls would no longer have to do the laundry by hand. There was a new hydro extractor and a rotary gas iron in the laundry, and he purchased coke-burning hot water services for each of the Cottage Homes. Mr Butler even had the name changed from the Melbourne Orphan Asylum to the Melbourne Orphanage, and had a radio installed. He told the children that it cost a hundred pounds. The master radio set was in the senior boys' cottage and the programmes relayed through loudspeakers in each of the other cottages. The girls complained that they never got to choose the programme.

Molly held her breath every time the monitors distributed the post around the Cottage Homes. But months had passed and Molly had not received a single letter or postcard. She didn't expect to hear from her old friends at Kensington State School: she had left suddenly and never had a chance to say goodbye. Mum was ashamed of sending her to the orphanage, and didn't want anyone to know.

One day when she came in to dinner, Bonnie asked, 'Did you find your letter? I put it on your pillow. You weren't here when the monitors came.'

Molly raced upstairs, nearly colliding with Mrs Field. She

recognised Mum's handwriting: Molly Fairweather, C/-Melbourne Orphanage, Dendy Street, Brighton, S.5. Mum wrote that she missed her and that she promised to visit as usual the following Sunday. It was just a short note, but it made Molly feel special finally to receive a letter of her own.

'Did Robert Hepper really run away?' Bonnie asked.

'Yes, he did. Lillian said so,' Molly told her.

'Well, Lillian wouldn't know. Lillian makes things up. Do you remember that time she said her father had let her drive his motorcar to a birthday party? Well, it turned out she had done nothing of the sort.'

'Really? How can Lillian be so wicked as to lie like that?'

'It's in her nature. My mother says that when a girl tells lies it is a sign of a wicked nature.'

Molly often heard stories of children who had run away. Usually they'd been given permission to stay with their mum for a holiday, and their mum had found them a job to earn money and hadn't brought them back. Molly happened to be sitting on one of the seats outside the administration building the following afternoon, when Robert Hepper was brought back. He expected to be punished, but after some time in Mr Butler's study he came out quite cheerful, not crying at all, and he went back to his cottage.

Molly loved school. She was nine and in fourth grade. In the playground, her teacher, Miss Ormond, was strict to all the other children, but nice to her own class. Molly loved the routines.

Miss Ormond had made her a monitor and Molly took her duties seriously, going into the classroom early to clean the blackboard while the others were lined up in twos outside.

So Molly let out a groan when, on one of her Sunday visits, Mum told her that she would be going home at last the following week.

'I thought you'd be pleased!' Mum said.

'What about the Lincoln Mills?'

'Oh, I don't have to go to that old place any more!'

'Why not?'

'I stopped working there ages ago! Didn't I tell you?'

'Where do you work now?'

'I don't have to work.' And just then, Mum looked guilty. Over the past few months, her appearance had changed. She wore dresses in the new, looser style that made her look younger. She smiled more, too.

Molly had read about falling in love in magazines, and overheard the older girls whispering about it.

Mum said, 'I thought you'd be happy to come home to me and Teddy and Olive.' But after nearly two years, the orphanage was Molly's home. She was happy here among her friends. Her dormitory wouldn't be *her* room any more. She would not see Miss Ormond or Bonnie or Mrs Field.

Several times at school that week, Molly started crying. Miss Ormond asked her what the matter was. Molly's group was to put on the play the following week and the realisation that she would not be here to participate was the thing that upset her. But it wasn't just the play; it was the feeling that she would be missing from her familiar world, the everyday life that was hers. It was all she knew now.

On the Friday afternoon, Miss Ormond organised a going-away for Molly. At lunchtime while the children were playing in the yard, Miss Ormond decorated the classroom with coloured streamers, and there were plates of cakes she had baked and bottles of Ecks lemonade. At the end of the party, Miss Ormond made a speech and gave Molly a present, wrapped in bright paper and tied with a pink ribbon. Mum's presents were never wrapped in such magnificent paper! Molly opened the present in front of the class. When she saw what it was, she felt like crying with happiness. A brand new Bible, with her name inscribed on the first page. Miss Ormond had signed her name and written, 'Remember us, Brighton, 1928'.

Suddenly it was Molly's last day. In the morning, girls came up to say their goodbyes. All her friends made an appearance, except Bonnie.

She found Bonnie sitting by herself in the storeroom. 'Have you been hiding up here all this time?' she asked Bonnie. She could see Bonnie had been crying. They had been friends for so long, but now Molly was going away, it was difficult to talk to each other.

'I'll miss you.'

'Please, don't cry!' Molly said. 'I'll come and visit you.'

'It won't be the same.'

'Why not?'

'Because if you come and visit, you won't be one of us any more.'

'Oh, give me a kiss!' Molly stretched out her arms and Bonnie allowed herself to be hugged and gave Molly a kiss on the cheek.

'Now, see, that's better, isn't it?' Molly said.

Bonnie laughed and nodded, and tried to look cheerful, even with her blotchy face.

Molly was going home to her family. But she was also leaving her family.

Molly

FOOTSCRAY, 1928

MUM AND BILL Williams fetched her from the orphanage
in Bill's car and drove to the house in Eldridge Street.

It felt strange that Mum and Teddy and Olive had moved
into Bill's house when, all the time she had been at the
orphanage, Molly had continued to think of them still living
in Eastwood Street, Kensington. Before that, the family had
lived in Seddon. And before that? There was no before that.
Teddy and Olive took her for a walk and showed her the house
in the next street, Empire Street, where they said they used
to live before she was born, but it didn't mean anything to
Molly.

At one end of Eldridge Street was a rope works; the ammunition factory was at the other end. There was a lane at the back
of Eldridge Street, above the quarry. Inside the fence, next to

the lane, Bill kept his chook run. He sold chooks and turkeys to people from all over Footscray.

Bill had black glossy hair with a part down the middle. His thin lips gave his face a cunning look, though he was always gentle and considerate towards Molly. Mum sometimes said, 'That Bill Williams! He's a bit of a rogue.' She also said, 'Bill doesn't let his left hand know what his right hand is doing.'

Inside the house everything was a variation on brown. Walls, wainscot, doors, blinds, the wooden floor—all of it was beige, brown, fawn. Along the hallway was the sitting room where, soon after she arrived, Teddy made her try his cigar and she was nearly sick trying to spit out the taste.

Molly went to Footscray State, her third school. She was in the fifth grade. In the afternoons, the kids all played together in the street. The girls played hopscotch and jacks, and the boys had their bags of marbles. Molly quickly learned the names of the kids; she had already forgotten some of the children at the orphanage. She remembered Bonnie, though, and they wrote letters to each other for a while. But then, for no particular reason, the letters stopped.

When Molly told the kids at school that she had lived in an orphanage for two years, and when she saw the dark cloud pass over their faces, she was quick to assure them that she had been happy there. None of them believed that a child could be happy at an orphanage, even though she told them about the swimming pool, the cows in the paddocks, the big garden, the trips to the beach.

There were times when Molly felt that she didn't really belong either at school or at home. Maybe this feeling came from living in the orphanage—she couldn't be sure. Her name was Fairweather, just like her brother and sister. But there was something different about her. She was blonde, while Olive and Teddy had dark hair. Their skin was darker too.

Olive was seventeen, Teddy nineteen. Teddy still worked in the sewers. Olive had a job at the Spotswood Bottle Works. 'I work on the line that makes beer bottles,' she told Molly. 'There are these big American machines that make the bottles. Once the bottles have been pressure-tested, my job is to sort them into crates lined with newspaper.'

Mum stayed home and looked after the house, because now she had Bill to earn money. He worked as a slaughterman at the Angliss Imperial Freezing Works and he had his chicken business as well.

Bill took Molly to the meatworks one day and showed her around. The first things she noticed were the bad smell and the lowing of cattle in the yards. It seemed to her like a miniature city. It had its own train track and siding. Bill showed her where the cattle trucks came in from the country, the yards, the chute where he worked, the rails along the passages where the lambs and sides of beef were pushed to the chillers. There were also skin-drying sheds, the boiling-down works, the cannery and meat-preserving works. She was shocked by the sound of the gun, and the way the cow's legs suddenly collapsed at the top of the chute. The men secured chains around the poor thing's legs, then it disappeared inside.

Every morning, Mum walked with Molly as far as Ballarat Road to make sure she got safely across. Once she was on the other side, she waved to Mum and ran the rest of the way to her new school by herself.

Back at the orphanage, she had made friends easily, but now

she often spent lunchtime alone in the schoolyard. If someone came up and spoke to her, she was friendly, and if some of the girls invited her into their skipping game, or to play jacks, she was happy enough to join in. She just seldom made the first move. On rainy days, girls had to stay in their own shelter shed, boys in another. Molly often thought of Bonnie, and missed the Brighton Beach State School. It was as though a part of herself had stayed there, and the other part couldn't feel at home in this new school.

Her teacher, Mr Bates, was strict, but Molly liked him. The children sat at their wooden desks with their heads bent over their exercise books, hardly daring to look up unless Mr Bates was speaking. Molly liked the classroom smell of the wood fire, pencil shavings, orange peel, sandwiches. Sometimes the smell of tobacco came from the staff room. She also caught a whiff of the leather schoolbags that hung on hooks in the corridor outside, as well as the smell of the incinerator in the yard.

There was a lot about Mum that Molly didn't know. She knew, of course, that Bill Williams was not their dad. And she knew that Mum was thirty-five years old and Bill was twenty-four, and that Mum didn't like people to know. There were things Olive and Teddy knew that she didn't know, because sometimes when Molly asked questions, they told her that some things are only for grown-ups.

She couldn't remember their father. Sometimes Olive mentioned him, but she didn't say much. Molly could often tell what Olive was thinking, because Olive had looked after her when she was small, and the sisters were close. Molly could never tell what Teddy was thinking.

Teddy was going out with Rosie and it was understood that soon they would be married. Rosie worked at Ball and Welch in Flinders Street and had sold umbrellas, gloves and handkerchiefs. Now she worked in the lace department along with twenty-seven other girls. The employees at Ball and Welch received a discount on purchases, and Rosie wore the latest fashions; she always seemed to have a new hat or new shoes.

Because Molly was shy and didn't talk much, the grown-ups sometimes forgot she was in the room. 'Did you see the way Teddy looked at her tonight?' Mum asked Bill. 'I think we can safely say that our Teddy's on the hook.'

'Rosie's a looker, all right.'

'As long as you're not looking, Mr Williams,' Mum said, but from her tone Molly knew she was joking. Mum often called Bill 'Mr Williams' and he called her 'Mrs Williams' even though they weren't married.

Olive had been to the pictures with a man who worked at Standard Quarries, and who everyone called Hoppy because of his fondness for the Hopalong Cassidy stories, which had been appearing in magazines for some years. He was mad about cowboy pictures, too. Olive and Hoppy went to the Grand or the Trocadero on Saturday nights, depending on what was showing.

Hoppy seemed always to be tired and dragged his feet when he walked: wearing his heavy quarry boots, even when he wasn't. Most evenings the two couples sat on the porch and talked. Teddy and Hoppy smoked. Sometimes Bill stuck his head in to say hello. Mum stayed peaceful in the kitchen, listening to the wireless, and helping Molly with her sewing or knitting.

'You know, my life hasn't been easy,' Mum told her. 'Well, that's nothing special, I don't suppose there're many people who haven't seen hard times. All my life I've spent jumping around from one place to the next, for one reason or another, and now at last I feel settled. I think this kitchen is my favourite place on earth.'

Molly liked to hide in the bushes and listen to the two couples on the porch. She could see their legs: their trousers, their stockings, their shoes. Sometimes they took the gramophone outside and practised the Black Bottom and the Charleston. If there was just one couple on the porch, and it was late, and they weren't talking, Molly could raise her head above the bushes to see them kissing. It was usually about that time she heard Mum calling her to tell her it was bedtime.

On Saturday afternoons after work, Bill's friends came and sat in the kitchen. Molly watched from the back door. Bill sat at the end of the scrubbed pine table with his hat on and a pencil in his hand, making marks on pieces of paper. The men counted out their two-shilling pieces, and sometimes Bill gave money back to them. They listened to the racing results on the wireless, and sometimes one of the men yelled in an excited way and Molly could not tell whether the man was very happy or very angry. She didn't like the cigarette smoke and the noise. She played in the backyard or with the neighbouring kids down the lane along the cliff above the quarry. Some of the kids in her street went to her school, and she had been to play at Louise and Jenny Talbot's house near the corner.

Late one Sunday afternoon, when Mum had gone out visiting and Teddy and Olive were out, too, Molly saw Bill in his gumboots and rubber apron, hosing out the killing shed.

As soon as she realised she had the house to herself, Molly went into Mum and Bill's room. She liked the feeling that there were secrets to be discovered. Mum kept a tin in the drawer of her dressing table. The tin was purple with a picture of violets on it. It had once contained chocolates. Inside the tin was a picture of a big house that looked like a farmhouse, with wide verandahs and a horse and cart pulled up out the front. Molly had looked at this picture before. On the back of the photograph, someone had written in ink, *Bellevue*. Molly had made up a story that once upon a time Mum was rich and used to live in that house. And maybe it was true. Why else would Mum have kept a picture of the house? It was a mystery, but of course Molly couldn't ask Mum about it without giving herself away.

There were no photographs of them as babies. Molly had been told that their dad had been killed in the Great War. But she had never seen a picture of their dad, not a soldier in uniform, or a wedding photograph of Mum and him, or his medals. She knew that soldiers who had been killed in the war got medals. In Louise and Jenny's house there was a photograph of a man in uniform on their mantelpiece. She didn't have the courage to ask who it was. There must have been pictures like that in many houses, Molly thought, photographs of faces, in lounge rooms where a father or a son or a brother should have been.

When Teddy came home from the Board of Works, he washed himself in the basin and changed out of his overalls. Teddy seemed like a giant to Molly. After he had changed into his trousers and flannel shirt, he sat at the kitchen table, smoking and reading the *Herald,* which he bought from the corner shop on his way home. If he found something interesting, he read it out to Molly. Late one afternoon when Mum was still at the shops, and Teddy had taken up his usual spot with the newspaper, he said to Molly, 'Listen to this. A lady was murdered in her orchard over in Mitcham. It says that her injuries were caused by a blunt instrument, such as the blunt end of an axe.'

'That's terrible!' Molly cried. She had never heard of such an appalling thing. 'Why don't the police put him in jail?'

'They're out looking for him right at this minute. But,' said Teddy, winking, 'if there's a murderer on the loose, you'd better watch yourself. You never know when he might be tempted to strike again. You'd better be careful, Molly. You're just the kind of little girl a murderer would be looking for.'

She knew Teddy was teasing her, but that night as she lay in bed, she could not get the thought of the Murderer out of her mind.

When she came home from school, Molly followed Mum from room to room, helping with the chores, sweeping and dusting. She also had her scrapbook with the pictures she had cut out of Mum's magazines, the *Australian Woman's Mirror* and the *New Idea.* There was her drawing book and crayons, her needlework and the collection of clothes she had made for her doll. Her favourite time was the late afternoon when the family was all home together, the smell of food cooking, and she knew that Mum was happy with Bill. Molly was happy too, even when Teddy tweaked her ear and told her stories about the Murderer.

Apart from the killing shed, there was another shed with an old car inside, covered in cobwebs and dust, with no wheels, resting on wooden blocks. Bill had bought it from a man, intending to fix it up one day. Molly was not allowed to go in there because Mum said that the bloody great thing was in danger of falling on somebody.

There was dirty glass in the windows of the shed and a hard, greasy dirt floor. From one of the roof beams a heavy rope hung from a pulley, two metal wheels bolted to the roof beam, the rope hanging from a hook. Teddy and Olive called it the 'hangman's noose', although there was just a loop of chain at the end of the rope, not a noose at all. Teddy told Molly that a murderer had once been hanged in there: 'That's what happens to murderers. Murderers get hung.'

When the girls in Eldridge Street visited each other's houses, they usually played indoors. Sometimes Louise and Jenny came to the front door and asked Mum if Molly was allowed to play. Mum almost always said yes, and Molly dutifully took them into the bedroom and showed them her dolls, her patterns and needlework, the pictures she had clipped from magazines. It was the groups of boys who ran wild out of doors. Molly was careful of the boys who came to play in the lane. They threw stones at you, and played complicated games where they took you prisoner and locked you in a crate in next door's shed. Even so, Molly liked to go off by herself down the lane. There were blackberry bushes, daisies in springtime, and holes in the wire fence where she could crawl through and sit on the very edge of the cliff and look down into the quarry.

Sometimes in the night—it must have been past midnight— the back gate creaked open and she heard the night man taking the can from the back of the outhouse, his quiet curses as he slammed it against the side of his cart and emptied it. The draught horse tramped on along the lane. Then she heard the sounds repeated as the night soil was removed from next door.

She remembered how scared she had been those first nights at the orphanage. But then she thought of how quickly those frightening, unfamiliar rooms, and the sounds from the other buildings in the night, had come to feel normal. She thought about Bonnie, and wondered if she was still at the orphanage, or whether some relative had come to claim her and she was living her life somewhere else. She decided to write to Bonnie again. If she had left the orphanage, Mr Butler would forward her letter to Bonnie at her new address.

After hearing the night man it was hard to get back to sleep and, lying awake in the dark, other thoughts came to her. She imagined the night man had a dirty face, like a picture of coalminers she had once seen in the *Argus*, their cheeks streaked, their eyes unnaturally big and clear. She wondered if the night man might have even been the Murderer himself.

One night Molly summoned up her courage, slipped out of bed and went outside. A breeze carried the stink of the night cart. She pulled her nightdress close around her and crept past the poplar trees, which Bill had planted like a row of soldiers, past the killing shed with its gutters that let out the blood, past the shed with the wheel-less car, and opened the gate beside the chook yard. It was too dark to make out much. She could see the bulk of the cart down the lane. She knew the draught horse was there by the sounds of its stamping hoof, and its snorting.

She dared go no further than her own gate. She was afraid she would fall down the cliff into the quarry. In the dark, that fear came close and she felt her stomach lurch as if she was already falling.

Back in bed, Molly closed her eyes and tried to fall asleep, but as soon as her eyes were closed there was something moving in the dark. She didn't dare look. 'It's only the draught horse in the lane, silly,' she told herself. But her terrified mind took her back to the lane. She heard a noise in the outhouse. Was the night man hiding in there? No, she reasoned, he had just needed to go in there to relieve himself. She smelled tobacco; he was sitting in there having a peaceful smoke while his horse waited in the lane and the rest of Footscray slept.

Suddenly the door opened and a man appeared, shockingly close, just a few steps away. He was still doing up his trousers. He went to the back of the outhouse, slid out the pan and hoisted it on his shoulder. His chest was rising and falling, as if from the exertion. He was wearing a khaki greatcoat and it looked wet from where he might have spilled a pan.

In that instant of her dream, he saw her. He looked at her with an air of indignation, as if accusing her of spying on him. He spoke in a low, hoarse whisper. 'Hullo, what have we got here?'

Teddy had told her once that the night man came with his horse and cart and collected little boys and girls and took them off somewhere. He did to them whatever murderers do. Chopped them up into little pieces, she supposed.

Now the man took a cloth from his pocket with his free hand and wiped the slime from his face. He was the night man, but he was also Teddy, having his wash after work, as he did every afternoon. Teddy came home from work in the sewers they were building under Melbourne, his clothes smeared just like that. It must be awfully dangerous work that Teddy did, Molly thought. The worst thing, Teddy had told her, were the wild animals that lived in the sewers. Down there he had seen lions and tigers that had escaped from the zoo.

'Real lions and tigers?' Molly had asked her brother.

'Oh, yes. They are very hungry. They'll eat little girls who go to the outhouse in the middle of the night,' Teddy had told her.

Then she remembered seeing the night man's face through the open door of a public bar once, when she and Mum had been walking past. He was standing with a gang of men, loud with their mates and their beer, their faces stretched into leering smiles. Molly remembered that afternoon because, pasted to the brick wall outside the pub, there was an advertisement for the Holden Brothers' Circus, and she had begged Mum to take her.

The night man must be so very tired, she thought. He went to work at sunset and came home at dawn. Molly could not imagine how weary he got, always more lanes to do, more pans to empty.

'Let's go,' he said, grabbing her by the back of the neck.

'Look here. My father is Mr Bill Williams and this is his house.'

'Your father isn't Bill Williams,' the man laughed. 'Your father is someone else.' The Murderer seemed to know everything about her. 'Look, here's what I'll do. I'll take you into town. Have you ever been to Luna Park?'

She supposed that the night man really was the Murderer, wanting to take her away with him on the night cart to where he lived, in Mitcham, she remembered. First he would have to tell her how he was going to kill her, wouldn't he? But where did he keep his axe? Molly was horrified by the fact that little girls' bodies could be hacked up like that.

She couldn't tell Mum, otherwise she would tell the policeman and the Murderer would be taken to the shed with the old car with no wheels and hanged. It must be like that in jail when a murderer is made to stand on top of a ladder and his head placed in the noose. She felt sorry for the man with the rope around his neck, who would be so frightened, knowing he was about to die.

Molly felt that she was always running away from someone in her dreams, ever since she had been sent to live at the orphanage. She had better not tell Mum about the night man. If Mum told the policeman, and the Murderer was caught and hanged, then wouldn't that be *her* fault?

Molly had never been to Luna Park, or to the circus. Once, she had seen the coloured tents, the carts and wagons in the paddocks near the Royal Agricultural Showgrounds in Ascot Vale. When she had seen the poster and asked to go to the Holden Brothers' Circus, Mum had said no.

Then, somehow, she was perched beside the man on the seat of his night cart, on their way to Luna Park.

He took her by the hand and led her through the open mouth of the face at the entrance of Luna Park. Then they were inside a room. A curved quarter moon hung against a background of stars and blue night. Molly and the Murderer were sitting together on the moon, having their photo taken.

A FEW MONTHS after she moved to Eldridge Street, not long after her tenth birthday, Molly sometimes got the feeling she was being followed home from school. When she turned and looked behind her, she saw nothing suspicious. She thought she must have been imagining it.

One afternoon on her way home, a man in a cloth cap rode slowly past on his bicycle. The face under the cap turned to look at her. Over the next few days, she saw the man again. The following week he was with a lady, parked in a dark green car across the road from school. The man smiled at her.

Molly kept it a secret. It seemed to belong to the imaginary world of her other secrets.

At three in the morning, she felt herself roar back from sleep and there was the man's face again, in her bedroom, waiting for her in the dark. Terrified, she pulled the blankets over her head. She tried to make him vanish through an effort of will. The trick worked, for a while. But the harder she tried to erase the face, the more firmly it became imprinted in her mind. Of course, *he* must be the Murderer! Why else would a stranger be interested in her?

This man, who had not yet spoken a word to her, who rode silently past on his bicycle, or parked in his car and stared at her, came to occupy her thoughts more and more. Those thoughts must have made their way into her face, because Mum had seen them. 'What's the matter, lamb?' Mum asked. 'Is there anything wrong?'

The next Monday after school, as she walked home along her usual route, the motorcar appeared, the man by himself this time. His head was round with nearly no hair. He gave her a little wave, barely moving his hand from the steering wheel, as if to reassure her. Molly walked on. When she turned again, she was startled to see how close the car was. The man made no attempt to disguise what he was doing. The Murderer was smiling at her, as though he knew who she was.

Molly started running, not stopping until she was at Ballarat Road, where Mum was waiting for her on the other side, in front of Kinnears. Molly ran wildly across the road, causing a truck to brake and swerve. 'Molly!' Mum yelled at her. Molly pushed her face into the fabric of Mum's coat.

'What's wrong?' Mum asked. 'What's got into my little lamb, today?'

'Nothing,' she lied. Molly thought that if she didn't tell anyone, the man might go away.

When they got home, Molly rushed to her room and lay on

her bed. She put her hands over her eyes, still trying to make the man's face go away. The blind was drawn, but the face was still there.

She got up and went to find Mum, who was stirring a pot on the wood stove. Without even turning to look at her, Mum told her to go and refill the wood box. She had a cake in the oven and she didn't want it to go flat.

'Ma?'

'Yes, lamb.'

'Why do men go bald and not ladies?'

'It's because they have a lot of worries.'

'How do worries make them bald?'

'Sometimes a man worries so much his hair falls out.'

'Don't ladies have worries too?'

'Yes, but we have different worries.'

'And our hair doesn't fall out?'

'No.'

'Never ever?'

'Hardly ever.'

Molly went off to play under the ironing board, her favourite place to be, the starched white sheets hanging down around her, the two flatirons Mum heated on the stove, the way the iron hissed as it hit the damp sheet and made the parlour smell safe and clean.

Mum often told Molly that she loved her. The feeling they both still had from her Sunday visits to the Melbourne Orphanage made their bond a special one. The years at Brighton had shaped Molly. There was something tentative and fearful in her expression, as though she was never sure when she might have to go back.

Molly had the chooks to talk to. She went down the back next to the lane above the quarry and imitated their clucking sounds, talking to them in their own language, telling them her secret about the man on the bicycle in the cloth cap, the man and the lady parked in the car after school, watching her. The intelligent eyes of the chooks seemed to understand. They clucked at her impatiently—they had heard it all before, those humans and their stories!—and returned to their grain.

The world had eyes now. At Sunday school at the orphanage, they had told her about God up in the sky looking down on all the little children. But this was different. Whoever it was watching her was inside things, like the objects themselves had minds and were having thoughts, and those thoughts were all about her. And even as she hid down the back in the chook house, she felt that the all-seeing eyes were the Murderer's.

It was her habit in the afternoons to walk down to the corner of Kinnears and meet her sister coming home from the bottle works. As soon as she saw Olive, the childish part of her wanted to run, but the grown-up part continued to stand there, just a shy wave, as though there was something to be ashamed of in displaying too much happiness. If she showed her love, then something bad might happen.

But this afternoon, Molly began to run blindly. She couldn't have stopped if she'd wanted. Olive had a surprised look on her face, half laughing, half worried. What was young Molly up to this afternoon? Molly's body met her with a force that nearly knocked the older girl over. Molly didn't even know why she was crying.

Olive took her hand and they began to walk together

towards Eldridge Street. Molly told her sister that she was frightened of the Murderer. She felt a wild excitement ripping through her: she felt light, dizzy, almost crazy.

'Whatever are you talking about?' her sister asked her. 'You shouldn't be frightened by Teddy and his talk. There isn't really a murderer, silly!'

'But there *is* a Murderer, there is, I know, I've seen him. I've seen the Murderer *and* his wife!'

Without meaning to, Molly began to speak those thoughts that had been dammed up in her mind all these weeks, the man on the bicycle, the man and lady in the car outside the school, those thoughts which always returned, no matter how hard she tried to squeeze them out.

Olive looked thoughtful and hugged her, but didn't say anything.

'Don't tell Mum,' Molly implored. Olive often told her that Mum had been through a lot, and that she didn't need any more problems in her life.

When they got home, Molly hid herself away down the back. When Mum called from the back step, her voice sounded normal. Perhaps Olive had kept her secret. Or perhaps it was just that Olive had not told her yet.

The door of the classroom opened and the headmaster appeared. As one, the children leaped to their feet and stood to attention beside their desks. They looked straight ahead, arms pressed to their sides, not daring to meet the headmaster's eyes.

'Mr Bates. Do you mind if I borrow young Molly for a moment?' The headmaster crooked his finger in her direction and she felt sick. This was the phrase he used when he came to collect a boy to be punished.

She had been writing in her ruled Vana exercise book, her nib following the lines in blue–black ink. The school ink was mixed by the monitors and poured from a bottle with a rubber spout into the inkwell in the corner of the wooden desk. The pen felt dry in her fingers. Some of the boys chewed the ends of their pens. Sometimes the steel nib broke and Mr Bates took out the box of nibs from his desk drawer. He took a long time, as if reluctant to part with a new nib. You could make the ink run in the grain of the wood in the desk lid. The wood felt smooth and waxy where the elbows of so many had rested and rubbed. Boys rolled up pellets of blotting paper and watched them sink to the bottom of the inkwell. When the ink was low, the bits of blotting paper in the ink clogged the nib.

Mr Bates was still looking at her, waiting for her to follow the headmaster.

She had never been to the headmaster's office. The oak door was usually closed. Now that she had been admitted to the room she saw a desk, a bookcase, the headmaster's overcoat hanging on a hook. And there, sitting in the armchair, was Mum! She was wearing her cherry-red coat. The room smelled of cigarettes and methylated spirits. The headmaster gave her a smirk, as if to say, 'Ha ha! Tricked you!'

Mum had come to take her home. Why? Molly stood there feeling frightened and foolish while Mum and the headmaster talked. If only she could stand straight enough, she might still be able to avoid the fate that awaited her. The hardest thing to know was where to put her hands. If they hung at her sides, her shoulders ached. Behind her back was not right either. That was for 'at ease', when the school was at assembly on the asphalt, and that came before the headmaster called the school to attention. Then, everybody had to stand up very straight and the boys saluted the flag and they all chanted together, *I love God and my Country, I will serve the King...*They had to form twos and march around the white line painted on the asphalt while one of the big boys beat the bass drum.

All Molly wanted was for Mum not to be here at school today. She wanted things to be normal. She wanted to go to her corner of the yard and eat her sandwich by herself.

'Your mother and I have just been having a little chat. Do you know what we were talking about, Molly?'

'No, sir.'

'No, Mr Curry,' he corrected her, and smiled. He nodded at Mum, as if to say to her, 'See? I was right.' At that moment, Molly knew that Olive must have told Mum about the man on the bicycle, the man and lady in the car.

And so she left school early that day with Mum, while everyone else was still in the classroom. The ordinary school day was going on without her. From the far end of the corridor came the sound of a piano being played.

It felt odd, walking home through the empty streets in the middle of the day. Still, she felt happy. As long as she was with Mum, no one could hurt her. All those things she had imagined were going to happen to her—that the man on the bike was going to steal her away and murder her—it all seemed silly now she was with Mum. And yet the fact that Mum was walking her home before it was home time told her that things weren't right.

She followed Mum around the house while she did her sweeping, but Mum was in a bad mood. 'Do you know why we don't talk to strangers?' she asked Molly.

'Yes.'

'Why don't we talk to strangers?'

'If the stranger was a murderer, he might try to kill you.'

'Or he might try to steal you from your family and keep you as his own little girl. Sometimes a girl is taken a long way away and she is given a new name and she grows up with the strangers as though they are her mother and father.'

Molly stared at Mum, her eyes wide. She could understand them wanting to kill her, because that's what murderers do, but why would they want to steal her away from Mum and Bill?

Mum said that she should never speak to that man and lady, even if they came up and spoke to her first, even if they were nice to her or offered her lollies.

Mum must have talked to Bill about it because he was particularly kind to Molly that afternoon when he came home from the meatworks. He was wearing his undershirt and grey worsted trousers held up by braces. He hadn't had a shave yet, but his black hair was glossy with hair oil. She sat on the back step with him, the smell of dead animals still on him, flecks of dried blood on his forearms. He carried deep in his skin the smell of his trade, the confidence of death-dealing mingled with fear. There were crimson patches on his hands where Mum had painted his sores with Mercurochrome.

He had brought out the treacle tin and he used a teaspoon to prise open the lid. He watched her licking the spoon even when there was no treacle left. 'So what's the matter?' Bill asked her.

'Nothing.'

'I know when my little fox is thinking chickens.'

'No chickens in my pocket.' Molly smiled at him.

Bill put his hat on her head so that she looked like a little man and walked her as far as the corner. He liked to take her with him and stop to talk to their neighbours, this happy blonde girl without much meat on her bones but a goodness in her heart that radiated out of her. Molly felt the same love for Bill that she felt for Mum, except that her love was mixed with something else: the fear of it being taken away.

Mum kept her home from school all that week. They went to the shops together. At Moran & Cato's the grocer gave Molly some broken biscuits and asked why she wasn't at school. On the other days, she helped with the housework, and in the afternoons she waited at the front gate for the others to come home from work. Mum found fault with the way Molly did everything. She could not even sweep the floor to Mum's satisfaction, it seemed. Since Olive had told her about the man and lady in the car watching Molly, something in Mum had changed.

Molly asked, 'Mum, do you *know* the Murderer?'

'Whatever are you talking about now? Has Teddy been putting that nonsense into your head? You wait until he comes home, I'll be having words with him!'

Mum wore thunder in her face, in the dark bruises around her eyes, in the way her mouth set hard, and Molly waited for the storm to pass. Mum sometimes needed to lie down with a cold compress over her eyes, she got so angry.

As Molly lay awake in bed at night, the smell of tobacco smoke came to her from the parlour and she could hear Mum and Bill talking. She heard their words—but then something happened that kept her stupid and she couldn't understand what the words meant. There was something in herself that wouldn't let her hear the words. There was a secret she wanted to know, yet didn't really want to know. She heard Bill say, 'It's only natural for the girl to be curious. She might even remember him from when she was little.'

They were only voices. There were always voices in the house at night, especially when Teddy and Olive stayed up late. Molly only really paid attention when they were shouting, which didn't happen often. But now Bill's words remained stubbornly in her mind. *She might even remember him from when she was little.*

Remember *who*? Was it someone she was supposed to *know*? Was it someone Molly had been keeping a secret from herself?

Mum was saying, 'I'm going to the police if he doesn't stop.'

'The police can't do much, seeing as he has a legal right.'

'A legal right to what?' Mum howled. 'A legal right to follow her around the streets and frighten her half to death?'

She now understood that Mum and Bill did know the man and lady who were following her. She felt relieved, but then a sense of disappointment, as though it was the Murderer she had wanted after all.

She heard Mum say, 'Well, if him and his floozy think they're going to get their hands on her, they've got another think coming.'

'We could go to court and ask the judge to give Molly to

us once and for all. You could ask the judge to have Alfred completely ruled out of it.'

Alfred? Who was *Alfred?*

'But *would* they rule him out of it? He might have some claim on her that we don't know about. Just because he didn't pay me a penny when I needed it most doesn't mean anything. What if the magistrate comes down on Alfred's side of the fence? Or what if he sends a man to look into aspects of my life and things come out in public I would rather keep to myself?'

'How much does she know, do you reckon?'

'Not much. But she has been asking questions.' Mum made a noise like a sigh or a moan. 'I suppose I have always known at the back of my mind that something like this could happen one day.' Then there was the sound of Mum sobbing. She said, 'Oh, Bill, what am I going to do?'

'She can't stay home from school forever.'

But Mum still wouldn't let Molly go back to school. She wasn't allowed to go out into the street by herself now, even to meet Olive after work. She was afraid that everything in her life was about to change again. Perhaps Mum was going to send her back to the orphanage? Alone in her room, she opened her Bible and stared at the first page, Miss Ormond's autograph and 'Remember us, Brighton, 1928'. She felt sad that Bonnie had not replied to her last letter. 'She doesn't remember me,' Molly thought. 'None of them do, not even Miss Ormond. As far as they're concerned, I no longer exist. I am no one.'

That Friday she sat and played with her doll and tea set on the front verandah. Mum brought out a plate of sugar sand-wiches with the crusts cut off. Molly poured a cup of tea for dolly, and one for herself. There was only her and the quiet weekday street. The sun was bright on the grass and it was cold in the shade. The sound of Mum washing the dishes came to her. From the way she was banging the pots and pans, she must have been furious. Molly felt a knot tightening inside her. It was *her* fault for causing Mum all these worries.

A shiver passed through her body. It looked like it was about to rain.

'Put on your coat,' Mum said. 'We're going out.' She was already wearing her own coat and carrying an umbrella.

'Where to?'

It was four o'clock in the afternoon.

Mum looked like she was choking with anger. 'We're going to get this settled once and for all.'

On their way out, they passed Hoppy sitting on the verandah, rolling a cigarette, his scuffed, never-polished quarry boots unlaced. His hat was pushed back on his head. 'You seen Olive?' he asked as they passed. Hoppy was a nice man but life had already defeated him.

The front gate shut with a thump behind them. It was raining softly, the light flooding under the clouds. It was one of those afternoons in Melbourne when the weather seemed to be going against nature. Inside some of the houses, the lamps were already on. Individual drops of rain made light tapping sounds on the leaves in the gardens they passed.

'Where are we going, Mum?'

Mum just kept marching, eyes straight ahead, and gave no answer. Molly could see it all already: they were going to see the Murderer and his wife. Mum would take her to their house and the Murderer would kill them with *a blunt instrument, such as the blunt end of an axe.*

They took the tram to Footscray Station, then the train into town. From there they got on another tram and went along streets Molly had never seen before. For a while she was afraid they were going back to the Melbourne Orphanage. On the way, Mum told her that they were going to Coburg, not that far from where she used to work at the Lincoln Mills.

They went along Nicholson Street. Then they walked up Glengyle Street, until they came to a small, double-fronted weatherboard house, indistinguishable from its neighbours.

Mum opened the gate and marched up the path. On either side were geraniums planted in square kerosene tins. The front door was wide open, as if whoever lived there was expecting someone. From inside the house came the sound of a woman singing.

Mum knocked on the wall beside the open door. Straightaway the man appeared. 'Hello,' he said in a pleasant, friendly way. 'Who have we got here?'

He was standing in his shirtsleeves and braces, blinking at them. He looked as though he might have poor eyesight. Perhaps he had been expecting someone else. He looked more ordinary and vulnerable, standing in the doorway of his own house, than when he waited for her outside school. Inside, the woman had stopped singing.

'You can forget about Molly,' Mum said.

It was an animal instinct, a finely tuned intuition that made the hair prickle on Molly's skin as she sensed danger approach. It was as though she had always been standing here in this doorway, facing this man who was a stranger and not a stranger. A woman's voice from inside called, 'Alf? Who is it?' The speaker's face appeared, at first hopeful, then dark, then it disappeared. The woman did not say any more.

'Why don't you come in?' the man said. Then he called through to the woman. 'Gert! Put the kettle on.'

'Oh, we're not stopping,' Mum said, but she made no move to leave. After a minute or so, she said, 'So I hear you two got married last year.'

The man stopped smiling. 'Where did you hear that?'

'A little bird told me.'

'Yes, we got married last year and this is our place.'

'What suddenly brought that on, Alfred? You two have been living together for years.'

Alfred listened to her reasonably. He might have been thinking things would still turn out all right.

'I know you've been following her home from school,' Mum said.

'I just wanted to get a look at her.'

'Well, here she is,' Mum said. 'Happy now? Happy that you nearly frightened the wits out of her?'

Alfred looked at Molly. He nodded at her then looked away, ashamed. He put his hands in his pockets and kept them there. His lips were pursed as if he were about to whistle. 'Look,' he said to Mum, 'I've stopped going to the school.'

'Why the sudden interest? You didn't want to know before. You didn't want to pay maintenance or do anything else to support her. Now you listen to me, Alfred Lovett. I won't have any more trouble about the girl.'

'Trouble? What trouble?'

'You didn't want to know anything about her until Gert got that idea into her head.'

'What idea?'

'You buggers want Molly, that's what.'

Alfred didn't say anything; he just continued to watch them with his frightened eyes. Molly stared back, paralysed. They want *me*?

'So why did you two get married all of a sudden?'

Alfred did not answer.

'I'll tell you why. Because she can't have children. So now you go and decide you want your daughter back after all this time!'

Mum took a step forward towards him.

'Easy now,' Alfred said. 'Easy.'

'You want Molly because Gert can't have one of her own.'

The rain had stopped, and the crickets were loud. Molly pressed close against Mum's coat, waiting for the trouble to pass. She didn't like being here. She wanted to go home. Mum grabbed her hand and they had already started along the path, when she turned back. Alfred was still standing at his front door. Mum raised her voice so that even the neighbours would hear. 'I'll never give up Molly!' Then she yelled again, louder. 'Do you hear me? You'll never get Molly!'

On the way home, Mum said that they must keep all this a secret, as it wasn't any other bugger's business anyway, and besides, if people knew, they might call Molly names. Mum explained everything to her—who Alfred was, where Molly had been born, all the things that had happened later. She said she had known for some time that Alfred and Gert were living together, but she had discovered only recently that they had got married at the Registry Office. Mum said they had married so they would seem suitable parents if they were to apply to a court to obtain custody.

So Alfred was her father! She had been born in the very next street! The same house Teddy and Olive had pointed out to her in Empire Street, where they said they used to live. It was just an ordinary house, peeling paint, rusty roof. How many times Molly had walked past that house!

When she got home and looked in the mirror she saw the face she didn't want to recognise. She had his nose, his mouth, the same crease in her upper lip. If this man who had been watching her really *was* her father, and he and his wife really *did* want to steal her away, then wouldn't they keep trying to get her? It was as though Molly had been living another girl's life. Her own life here with Mum and Bill and Teddy and Olive was a fraud. For years and years her brother and sister had known the secret about her and neither of them had said a word about it! She hated them when she thought of that—*hated* them! Molly felt they weren't really her brother and sister anymore, but strangers who had lied to her and tricked her. So she had belonged in the orphanage, after all. Now she felt she didn't belong anywhere.

IN A HOUSE where, as far as the men were concerned, every second word was bloody or bugger, the one 'b' word that no one was ever allowed to use was *bastard*.

As she grew older, Molly spent most of the hours after school and on Saturdays and Sundays indoors. The business with Alfred kept Molly close to her mother, not in the street where there was a rawness to life that went against the girl's quiet nature. Molly felt she could only be at peace when she and Mum were in the same room.

By the age of twelve, when she was in 7th Grade, Molly could hem a dress as well as anyone. At thirteen, she knitted a jumper for Teddy's birthday. Well, at least she knitted the body and the sleeves; only Mum knew how to knit the neckband.

Molly left school when she turned fourteen. She had

completed 8th Grade and the Merit Certificate. With the stock market crash and the Depression, lots of people were out of work, but Mum still managed to find her a job at the Australian Woollen Mill in Barkly Street, behind the Western Oval. It was only a mile to walk to work, though Molly sometimes took the bus.

The whole business with Alfred had a bad effect on her. Molly went out to work and to the shops but she kept to herself and made few friends. At the weekends and in the evenings, she preferred to stay at home with Mum. She lived penitentially, hoping this might ward off the evil she always felt lay just ahead. She steeled herself against the possibility of coming across Alfred in the street. Even so, she sometimes walked past the house in Empire Street and lingered there, searching for spectral traces of the people who had once lived there, guessing at the events that had taken place under its roof, the other possible lives that might have been.

Mum had said to her, soon after it happened, 'Promise you'll tell me if you ever see that man and lady again.'

'They don't come looking for me any more, Mum.'

Alfred existed only in the corners of her thoughts now, in the shadows of her dreams and sometimes in her nightmares. But also, in a way, everything the family did now was directed towards one purpose—'to stop Alfred from getting Molly'. Alfred was at the core of the vague fear Molly carried in her belly when she walked along Gordon Street every morning on her way to work.

The years of the Depression passed. The family survived the hard times. Bill liked to say that he had invented the lay-by system in Eldridge Street, letting people pay for their Christmas chickens and turkeys on the instalment plan.

Teddy and Rosie were married and lived nearby with their daughter. Olive and Hoppy were married, too. They'd bought a house a few blocks away; they had no children. The family all got together at the house in Eldridge Street on Friday nights after work, the men sitting outside drinking beer, the women cooking.

By the time Molly was seventeen, in 1935, Alfred still haunted their thoughts, even though he hadn't been seen or heard of for years. Every family has its secrets, but the Alfred who could not be put into words became like an illness, a malady. He was so deeply the enemy that his name could not be mentioned, for to name the devil might have been to summon him up. He became more monstrous in imagination than he ever was in life.

Alfred continued to live on in the silences, in the looks that came into their faces at certain moments, though no one uttered a word about him. But every time there was a knock on the front door, for an instant Molly had the reflex thought that it might be Alfred.

As she grew up, Molly developed a wary expression in her eyes, wondering if this invisible father might one day return to claim her. For the rest of her life, the eerie feeling would suddenly come over her, that someone was following her, trying to steal her, and that, one day, when she had a child of her own, the Murderer would return and try to steal him, too.

At the Australian Woollen Mill, the girls sat all day at their machines. Molly kept her head down and worked hard. The foreman always praised her. She got on well with everyone, but she was selective in the company she kept. She disliked the insults the other girls hurled at each other, their rough ways, their dirty talk. She didn't like the way the girls laughed when men were around, and tugged at the hems of their skirts and smoothed them over their thighs and combed their hair, and looked into the compacts they carried in their handbags. Some of the girls talked at dinnertime about things she did not want to hear. She knew that men were not saints. But she didn't know much more than that. Molly didn't want her own life to turn out the way her mother's had, full of trouble and turbulence.

One evening in the winter of 1937, Molly had just come out of work and was walking along Barkly Street when she watched a young man dismount from his motorcycle outside a bike shop. He wore a leather helmet that fitted snugly around his head, and goggles. When he took off the helmet, he caught her looking and smiled. He came across to talk to her. He had just finished work too: around the corner in Cross Street, at the Olympic Tyre and Rubber Company.

His name was Percy. His father sold bicycles and did repairs. Footscray was still a suburb of bicycles. There were always rows of bikes outside factory gates. The family lived in rooms above the shop.

Percy was eight months older than Molly. He had finished his apprenticeship as a draughtsman at Olympic. Now he was studying Mechanical Engineering three nights a week at Collingwood Technical College.

He asked Molly out to the pictures on Saturday night. They sat in the comfortable seats at the newly refurbished Grand

Theatre in Paisley Street. The film was *The Texas Rangers*, with Fred MacMurray. Molly was nervous; she had never been out with a boy before.

Percy tried to explain the subjects he was studying: algebra, trigonometry, calculus, physics, applied mechanics, engineering drawing—things Molly had never even heard of before. She allowed Percy to put his arm around her shoulders and they waited for the lights to fade and the curtain to go up.

Percy got a job at the Central Drawing Office of the Department of Defence Production in Maribyrnong. Molly stayed on at the Australian Woollen Mill.

They were married in the Barkly Street Methodist Church by the Reverend Rex Dakers in 1939. Mum helped Molly make her own dress. Bill gave Molly away. All the family were happy for Molly. At the wedding, Teddy looked handsome in a dinner suit and black tie. Olive and Rosie helped with the catering. On their honeymoon, the couple stayed at the Grand Pacific Hotel in Lorne.

The following month, Hitler invaded Poland. Percy wanted to enlist but he was now in a reserved occupation.

They bought a block of land in Essendon, still mainly paddocks, and lived with Percy's mum and dad above their new shop in Ivanhoe. They had sold the bike shop by then and bought a milk bar. Molly and Percy fitted a sidecar to his bike, joined the Ivanhoe Motorcycle Club and went on outings at weekends with the other couples.

In October 1940, Mr Harvey, the builder, made a start on Molly and Percy's two-bedroom brick veneer house. The following April it was finished and they moved in. They had a mortgage with the State Savings Bank of Victoria. Molly left her job at the woollen mill to look after the house, as they planned to start a family.

There was a lot to do. They did the painting themselves, all the walls and ceilings and doors inside, the fascia boards and window frames outside. Materials were in short supply because of the war. Even floor varnish was hard to come by. When they came to do the floors in the dining room and living room, they varnished only those floorboards that showed at the edges of the carpets.

Molly worked beside Percy on weekends, laying out the paths and rockery beds in the back garden, deciding which flowers and shrubs to plant. They bought a young silver birch and planted it in the middle of their front lawn. Soon the tree was spreading its branches. In summer, Molly watched the morning light on its leaves outside their bedroom window.

Molly and Percy rode to Ivanhoe on Saturdays to help out at the milk bar. Molly was popular with the customers—blonde, slim, smiling. There were bottles of coloured syrups lined up on shelves in front of the big mirror—strawberry, pineapple, lime, blue heaven—and a glass malt-dispenser and a row of machines for mixing the drinks in metal beakers.

American soldiers who came to the shop from their camp at nearby Heidelberg said that they made the best milkshakes in Melbourne. The shop was crowded in the evenings, the Americans polite and friendly, smoking cigarettes, flirting with the local girls. Molly and Percy sometimes stayed the night in

Ivanhoe and on Sundays they went for rides with their old friends from the motorcycle club.

In 1943, Percy was promoted at work. He supervised the installation of the plant at one of the explosives factories. The following year, he designed and supervised construction of a forty-ton floating crane.

After the war, the Central Drawing Office turned to civilian projects. Percy designed the manufacturing plant for Westminster Carpet. By July 1952, Percy was Head of Section, in charge of ten men with their heads bent over their drafting boards in the large, well-lit room at the end of the tram line in Raleigh Road, just across the Maribyrnong River from their home in Essendon.

In the evenings, Molly and Percy listened to the wireless or played records—big bands and musicals, Glenn Miller, Rogers and Hammerstein. They loved *Oklahoma!*, *Carousel*, *South Pacific*. Every fortnight, they went to the local record shop in Buckley Street and added to their collection.

Percy was everything any woman could want in a husband. He was attractive, athletic. No one in his family drank or smoked. Molly was proud of him. He was a hard worker. They had their own home. He was still going to night school and soon he would qualify as an engineer. She believed in him with every bone in her body. But through these happy years, there was something missing.

They still had their motorbike and sidecar. One Sunday, on a run along the Great Ocean Road to Lorne, one of the motorcycles broke down. The men spent the afternoon fixing it. The women sat on rugs with their thermos tea. Bette Reeves said, 'I know a couple who adopted a baby. They didn't have to wait long at all. If you want a girl, it takes longer. But if you want a boy, you put in your application and a few months later you've got your bundle of joy and he's yours to keep.'

It had been a long time since anyone had asked Molly, 'When are we going to hear the patter of little feet?'

Part Two

Anna

NORTH FITZROY, 1952

IT WAS LATE, late, in the wobble of the night. Her brother Robert had driven his car around to the lane earlier and left it parked there so they could go out through the back without being seen by the neighbours. She was awake but it felt like she was dreaming. Her heart was pumping in a slow, squelchy way. Mum said it was just a tablet to help her feel calm, like a sleeping tablet. 'You're going away to a home for girls for a spell, Anna,' Mum said. 'It's all for the best.'

She looked out the car window. It had been raining and the night was still slippery. They drove along Melville Road, past all the innocent houses with their lights on inside.

Dad sat in the front next to Robert. Mum and Anna sat in the back. The inside of the car smelled like new shoes. When they turned into Brunswick Road, Robert made the tyres squeal, deliberately, as if he were angry. 'Now, Robert,' Dad said mildly. Robert wasn't saying anything, just driving. They came to a stop beside the Edinburgh Gardens. It was windy and Anna could see the big trees thrashing around, laughing and rolling. Oh, the trees were having a great time!

'Is this the place?' Robert asked, though he already knew. His voice sounded different from the way he usually talked.

'This is the place, son,' Dad said. Mum and Dad had already been here to make the arrangements.

'This is the Haven, Anna,' Mum said, and her voice choked. Anna had seen that she'd been crying without making a sound all the time they were in the car.

'What haven?'

'The home for girls in your situation.'

It.was a big stately house of two storeys set in a large garden, with a high fence. The front windows were dark. A single bulb above the front door leaked weak yellow light.

Mum took Anna's hand and squeezed it. They opened the heavy iron gate and walked up the path. Dad carried the suit-case. The front door opened straightaway; they were expected. The woman standing there in a white uniform was so short, she might have been a dwarf.

Mum and Dad were not allowed inside. Anna said goodbye to them in tears on the front step—she was certain she would never see them again. The nurse carried her case up the stairs into the upper regions of the house. Anna followed her with difficulty, climbing the stairs one at a time. It was the first time in months she had left her family's home. She wasn't used to walking. She felt that she had come apart in the middle. Her legs were obediently following the dwarf through the entrails of this strange hotel, while the rest of her body was still at home in West Brunswick.

The woman went ahead down a narrow hallway. There was the faint smell of cigarettes. They passed an open door; the light was on, the globe dim, a row of beds, a girl's body lying on a bed, a pair of eyes meeting hers.

At last they came to her room. Eight beds were lined up against the walls. The nurse placed her case next to the window, beside a bed with a cream-painted iron bedstead. Anna thought there were bodies in most of the beds. The nurse withdrew without a word and she was left alone with strangers.

The girls were lying quietly. None of them spoke to her. Their quietness made Anna fearful. She knew she wouldn't be able to sleep. From hour to hour a clock chimed somewhere in the night: the house was reminding her that she was still awake. She felt her body floating above the bed, escaping the Haven, floating above the sleeping trees in the Edinburgh Gardens. In these uneasy, wakeful hours she was free of her body, free of her *situation*...she was primitive, unattached, a vagabond of the spirit. It was the way she used to feel at Cockatoo, with Neil. She had been a lively, happy, solid girl with brown hair and blue eyes; her mouth had been relaxed and smiling back then, not this compressed line of worry she'd seen in the mirror these past few months.

The Haven at night was full of stifled weeping; she did not hear anyone crying out loud. Anna had been brought to a place where the girls were like shadows, wounded. Even when it was quiet, it was never entirely quiet. The girl in the next bed was breathing harshly in her sleep. Every breath carried the force of emotion—not tearfulness, but a deep shuddering that seemed to touch the limits of existence. Her shallow, helpless snores filled Anna with pity for her. The whole of the Haven was grieving in the night, the girls part of some vast exhalation going on deep in the building. She felt as if the old house was weeping from all the terrible things it had seen.

The bedroom smelled of disinfectant. She remembered the time she had had her tonsils out in hospital. There had been the same smell, the ether mask coming down over her face, and her thoughts stretching into other thoughts that moved with the steady percussion of a steamboat making its way along a green river. Now, in the night, the sound came to her again, the *putt-putt* of Bogart's dirty little steamer in *The African Queen*, which she had seen with Neil earlier that year.

Next thing she heard was birdsong just before dawn. She must have slept for a while. Then another sound: the tramping of boots, the opening of doors, and someone shouting 'Good morning!' Their door opened and a hand switched on the sick yellow light.

It was six o'clock. None of the other girls said anything or made any sign of moving, so Anna just lay there, too. The boots marched on.

The weak light seeped into her.

The girls got dressed for morning prayers. Anna had to change from her own warm nightgown into a coarse tunic made from thick cotton that felt stiff and uncomfortable against her skin. The tunics were shapeless coveralls, and although they were allowed to wear their own dresses underneath, if they had one that still fitted, the tunics felt damp in the unheated building.

Matron and the nurses in their starched white uniforms also attended prayers: they were part of the Salvation Army, not just employees. It was something more than the usual strictness of nursing routine. They had to say a prayer to the Redeemer, and sing hymns.

After prayers, there was breakfast, porridge. They were allowed to pour on their own treacle and milk. When it got light, there was mist in the trees, and the grass in the Edinburgh Gardens was white. Anna stared out the window at this ghostly world she had been delivered into.

The dwarfish nurse who had admitted Anna now gave her a perfunctory tour of the place. Apart from the main building, with its imposing facade and its cast-iron balcony, there was a separate laundry and a maternity wing off the asphalt courtyard at the back. As they came down the side path and returned to the front door, Anna noticed the emblem, which she had missed in the dark on the previous night. There was a large 'S' snaking around a crucifix, two crossed swords, and the motto, BLOOD AND FIRE.

The girls had to work hard at the Haven. Anna was put on the roster and told to scrub the wooden floors. There was supposed to be a wage, but she never saw any money. She cleaned the wards where the mothers and their babies were kept. She also worked in the laundry. The loads of linen never stopped coming.

'Who's this?' asked the cook, that first morning, when Anna appeared in the kitchen with her tin bucket and scrubbing brush. Anna was too afraid to reply.

'Speak up! What's your name, girl?' The cook, a big woman whose name was Margaret, had a gruff manner, but kind eyes.

'I'm Anna. They told me to do the floor.'

'Anna? Is that the name Matron gave you?'

'It's my name. I haven't seen Matron.'

'Oh.' Margaret nodded. 'You girls are not allowed to use your real names here.' Anna was too nervous to ask what she meant.

She lowered herself carefully onto her knees and dipped the scrubbing brush in the soapy water, with its strong smell of pine disinfectant. Margaret watched her, smiling. 'Don't worry,' she told Anna. 'You'll soon get used to it.'

It was October, she was nearly six months pregnant, and getting down on her hands and knees was difficult, with her belly in the way. Anna kept trying to get up a scrubbing motion, but it was hopeless. Margaret put down the stainless steel bowl in which she was beating flour and water, went to the broom cupboard and brought out a mop.

'Here,' she said, offering it to Anna. 'Use this, if you can't manage the brush. But you'd better start next door in the dining room. I don't want that Pine O Cleen smell getting into my dumpling batter. You can come and do in here when I'm finished making the dinners.'

The dining room would have been the grandest room in the house when it was built, perhaps even a ballroom, Anna imagined. As she was mopping, she saw, in a crack between the wooden parquetry, a tiny gold pin, almost hidden by the grime. It might have been dropped there and forgotten at a party or ball during the Haven's former life as some rich man's mansion.

She had almost finished when Matron appeared, and immediately went to the kitchen door and said to the cook, 'What's she doing with a mop? I want to see her on her hands and knees.'

Margaret did not say anything. She looked down into her bowl and beat the batter for her dumplings more resolutely. The physical effort pulled her mouth tight. Matron took the mop out of Anna's hands and returned it to the broom cupboard. She waited only long enough to see Anna begin to lower herself.

Matron came back half an hour later to check on her. When she saw Anna scrubbing, she said to Margaret, 'That's better. Down where she belongs. She's a sinner and she needs to beg Our Lord for forgiveness.'

Anna had been raised in the Church of England and, since her sixteenth birthday, she had taught at Sunday school. She sang with the children, 'Gentle Jesus Meek and Mild', and she taught them about forgiveness. On the postcards she handed out to the children, Jesus looked kindly, too. These Salvation Army people, Anna soon realised, were made of sterner stuff, with their military uniforms, their brass bands.

Where was the forgiveness in that? They were yelled at, called names, told they were 'street girls', not decent girls, not 'good girls'. It seemed to Anna that the Salvation Army was a punishment machine, and even those among the staff, like Margaret, who were kind to the girls were afraid of being caught out by Matron.

You had to do what you were told. You went to chapel on Sunday morning, you went to the altar and got down on your knees and admitted you were a sinner and begged the Lord for forgiveness. Then you were free for the rest of the day to receive your visitors in the downstairs sitting room with its

147

dark wood-panelled walls and mismatched furniture. Occasionally, the girls were allowed to take the tram into the city on Saturday mornings, before the shops closed at midday, to purchase personal items. These privileges, it was made clear to the girls, could be withdrawn at any time.

Those who were lucky, like Anna, had parents who stuck by them, and promised to visit each week. Many of the girls from the country, and those from other states, had been sent to the Haven precisely because it was far away and the family could avoid embarrassment. Those girls had no one.

Every day as she struggled to get her work done, one idea kept floating back into Anna's thoughts—a hope, a dream— that Neil would come and take her away from here, and they would be married, and they would have their baby together. He would be her knight in shining armour, like he used to be. *They would have their baby.* There, she had said it. This new life that was swelling inside her was at once the most beautiful and the most terrifying prospect.

Sometimes she heard the sound of a baby crying in the maternity wing. A piercing scream, the baby hungry or in pain, calling for his mother. And if his mother did not come? I would not let my baby scream. I would always come to him, Anna thought. Her baby was always a boy in her mind. Even though the little thing has brought me all this trouble, how could I not love it? Yes, I am beginning to love him already, she thought. And when he—or she—is born, when I see him and hold him in my arms, that love I feel now will be ever so much stronger.

When she thought of the difficult months and years ahead, however—finding money to keep her baby, living as an unmarried mother—she wasn't able to see anything clearly. She was frozen with apprehension, sick with self-pity. The baby was no longer something new and delightful coming into her life. It was something that made her disgusted for letting herself end up here at the Haven, a victim.

Everything could be fixed, if only Neil would come for her. A ring on her finger—that's all it would take. The daydream returned to her, day after day, and she knew that these hopeful feelings came because they were the only way she would be able to survive in this place.

Outside, it was springtime. Morning sunshine shone through the stained-glass panels at the sides of the windows and doors. For precious minutes, those colours were for Anna the only living things in this dead world. The dust motes floating in the shafts of sunlight made her nostalgic. She remembered how much she loved the golden wattle coming out in spring at Cockatoo. On Sundays she used to like to go to Station Pier to watch the ocean liners pull out, all the friends and relatives throwing streamers. But now those happy memories felt like old sorrows.

One day during her first week at the Haven, after their midday dinner, she was sent to work in the laundry with a girl called Leanne. She was further along than Anna, about eight months, by the look of her. She told Anna that her real name was Jennifer, not Leanne—that was just the name Matron had assigned her on admission. She explained what Margaret had hinted at: that all the girls were given false names.

She looked like a Leanne, though, with her dark brown,

almond-shaped eyes, a mop of coarse black hair cropped straight across in a fringe. A farm girl, a childhood spent in the sun. She told Anna that she came from Leongatha; Anna wondered if 'Leanne' was just the first name that had come into Matron's mind.

The work in the laundry was demanding: lifting the wet sheets, hanging them out on the lines that crossed the building's internal courtyard, taking them down again and folding them. And they had to wash, dry and iron all the laundry from the hospital wing.

'Do you think it would kill them to let us have an orange sometimes?' Leanne asked.

'I can ask my mum to bring in a bag. I'll ask her on Sunday.'

Leanne was quiet. Her people, she'd told Anna, had sent her away and disowned her.

Anna looked down into the trough and watched the way the bag of Reckitt's Blue leaked out into the clear water, faint membranes of stain spreading like a cloud, or a jellyfish.

The pregnant girls did most of the work at the Haven, under orders from Matron and the other Salvation Army women. The Salvation Army men never came in here. It was a women's world, this house of shame.

The family had to pay board each fortnight and the girls had to work hard right up until the day they went into labour. Anna still hoped that she would be gone from here by then.

Matron's office was in a low brick building off the courtyard at the back, between the old house and the maternity wing. As Anna was crossing the courtyard one afternoon that first week, the flap in the shiny green door opened and Matron looked out. She gestured for Anna to come into her office.

Matron had returned to her desk and was reading a file. It was a small windowless room, the only light coming from a lamp. Matron's desk was against the wall, and there was hardly room for the wooden cabinets and shelves of files. The desk was piled high with documents. On the wall there were two pictures: a framed coloured print of Jesus on the cross, and an old black and white photo of a hulking Gothic building with turrets, and the legend beneath it, THE CITADEL.

'You're Anna Ross, aren't you?' Matron asked, without looking at her. Then she slowly swivelled in her old wooden chair and faced Anna. She had a brooch where her uniform buttoned at the top, and there were black flashes with a large 'S' on both collars. She was a Brigadier in the Salvation Army.

'You're going to be needing another name,' she said.

Anna had been expecting this. She said calmly, 'I have a name already and I don't see why I should change it.'

'Oh,' Matron said, and looked at her hard. 'I'm not used to girls talking back to me.'

Anna stood in silence, Matron's words hanging in the air.

'We have our reasons for getting the girls to use different names.'

'What reasons?'

'Privacy reasons. In case one day you should come across a fellow inmate and recognise her. It should be as though your time here never happened.' Matron looked at her brightly. 'I'll tell you what—you can be Violet or Daisy. The name of a flower. There—I'll give you a choice, which is more than I do for most girls.'

151

'I don't want another name.'

'This topic is not open to discussion.'

'Well, if I'm to have any say in the matter, then call me Elizabeth.'

Matron's eyes came alive behind her glasses. 'Why Elizabeth?'

'After our new Queen.'

That tickled Matron's fancy. 'After Her Majesty the Queen, eh? That's a good one. So that's what you think you are, is it? A queen? Well, I'll tell you something. For one, your name here will be Violet. You seem like a nice quiet girl to me, and your parents seem decent and hardworking. But what you've done is lowered yourself. You're not like some of the street types and the gutter types we get coming in here. But there are consequences to your actions, my girl, and if you think you can come in here with your head held high like a queen, then you've got another think coming. You'll get on your knees like the rest of them and ask Our Lord for forgiveness.' Matron looked down at a file. 'How old are you?'

'I'm twenty.'

'Where did you work?'

'Victorian Railways.'

'What job did you do there?'

'I worked in the pay office.'

'When did you leave?'

'I kept working until people started getting suspicious about me putting on a little weight. My doctor gave me a certificate stating that I was having a breakdown, that way I'd have a job to come back to. But the Railways said I had to present myself to their doctors, and by this time there was no disguising what my problem was, so I resigned.'

'Well, you see, you had done a very bad thing,' Matron said.

'Do you think I am a bad person?' Anna herself no longer knew the answer.

What Anna would not admit to anyone was that secret place in herself where hope was still alive. If she revealed that, it might be taken away from her. True, when Neil was supposed to meet her in the city, to go to the doctor's, he had sent a note with a friend, saying that he was ashamed and please don't tell his parents. But that might just have been a moment of weakness when fear got the better of him. One day soon, the Neil she knew would come back, the pure and good Neil with his smiling blue eyes, and he would tell her he wanted to marry her and take her home and they'd have their baby together.

'You will give birth to a baby who will have the stigma of illegitimacy all his life. And if it was your purpose to bring about this state of affairs, then I can only think you are a very wicked girl. And yet, I do not believe you to be that kind of girl. Tell me—who was he, this boy?'

'A man,' Anna said quietly. 'He is not a boy.'

She felt uncomfortable talking about Neil, but at least if she talked about him, then she wouldn't have to talk about other things. Anna knew, even before the battle had begun, that they would try to talk her into giving up her baby.

'Well, he must not be much of a man, if he gets you in your present situation and then disappears. Where is this man of yours now? Is he prepared to marry you? Is he walking you down the aisle?'

'It doesn't make any difference.' Anna had made up her mind that she was going to keep her baby. No one—not Matron, not anyone else—was going to convince her otherwise.

'The difference is that you are a resident here and he is let off scot-free. In all likelihood he is, at this very moment, out sweet-talking some other foolish girl into trouble.'

Matron leaned back in her wooden swivel chair, and her face seemed to relax. She was like an employer who, after hours, tried to earn the trust of his worker. 'Tell me about this boy—this man—of yours. He has a name?'

'His name is Neil Glass. He is a trainee accountant.'

'And where did you meet this gallant Mr Neil Glass?'

'His family own the farm next door at Cockatoo.'

'At Cockatoo! But I have your address written down here as Brunswick West.'

'We have a little weekend place up at Cockatoo.'

'Cockatoo!' The place name seemed to amuse the older woman. 'Your Mr Neil Glass is a very helpful neighbour to all the girls in the district, no doubt! A very popular young man with the girls of Cockatoo, I shouldn't be surprised to learn. Well, then. How many times did you do it?'

'Do what? It was humiliating for Anna to have Matron ask such personal questions of her: how many times they had done it, whether she had enjoyed it. 'I don't want to talk any more. I have a sore throat.'

'A sore throat! I hope your sore throat is not of the infectious kind. You can imagine how any kind of infection roars through this place, with the girls living at such close quarters.'

'His family are straightforward, hard-working people. I don't want to speak ill of him or his family.'

'A trainee accountant, you say.'

'That's right. He works for a firm in the city and does his studies at night.'

'A pleasant-looking young man, I imagine?' she asked.

'He is serious about his studies. But he loves to play sport. He's tall and strong, very good at football and cricket.'

'Ah! But he has forgotten all about the poor girl he got into trouble.'

A scalding feeling rose from Anna's chest into her throat and she breathed pepper.

'It is not difficult to know what a man wants. All men are prey to the carnal urges. The devil knows very well how to twist a man's soul by tempting him with a comely girl. The difficult part for the girl is knowing how to avoid giving in. That is a matter of morals.' Matron's tone became sharper. 'Where did it take place, this intercourse with the boy from the neighbouring farm?'

'In several locations.'

'You mean the barn, the haystack, and so forth?'

'Is this really necessary?'

How could she tell Matron that they had done it in the back of a Bedford truck? In the deserted Shire Hall where, just the previous evening, the Cockatoo gang had watched a screening of *The African Queen*, the steamboat chugging along the vast river?

'An acquaintance with your circumstances is absolutely necessary. See, here on your file—I am required to make notes regarding your moral character.' Matron stabbed a finger at some papers on the desk. Anna leaned over to peer at a foolscap manila folder to which was attached a file card with a paperclip. The card was marked BFA. 'What does that mean?' she asked, pointing.

'That's not something that need concern you.'

'But this is my file. I have a right to know.'

'This file is confidential. It is not for your eyes.' Matron turned back to her desk.

'What does BFA mean?'

Matron ignored her, but Anna had guessed. 'There's a mistake,' she told Matron. 'Who marked my child for adoption?'

Matron remained silent.

'It's my baby. I'm not signing anything that gives you power to decide what happens to my child.'

'You think you know it all, don't you?' Matron answered without turning. 'But let me tell you something. You girls are brought in here because of what you don't know.'

Anna looked away and said nothing. She felt hopeless.

'If only you had stayed at home and helped your poor mother at her chores like any number of good girls! What age are you now?' Matron consulted her papers. 'Twenty. Well, a girl of twenty ought to know the difference between right and wrong.'

'I do know the difference.' Anna felt unjustly accused.

'My dear, as I like to tell every girl who comes in here, what is at stake is not only the unborn soul you are carrying, but the stain you have put upon your own soul in lying with the boy, this neighbouring farmer boy or this accountant or this excellent cricketer or footballer. You see, God hates pregnant girls. He hates unwed mothers. The only way to cleanse the stain is to repent. I like to think of the Haven as a factory of redemption. Girls are brought in here to cleanse their souls. It's only through suffering that a girl might come sincerely to ask the Lord's forgiveness.'

A weight sank through Anna. She realised once again that it was a kind of prison she had been brought to. 'I'm not signing anything,' she repeated, in a determined voice.

'My poor child, the truth is that if you truly repent, then you will come to see that the right thing is to give your baby to a deserving married couple who are unable to conceive of their own. That way, you see, you will be passing on God's gift to them. An open and generous heart would see the truth in that. You will be doing God's work.'

God hates pregnant girls. God hates unwed mothers. God wants your baby to go to a good home.

The Salvos seemed to know a lot about how God thought and what God wanted. Anna tried to see the lighter side of it all: Matron was carrying on as though she sat down with Him for a cup of tea every afternoon and had a good natter about the sinners who had been brought here.

But Anna thought she *was* a person with morals. She knew that there was good and bad, right and wrong, and that what she had done with Neil was both bad and wrong. But it was also more than that. Wasn't there something pure? Something like love? To the Salvos it was all so cut and dried. The feelings a girl had were made to feel cheap and dirty.

Anna thought she might form a great hatred for Jesus Christ, here at the Haven. She might, instead of being 'saved', on the contrary, be filled with anger and plans for revenge. These Salvos really were an army, and the war they were fighting was not against the devil and sin, but against the girls themselves. It was the girls who were the enemies of God. Anna understood now that they were to be deprived not only of their liberty, but also of their personalities. When Matron said that the girls had been brought here to cleanse their souls, she meant, to break their spirits.

If only Anna could keep her nerve for long enough. If only she could grow a skin to protect everything that was precious in her thoughts and feelings, then she might survive and get out of here with her baby.

'I shall never, ever give up my baby,' Anna said in a low voice.

Matron's face went hard. 'Think of your poor parents. But think above all of your baby's future. If he or she is to go to a deserving couple who can give him every advantage in life, who can give him an education—' She paused a moment, then went on. 'Look, I feel very sorry for you. We can be friends, can we not? Let's go to chapel and pray together. I'm sure that you'll come to accept God's will. You will come to see the wisdom in what I have told you.'

'So you say. But I don't believe you.'

'Ah!' said Matron, shaking with irritation. 'I see that the devil has got into you. So stealthy is he, that enemy of Christ; he settles into a poor girl's soul and even the most experienced Salvationist might miss him. But I can winkle him out, that old reprobate. I can look right into your soul and see him there, Anna. You might think the only blot on you is the babe in your belly, but there is also a stain on your soul. The devil entered you on that first day you gave in to temptation with this excellent accountant and cricketer.'

She added, not unsympathetically, 'My poor girl! It is something I see all the time. A girl comes in thinking herself just unlucky, whereas luck is the least of it. Almost every day I admit another girl in your position. It's only the stubborn ones who have to be dealt with firmly. They are the selfish girls who think they might find a way to keep their baby. But I am sitting here before you to tell you plainly—there is no way for you to keep your baby.'

Anna didn't have to say a word. Matron knew the secrets in her soul. She knew how hard Anna would fight to keep her baby. Maybe there really *was* a stain on her soul, the devil inside her body. Was she in fact not at all the person she thought she was? Perhaps, after all, Matron was right, and she could never be a proper mother to her baby, and the Salvation Army should give her baby to a real mother. But Anna knew in her heart that the baby inside her was not a mark on her soul. He was part of everything that was good about her.

Matron kept telling her off for a considerable time and Anna felt the back of her throat burn, but she was determined not to cry. 'You are the stubborn type, but you will come to heel. You see, we have the power of the Lord on our side, and you will repent and ask for forgiveness, one way or another.'

Anna said quietly, 'My mum told me she is going to stick by me.'

'Ha!' Matron hacked out a bark. 'I'll tell you what your mother said to me when she came here begging me to take you in. Oh, you should have seen how grateful she was. She actually cried with relief, you know! Promised that your father would come every fortnight to pay your board here straight out of his wages. Your poor mother's last words to me as she was leaving were, "If you can't convince my girl to have that child adopted, then tell her she can never come home again."'

'My mum would never say a thing like that!'

'You can think what you like.' Matron turned back to the

stack of files on her desk. Like the rest of the Haven, Matron's office had dim light globes, though whether to save on the power bills or to keep the place worshipful and sepulchral, the patina of sin on them all, Anna could not decide.

'If you love your baby then you will give it up for adoption,' Matron declared, her back still turned to Anna.

On Sunday, Mum and Dad arrived with fruit in a brown paper bag, some barley sugar and magazines. Mum sat with Anna in the downstairs sitting room while Dad went out the back to Matron's office to pay for her board. As soon as Dad was out of the room, Anna asked, 'Did you tell Matron that if I don't adopt the baby out, I can never come home again?'

Mum's face changed. 'That's not what I said.' But from the look on her face, Anna knew she must have said something like it. Anna felt something inside herself turn hard, bitter. Was there no one she could rely on now?

'Through thick and thin—that's what you told me,' Anna reminded her, her voice straining.

'And I meant that, too, I really did. I still mean it. It's just that things are not always as simple as they seem.'

'Not as simple? I think my situation is pretty straightforward. I am going to keep my baby.'

All the pain of these months came into Mum's face. She went to put her arm around Anna, but Anna pulled away. Mum said, 'You know Dad and I love you and we'll always stick by you.'

'Through thick and thin,' Anna repeated. 'You promised. And now you're going back on your promise.'

'No,' Mum said. 'We're going to stick by you.'

'If you could look after the baby during the day, I could find a job. And there's the insurance policy with AMP. If we could cash that in, it would keep me going for a while. Or if I could find a job at a place where they have a crèche...'

'Look, Matron did ask for my help to try to convince you. I said I would talk to you—that's all. I did not say you can't come home if you keep the baby.' Mum looked and sounded suddenly very tired.

Anna felt anger surge up inside her. She thought that Mum was going back on what she had promised her, but she wasn't able to admit it.

'Anna,' Mum said, and now her voice was imploring and pathetic. 'We're on your side, you know. Dad and I love you so very much, no matter what has happened.'

'I know you love me. But I want to know if you'll help me with the baby.'

'Yes,' Mum said, at last. 'I'm going to help you keep the baby.'

Just then Dad came back. Anna and Mum hastily rearranged themselves, as if to conceal the topic of their conversation. He lingered in the doorway with his sheepish smile. 'How are they treating you?' he asked Anna.

'Most of the people are nice.'

'How's the tucker? You getting enough to eat?'

'Brisket and potatoes. It doesn't change much.'

'Mum and I and Robert went for a drive up to Cockatoo yesterday,' Dad told her. 'The wheat's coming on, and there are already cherries on some of the trees.' He did not mention the Glass farm, or Neil, or what his family was up to.

'What do they call you here?' Mum asked. Matron must have told them about the other names.

'Violet.' Anna made a face. She felt ashamed. She did not even own her name any more, the name that Mum and Dad had given her. 'I wanted to be called Elizabeth.'

When they were leaving, Mum whispered, so that Dad couldn't hear, 'We will stick by you, Anna, I promise. You're still our little girl.' Now Anna was determined to believe her. Mum and Dad would let her bring her baby home.

Mum and Dad never missed a single Sunday. Robert drove them, or they caught the tram. Her brother didn't come in, but stayed sitting in his car, or went off for a drive by himself. Anna supposed he was frightened of the Haven, the atmosphere in there, the feeling of the girls being shamed. He had girlfriends of his own, and maybe he saw their possible futures. For Robert, it must have been like the feeling you got when you drove past the dark walls of Pentridge Prison.

Dad never had much to say. He'd been in New Guinea during the war, and Anna felt that the Haven sent him back there, somehow, that it brought out an emptiness in him and made his thoughts dry up.

Her parents didn't see the real Haven; they only saw Sundays. They wouldn't know about girls crying in the night, Anna lying awake hour after hour, her thoughts caught on a merry-go-round of worrying. They wouldn't know what the girls talked about in the bluestone lane as it was coming on dark, with the tobacco smoke and the smell of cooking in all the kitchens of all the houses in Fitzroy.

One Sunday, Mum brought in a piece she had cut out from the *Sun*, announcing Neil's engagement. It was another blow, another betrayal. Anna's last hope for Neil faded. There would be no one coming to the Haven to rescue her.

Anna didn't know the girl. It might have been someone who worked at his firm in the city. Or someone else. She must have been a 'good girl', who hadn't fallen into misfortune. Or maybe she had, and he couldn't get out of it this time. Anyway, he was going to marry her.

Mum was looking at Anna, trying not to say his name. There were some things that could not be said.

Anna handed back the clipping without a word, determined not to reveal the fact that she had harboured secret hopes. Mum carefully folded the piece of paper and returned it to her handbag.

Mum and Dad would only stay for a while. Like prisoners, the girls here learned to be numb. Anna could tell that it hurt her parents to see her going numb, too. You're a little girl, you're safe in your childhood, you think it will never change. Then one day something happens and you realise that life is foreign to the world of feelings. Your own puny existence doesn't matter much to the great world.

Anna knew that Mum and Dad loved her, but she felt bad she had brought all this on them, and in a way it was a relief when they went home, though the emptiness stabbed deeper for a minute. The only thing she had left, the only thing she was sure of, was her baby.

New girls arrived, wrapped in blankets and overcoats. Some of them arrived alone at the Haven, each carrying her own case. Others came with their mum or dad, or both of them. More than one girl told Anna a story similar to her own: of a mother giving her daughter sleeping pills without her knowing, and the girl waking up in the car outside.

They had been uprooted from their normal routines and family homes, their brothers and sisters, their boyfriends (those who stuck by them, though they were not allowed to visit, wrote letters), their own interests, their personal possessions. Quite a few girls were from Tasmania. Some of them had arrived by plane at Essendon aerodrome. Others came from towns Anna had never heard of before. Jerilderie. Taree. Narbethong. They were driven to Melbourne by their families, so that no one in their district would know.

Some of the girls, rich ones from big farms and sheep stations, had never done a stroke of work in their lives. It was a new experience for them to have to scrub the floors, or work all day in the heat of the hospital laundry.

Every day, every hour, brought another test to be passed. Even on Saturdays when they were allowed to go to the shops in the city, there could be no more than two in a group. The local citizens didn't want to see a gang of them walking along the footpath, bellies bulging, laughing and raucous, unrepentant. If they went in pairs they caused less staring. The Baby Factory, people called the place. There had been complaints to the administration from homeowners in the area about the girls 'walking the streets in their state'. Pregnant unmarried women should not be seen in public, at least no more than necessary, so if they were in the streets on Saturdays, it meant that Matron was failing in her duty.

The girls gave each other nicknames. Anna was The Mouse because she never said boo. Leanne was Blacky. Elizabeth, a tall girl, was Stalky. Lorraine was Dish-mop because of her unruly corkscrew curls. Lorraine liked all kinds of pranks, and if ever there was a squealing laugh to bring Matron running, it was Lorraine's. She was one of those girls always out of favour with figures in authority. Anna imagined Lorraine at school, always in trouble with the teachers. She was seventeen, though she looked older. Her greatest pleasure was smoking, which was frowned on at the Haven. Smoking was a vice, an abomination against God, an example of intemperance. Anna didn't smoke, but for the company she went out with Lorraine and Leanne and the others to the back lane when they had finished work for the day.

To get to the lane they had to go through the courtyard, past Matron's green door with the little flap that opened. Matron turned a blind eye to these unofficial smokos—without them the girls might have gone mad. They had to work twelve hours a day, from six until six, with only an hour's rest at half past one, and these stolen half-hours in the back lane were a release from the drudgery. Inside the Haven, they were unsmiling ghosts. In the bluestone lane with a packet of Turf, for half an hour the girls came back to life. Springtime in Melbourne, not yet dark. Raucous voices and the smell of tobacco. Lorraine and Leanne always offered Anna a smoke, but Anna always refused.

Some of them were real chatterboxes, like Stalky, who told Anna she had owned a horse in Box Hill, and when her parents had found out she was pregnant, her father had walked down to the paddock where the horse was kept and, without saying anything, shot it with his .303 rifle. Stalky had heard the sound from her bedroom, a single shot, sudden, puzzling, followed a few seconds later by a second shot.

She told the story without emotion, the way people talk when something still hurts too much.

The 'Knocked-up Club' the girls called themselves, and there was a kind of hating themselves as well as laughing at themselves in that. When the girls sat together in the lane at six o'clock, it was the one clean half-hour in a dirty day. Pearl was a tough nut. She despised that belly of hers and cursed it and called it names—the hump, the bump, the lump. But maybe she was one of those girls who didn't like herself to begin with, Anna wondered, and there must have been a reason for that.

'You gonna keep the bub?' Pearl asked.

Leanne turned her head with interest.

'Oh, yes!' Anna said. 'My mum said she's going to stick by me.'

She was surprised to hear the vehemence in her own voice. After all, she was just stating something that Mum had told her. But Anna really needed to believe those words: she could not bear to think of the consequences otherwise.

'When it first happened,' Pearl said, 'when I told him I was late, we were going to get married, Charley and me. We even went to look at a little place for rent near my mum's in Newport. We were in love, me and Charley. But now he's with my best friend, Colleen. She'd better watch out, when I get out of here. Anyway, he'll probably put her in the family way as well. He must have potted me the first time we done it. My dream was me and Charley. Now he's with Colleen.'

Once, Anna, too, had dreams. A wedding in white. Buying a house with Neil, buying the furniture she'd like. They used to plan their future together. Now she would have to find a

166

house to rent for herself and her baby, once she had found a job and they had moved out of Mum and Dad's.

'Me and Charley, we used to talk about buying a block. He said he knew where some land was going cheap, and we used to talk about the kind of house we'd build, and what we would see out of our window, lying in bed together on the weekend. Now he's probably telling it all to Colleen.'

'I saw the Crows arrive before,' Leanne said. They were finishing breakfast on Sunday morning, semolina porridge as usual, its texture like fish scales. A jug of bluish milk. There was lukewarm tea in the pot.

The Salvo women were dressed in black, with black bonnets. The Salvos in uniform only came on Sundays.

'I've had a gutful of those prayers of theirs,' Leanne said. 'I'd nail the Crows to a cross if I had half a chance.'

Once, Anna might have objected to this kind of violent talk; now she went along with it. She hated the Salvos, too.

After chapel, there was a rest period while they waited for their midday meal. In their room, the girls talked and shared sweets and magazines. They weren't allowed to have a wireless or to play records. The *Women's Weekly* was full of pictures of the new Queen, photos of coaches and crowns, news about preparations for the coronation. Anna always said she 'read the print off the pages' of the *Women's Weekly*. It came out on Wednesdays, price 9d. Anna waited eagerly for Mum to bring it to her on Sundays. She enjoyed the Fireside Reading, the short stories, and the Social Jottings. She asked Mum to bring her the old issues, too, a year's worth—she knew Mum kept them in the bottom of the linen press, to save the knitting patterns and recipes.

The *Women's Weekly* took Anna away from the Haven. Through its pages she stepped into another life, the life she might have lived: a married woman, a mother, a housewife. She stared sightlessly, disappearing into the lost world she might have had. In the pages of the magazine, she allowed herself to remember feelings she had had to kill off—her dreams of a future with Neil. She spent hours staring at the advertisements for Jantzen bathers, Actil sheets, Hoovers, and she allowed herself to inhabit an ideal world quite different from her days at the Haven.

She kept her magazines in a pile under her bed, and often flicked through the pages of old issues in spare moments. There was a picture of a baby with blond curly hair, playing with a bubble pipe, on the cover of an issue from earlier that year. In July, there had been *The Great Gatsby* by F. Scott Fitzgerald, complete in one issue. But the topic Anna always returned to was the Queen.

Even before her accession to the throne back in February, Anna had liked looking at pictures of Princess Elizabeth in military uniform on horseback. There had been photos of her with yellow roses, wearing a tiara, on her birthday in April. In June, there had been photos of Prince Charles. The cover in September had a new portrait of Queen Elizabeth.

'When did you first do it with Noel?' Pearl asked.

'Neil,' Anna corrected her.

'With Neil, then. Did you let him put it in right away?'

Anna didn't like to talk about sex in the rough way the other girls did.

'Did it feel nice?' Pearl asked.

'Oh, yes!' Anna said. But the way it had come out sounded silly. It wasn't something that should be talked about. Not because it was wrong or vulgar, though she supposed it was, but because Anna had been hurt so much in these months since, and to revive those memories made the wound raw again. She couldn't talk about it because those days and nights at Cockatoo were hidden away inside her. As long as she kept her secrets and never talked about them, that life continued to exist in the place where she dreamed.

Pearl was still recounting her adventures with Charley, adventures he was no doubt repeating with Colleen, but Anna had stopped listening. She was safe with her own thoughts. She felt Neil's body close to her, the feelings he had given her. The way he used to drive his car fast on the corners of the dirt roads up at Cockatoo, smiling and turning his head to her when he made her squeal. He liked to make her laugh, too. The way he grabbed her waist, which she liked, because he was tall, broad-shouldered and strong from playing football. Neil had been special. She would not have him compared with Charley. He was not just another boy who wanted to feel her tits.

Now Anna supposed Neil loved this girl he was marrying. But she was certain he had loved her, too, once. That kind of thing couldn't just go away, could it?

Her memories of weekends and holidays at Cockatoo were too precious to give away to the other girls in idle talk. Sometimes she would find herself visiting Neil again in her mind—Neil as he had been, not Neil as he was now, not the Neil who was engaged to another girl.

Anna had met Neil in 1951, when the Glass family bought

the farm opposite at Cockatoo. Don, the youngest son, worked for his dad. When Anna's family was there, Don would come over and see them in the evenings. May, the sister, worked hard, had never married, ran poultry and grew vegetables. Neil, the middle child, was pursuing his studies and working in the city. He used to come home for weekends and holidays. They all became good friends.

Then, suddenly, at Easter the following year, it had begun.

Anna had arrived at the shack by herself on Thursday afternoon, to get the place ready. Since the wages had been paid early that week due to the holidays, the staff at the pay office were given the afternoon off. At lunchtime, she used her staff pass to take the train from Flinders Street to Ferntree Gully, where she changed to the narrow-gauge train to Cockatoo. Dad and Robert had to work all day; they would drive up with Mum the following morning. Neil had already driven up from Melbourne and, seeing the light on at the shack in the evening, walked over to say hello.

She knew something was different about him. Neil was, as usual, smiling and friendly, but there was a teasing look in his eyes, the look of someone who had a secret. For the first time, Anna felt self-conscious in his company. They had been talking about Easter, the funny names. 'What's good about Good Friday?' Anna joked.

'And what does Maundy Thursday mean?'

'I know it's today. Thursday was when Jesus had the Last Supper and washed his disciples' feet.'

'You can wash my feet, if you like,' Neil said, his usual smile, that teasing look.

She pretended to fetch the enamel basin, picked up the soap,

Neil laughing at her. Somehow, they had ended up in each other's arms.

After that, every weekend in April and May, they were inseparable. When she was with Neil, Anna did not feel it was dirty because she was convinced of their destiny together. They would get married, they were part of a greater moral purpose. She traced the contours of his arms and shoulders, the muscles of his back, and she felt herself go weak with need for him.

Mum did not understand that, of course. She had guessed that Anna and Neil were having sex and, one Saturday afternoon at Cockatoo, when Dad and Robert were out in the paddock, Mum had sat Anna down and tried to talk some sense into her. 'Wait until you're married,' she implored. 'There'll be plenty of time later.'

'Oh, Mum.' Anna stopped herself from saying anything more.

'I always thought you were a good girl.'

They were sitting in the tiny lounge room of the cottage. Anna remained in her place near the wood stove. Mum went through the doorway into the skillion kitchen. 'It isn't that I like having to say these things to you,' Mum said from the kitchen. 'We never talk any more. Not the way we used to. Remember the way we used to laugh so hard we cried?'

Anna had felt a lurching sob pass through her body. She was fond of those lost, innocent times, too.

'Now you hardly say a word. I don't know what's got into you.'

'Nothing's got into me,' said Anna dully.

'It's that boy who's changed you. It's Neil Glass, with his big ideas about himself. His accounting firm in the city, his triumphs on the football field. I don't blame you for falling for him, but just be careful, that's all.'

'We are careful.' There, it was out. Anna hoped that would be the end of it. Even as she said it, she knew it was a lie.

'I'll tell you something. You don't want Dad to find out that boy is not treating you right!'

Anna felt her face burning from sitting next to the stove. She got up, and started towards the front door and the verandah.

'Don't just walk away when I'm talking to you.'

'I can still hear you, Mum,' she said in an exasperated, sing-song voice. The last thing she wanted was a row.

'And don't take that tone with me, either.'

'What else can I do?' Anna asked her mother. She felt suddenly hopeless.

'Will you do something for me and Dad?'

'If it's not seeing Neil, the answer is no.'

'My heart will break if that boy does anything to hurt you.'

Anna felt bad that she had disappointed her mum. She had put that 'little talk' with Mum out of her mind. The hard thing for Anna to admit now was that Mum had been right.

And yet…Anna couldn't stop those memories returning. She would feel like her old self for a while, then Neil's face would appear before her and her head would fill with a powerful whooshing sound like the beating of wings. She could not tell anyone about it. They would say she was mad.

It was as though she and Neil, on those cold weekends in April and May, had been engaged in some grand noble enterprise. There was a purity in their love that others would not have seen. They had made their promises to each other. Neil had said he would not let her down.

When it had first happened, being late, she had been so afraid of telling him. And then Neil had sent that stupid note. Still, he'd said, they would continue to love each other in that other world that was forever Cockatoo. Now, after seeing the engagement notice, she knew she shouldn't have believed a word of it.

Sometimes the sound of a girl's screams carried from the hospital wing at the back of the Haven. If that was childbirth, the pain of squeezing forth life from life, Anna dreaded what lay ahead of her.

She heard all kinds of rumours. She heard that girls were made to sign papers and then their baby was taken away. The girl left quickly, it was all arranged, sometimes without even saying goodbye. The birth certificate was changed so that you could no longer have any contact with your baby, or any way of finding him. There were rumours about the drugs they used on you. Sedatives to knock you out, so you wouldn't be aware of what they were doing. Barbiturates. Anti-psychotics. And after the birth? She heard the stories about stilboestrol to dry up your milk, the binding of the breasts with a calico cloth secured with a safety pin. When a girl was uncooperative, she was shackled to the bed in the labour ward. Anna also heard that sometimes, when you were giving birth, they put a pillow over your face, or put up a sheet, so that you couldn't see your baby. The unmarried mothers were not supposed to see or touch their babies. A married woman whose own child had been stillborn might be offered a child for adoption in its place. Where had that baby come from? There were rumours that some single mothers were told their baby had died, when in fact the child had been taken for a 'rapid adoption'.

Anna did not yet know what really happened; in a way it was worse to imagine it.

She would take her baby home to Mum and Dad's, and somehow they would survive. They had said they were going to stick by her. *Through thick and thin.* The thing Anna was most afraid of wasn't the Welfare, or the Salvos, or even that Mum and Dad might change their minds, but a part of her own mind that she did not trust. It was a black despair that sometimes bloomed and spread through her thoughts: the part of her that wanted to be defeated, that just wanted to give up. Even when she steeled her mind against the Salvos, Anna was not always able to block out the poisonous phrases they repeated to shame her, make her passive, steal her personality. Her old life wasn't hers any more. She was living someone else's life here.

There were moments at the Haven, with the eleven o'clock sunshine coming through the laundry windows, when her thoughts floated free for a while, and she forgot to feel afraid. But then the thought always came back, about what might have been if Neil had stuck by her, and she always ended up feeling frightened and alone again.

'Christ, you're a mess,' Leanne said. 'Just take a look at yourself in the mirror.'

Anna stared: red eyes, red face, hair everywhere. She had been crying, long sobs ending in a shudder. 'I like crying,' Anna said. And they both burst out laughing because it was a funny thing to say.

'Don't be a sook,' Leanne said. 'Come out to the lane with me while I have a fag.'

They crossed the courtyard and went through the gate behind the laundry, making sure there was no face at the flap in the door of Matron's office. Leanne sucked on a Turf cork-tipped. 'You know the house next door? That one there—on the other side of the wall? Well, sometimes I see a man standing at the upstairs window, looking down, watching me.'

Anna took in a sudden sharp breath of air. 'Is he watching us now?'

'No. But I often see him watching. He must be a millionaire to live in a big house like that. He's always wearing a red waistcoat and standing at that window, smoking a cigarette. He has this funny little smile on his face. I can't make up my mind if he's laughing at me or if he feels sorry for me.'

'You'd do well to ignore him.'

The sky was heavy and grey; it was going to rain. Leanne said, 'I tell myself he has fallen in love with me and one day he'll come and take me away.'

'That's a pretty fairy tale!' Anna laughed.

'Pathetic, aren't I?' Leanne screwed up her freckled face and took another drag on her cigarette. 'Still, I will be going away from here one day, me and the baby. After the deed is done.'

'So you're going to keep your baby, too?'

'My mum and dad wouldn't let me back with the baby. They'd be too worried about what people would think.'

'So what are you going to do?'

At the sound of the bell for the evening meal, Leanne stepped on her cigarette butt and they moved towards the gate.

Leanne said, 'Well, I'm going to keep my baby. That's what I'm going to do.'

They had reached the steps up to the familiar back door, and from there they made their way to the dining room. Most of the girls were already seated at the scrubbed tables. The two latecomers found their places.

'I want to ask you something,' Leanne said.

'I'm listening.'

That night they were having cutlets, a better meal than those Margaret usually served up. She must have been on good terms with the butcher, or perhaps he was sweet on her at the moment.

Eating her meat and drinking her tea, Leanne smiled a crafty smile. 'You know the Women's Hospital in Carlton? Well, I've heard they take unmarried girls for their lying-in. Come closer. I don't want anyone else to hear. So I reckon if I pretend I'm going to the shops with you one Saturday, I just might not come back. If that happens, and they ask what happened to me, tell them you don't know. Just say I must have got lost in Myer's.'

'I have an idea,' Anna said. 'What if we both got lost in Myer's?'

'Would you really?'

'You don't think I have the guts to do it?'

Leanne seemed to consider the idea for a moment. Then she said, 'Sure you do.'

'Hang on, what would we do for money?'

'I'm pretty sure they take in charity cases.'

'Well, we have to give it a try.'

Anna held out her hand under the edge of the table. 'We

have to stick together,' she added, and they shook on it.

The two girls continued to talk about how they would keep their babies. One of the Crows must have overheard them, because later she sought Anna out. 'You foolish girl! You think you're going to keep your baby. But let me tell you something—in the end, girls like you always have to give them up.'

Anna felt the rising urge to slap the woman's face. She struggled to control herself. Since she had come to the Haven, Anna had tried to hide behind a docile manner. If I don't make trouble, she had thought, perhaps they will go easy on me. But belonging to this company of girls was more complicated than that. You couldn't hide by being docile. The Salvos had a way of finding you out, even if you never answered them back, and didn't dare to look them in the eye, and even if you joined in singing their Glory Bloody Hallelujah.

Stupid girl, *foolish* girl, *wicked* girl, *sinful* girl. Anna heard herself called these names so many times she came to believe them.

At prayers in the chapel, the girls were harangued. 'Get on your knees, girls! God knows what you did! Do you really think you can keep secrets from His all-seeing eye? He will take pity on a poor sinner if only she will repent.'

Well, I ain't sorry for you no more, you crazy, psalm-singing, skinny old maid!

Bogey appeared in the chapel and gave Anna that shame-faced, apologetic smile of his. Charlie Allnut was his name in the film. Katharine Hepburn was the missionary, Rose Sayer.

Bogey appeared to Anna more and more at the Haven—in the chapel, and when she was in bed at night unable to sleep.

Things are never so bad that they can't be made worse, he told her.

When she was working in the laundry, she heard the sound of an engine. It was a mechanical sound—a steam engine. A boiler? The sound was meant for her and for no one else. It was as though the engine wanted her to do something. Then she remembered Bogey's dirty little steamboat in *The African Queen*.

The sound of the steamboat on the river was the beginning of the illness that saved her. Bogey looked at her. His grease-streaked face seemed to reassure her. He was going to rescue her. He was going to take her and her baby away from here.

It was the first week in December. Leanne must have been close because she had been taken off laundry duties that Friday. With her great belly, she had hardly been able to sit on the gutter in the bluestone lane. She was so far gone that they had not been able to pull off their shopping expedition on the Saturday.

'So much for our grand plans,' Leanne said at lunch on Sunday.

'Don't worry. Things will work out,' Anna told her. 'Just remember—whatever happens, don't sign anything.'

Leanne nodded, but Anna could see that she was demoralised.

At midday on Monday, Anna came in to have dinner and Leanne wasn't at the table. One of the girls said Leanne had gone into labour that morning and had been taken to the hospital wing.

There was no news of Leanne all week. On Saturday, Anna

heard that Leanne was back. When she went up to Leanne's dormitory, a shape in her bed was quietly weeping. 'A little boy,' Leanne said. 'I called him Jesse. They wouldn't even let me hold him.' Matron had injected her with something, then showed her the typed paper with her name signed. 'But it wasn't my handwriting!' she wailed to Anna.

Leanne was devastated. Anna tried to think of some way to comfort her friend, but how do you console someone when a thing as terrible as that has happened?

Leanne's people hadn't come to take her away yet. Maybe their car had broken down, or there was no train from Leongatha that day. But when Anna came back up after tea, Leanne was gone. She didn't have a chance to say goodbye.

Anna felt her whole being change, as though a new voice spoke through her with calm authority, an intelligence born of pure hatred for the Salvos and what they had done to her friend. So, Anna would wait to take her revenge on these Salvos. She would defeat Matron by being resolute. When she finally did get out of this place, it would be *with* her baby.

And in the years ahead? If she ever saw the Salvos on Friday nights with their brass bands farting out hymns on street corners, just let one of them come up and try to sell her the bloody *War Cry* and see what she gets! Anna could imagine it all. She would rip off the first black bonnet she saw. A bread knife in the belly. Split her skull open with a hammer. These homicidal fantasies warmed her and gave her a secret smile.

Anna let the demon enter her, that night after Leanne was taken away, the demon the Salvos had spoken about in their threats and prayers. How could anything in their Hell frighten Anna now? They had stolen Leanne's baby. They wanted to steal Anna's baby, too. What could be worse than that?

She realised only now how hard she was going to have to fight to keep her baby. She was determined not to suffer Leanne's fate.

That's what life is about, in the end, she thought: women keeping babies.

ONE MORNING ANNA woke to find herself bleeding. The doctor ordered bed rest. She didn't leave her bed for three days, except to go to the lavatory. One of the young Salvos brought her meals on a tray. Although Matron did not put in an appearance, she must have been aware of the situation.

Mostly, Anna slept. She would sleep all afternoon, wake for a few hours and lie there, then sleep all through the night. The other girls left her alone. She had begun to withdraw from the Haven into her own world.

Her illness was not feigned. Its symptoms were physical—her brain shut down and some power pulled her irresistibly towards sleep. Her mind had found a way to abolish the Haven and to silence the Salvos' songs. Her journey along the dark river with Bogey was her way of denying their god. Not just denying his existence, which might have been a childish way of taking revenge on them, but hating the God that had put her in the Haven. For the rest of her life, Anna was sure, she would never pass a church of any denomination without feeling a shudder of revulsion.

She wasn't always ill, unfortunately. There were days of relative normality, when she could speak to the other girls, when she could meet the curious eye of Matron and answer questions put to her, and do the bit of floor-scrubbing required of her in order for Matron to save face, or work for an hour in the laundry. There were always so many sheets to be washed, starched, dried and ironed, and Anna liked the warmth of the steamy laundry.

But then she felt the heaviness descend again. The baby inside her was the least of it. She sat down wherever she was, or lay on her side on the floor and went to sleep. Sometimes they had to carry her upstairs. Or she felt her feet moving towards the dormitory, towards her bed, without her having decided it: her feet knew better than she did.

Anna had discovered her weapon. But she would need further weapons to help her keep her baby. Sometimes she thought that on the river, behind that mechanical sound, Bogey was trying to whisper how she might go about it.

Doctors brought interns from the university to practise on the girls at the Haven. Anna felt herself being poked and prodded from every direction.

'This one's eight months gone, reported bleeding from the uterus, baby seems to be still kicking, though. Any ideas?' the head doctor asked.

'Could be a very late period,' one student said, and the others sniggered.

'Now, that's enough, Mr Parsons, this is no place for your questionable humour. Any others?'

'A lesion in the cervix?' another student tried. The students talked about her as though she wasn't in the room.

Some of the doctors told the girls to take off their clothes even if it was just to take their temperature or blood pressure, but Doctor Jericho was different from the others. He did not ask Anna to take off her clothes. He did not give her an internal examination. He was dressed differently from the other doctors, too. He wore a fine tweed suit, and he seemed compassionate. He was some kind of specialist, she thought.

'What's wrong with me, Doctor?' Anna asked. She began to shake and she tried to hold back her sobs.

'You're so wound up in your worries that your body has gone on strike.'

'Yes,' she said. She knew he was right.

'What do you think is going to happen?' he asked.

'I'll have my baby and keep it and take it home with me. I've got my mum and dad on my side. They've promised to stick by me.'

The doctor watched her face closely. 'You are exhausted. I'll ask Matron that you be excused from all work. It's essential for your own health and that of your baby.'

'You don't believe me, do you? You don't think my mum and dad *are* going to stick by me?'

He was silent for a long time. Then he said, 'I'm always very careful about what—and who—I believe.'

In her new state of mind, it was finally clear to Anna that Neil had done the dirty on her. She had even thought he might have been paying the Salvation Army for her board. She asked her dad on one of his visits. 'You don't need to worry about that,' he told her. 'Forget about Neil. He didn't have the moral fibre to do the right thing by you.'

Yet Anna could not give up her memories, even when sometimes they made her so miserable that she truly wanted to die. But at other times, when she thought about the man she had loved, the man who had betrayed her, the man she still loved, if truth be told, she felt she was back at Cockatoo again, it was all still happening, time did not exist.

Anna no longer listened to the Salvos. She was ill, but they had not broken her. In bed at night, she hugged her swollen belly and conducted silent conversations with her unborn child, telling him how much she loved him, vowing to protect him always. She could feel him moving inside her, kicking. She imagined holding him after he was born. With every last ounce of strength in her body she would stop them from taking him. Yes, she would have her victory over Matron. There would be nothing Matron could do, anyway, since Anna had Mum on her side.

The prospect that she might lose her baby, that she might have to go through the rest of her life searching for him, was unthinkable. She would keep her baby safe from these inhuman, baby-stealing fiends at the Haven.

Bogey would take her home and look after her. He would help her keep her child. In the chapel, with her eyes closed, she prayed not to Jesus Christ, but to Bogey. She called on Bogey to come and rescue her. But even as she was praying like this, she could still hear Matron's cold voice in her head: 'He won't help you—this is what you deserve for getting pregnant.'

She was full of chaos and uncertainty. Anna realised she was praying to Bogey because, deep down, she had begun to lose faith in Mum and Dad. She was terrified they were not going to let her take her baby home, after all.

There was a door at the end of the hallway upstairs that led to the balcony. Anna loved to go there in the mornings and look out over the Edinburgh Gardens. For a few minutes, out there, the heavy feeling vanished. One morning she went onto the balcony as usual, but something felt different. The sun was shining, a perfect, still day at the beginning of summer. She noticed that one of the oak trees was moving. The branches were trembling, light danced in the leaves, even though there was no wind. How could this be?

To Anna, God was something felt but seldom seen. But she was seeing Him now, she thought. This dancing green light belonged to some divine world, not to the Salvos with their sermons and psalms, and she was moved. She concentrated all her attention on that lovely light. She drew it into her body so she could hoard it there and let it nourish her spirit. For the first time she felt that what was happening to her had a purpose. The new life swelling inside her was connected to the same vast, unknowable power that was moving the tree.

Later, she lay on her narrow bed and closed her eyes. She

was alone, the other girls were still at work. Anna kept thinking about the mysterious light she had seen in the tree. She would always love her baby, she understood now, no matter who he grew into or whatever he did. This was something the Salvos could never take away.

She managed to get out to the balcony again in the early evening. The Edinburgh Gardens were now thick with shadows. Her soul was dark, like the gardens. The energy, the feeling, was gone. It was night-time again.

Visitors were allowed on Christmas Day, even though it was a Thursday. The girls' families arrived with their greetings and gifts; there was no one for those who lived too far away, or for girls who had been disowned.

Anna's parents arrived in the downstairs sitting room at eleven o'clock on Christmas morning. Robert came inside with them this time. He carried Anna's present, a one-pound tin of Cadbury's Roses chocolates. Mum had also brought in the *Women's Weekly*, of course. On the cover was MERRY CHRISTMAS from the Sara quads—four children in hats playing on a toy car with coloured streamers. Anna felt embarrassed that she had nothing to give Mum and Dad and Robert. After they left, there was Christmas dinner put on by the Salvos, chicken with stuffing, baked potatoes, plum pudding with custard. The girls pulled crackers and sang Christmas carols. Anna hated the sentimental atmosphere in the dining room that afternoon, the forced jollity, the institutional insincerity, and before long she went upstairs to the dormitory to be alone. She opened the magazine Mum had brought her. There was the young Queen smiling, wearing a diamond tiara crown, in her horse-drawn royal carriage.

In the spooky quiet of a hot Melbourne January, her incarceration continued. Usually in January she would be up in the hills, at Cockatoo. It was cooler up there; she remembered waking to the fresh summer mornings last year.

How long ago it all seemed! She remembered the time she and Neil had talked about a wedding, and the dam burst. All the old memories came flooding back: the bread and newspaper smell of the milk bar at Cockatoo, the films they had seen on Saturday nights, the first time Neil had taken her in his arms and kissed her—she had been lifted on a wave of desire she had never known before.

Even when she was well enough to work in the laundry again, she kept watch with a kind of sick excitement in her heart. 'He is coming to save me,' she told herself. 'Who?'

Not Bogey, not Charlie Allnut.

Neil.

Then, when her mind cleared and reason returned, she was disgusted with herself for giving in, yet again, to this desperate fantasy.

At least she had found a temporary escape. Every day she walked in the Edinburgh Gardens for a few minutes, for half an hour, and came back to life. No one tried to stop her. She did not ask anyone's permission. She simply walked out the front door, down the steps, through the iron gate and across the road. The long branches of the trees swayed in the wind, the summer leaves as thick as hair.

One hot afternoon when there was a northerly, as she walked under the trees, the fronds flapping at her mouth, she turned her head and saw a man standing at the edge of the park, beside a car, a guilty smile playing on his lips. She made an effort to control herself, to hide her delight, but it came out in her face by itself.

'Neil?' she called to him.

The man raised a hand in a surreptitious wave, then turned and got into the car. She had been mistaken. It wasn't Neil. Not even Charlie Allnut. It was some other man, a stranger, who had been watching her. She thought it might have been the same man who had watched Leanne from the upstairs window of the big house next door.

She turned sharply and walked towards the middle of the gardens. When she had gone a few steps, she stopped and watched the car glide off in the sunshine and disappear around the bend of Alfred Crescent. Anna gave a deep sigh and stared at the empty road.

The 4th of February was an unusually hot day. Even the interior of the Haven, usually so dark and cold, was oppressive that afternoon. Anna lay on her bed, sweating. On doctor's orders, she was again excused from work.

At five o'clock the other girls came in, complaining about the heat, grumbling to Anna about the events of the day. Anna got up to go to the window for a breath of air, and suddenly had a very strange feeling. It felt like a balloon popping inside her. A gush of warm fluid spilled from between her thighs, soaking her underpants. It trickled down her legs and spread around her feet on the parquet floor. 'Crikey, I've wet my pants,' she said. She felt so embarrassed. Every time she tried to move, another gush came out.

One of the new girls, Kelly, told her. 'That's not piss. Your waters have broken, that's what's happened!'

The girls helped her to change her clothes. They walked with her to the hospital wing. The first pains had started.

She was left alone on a trolley in a kind of waiting room. The nursing sister went about her tasks, ignoring Anna. The pains were coming regularly now. It seemed to be taking too long. Could something be the matter? Every few minutes, she asked the nurse, 'Is it time?'

'No, not yet,' she said irritably. 'Just wait quietly. We'll be the ones to decide when it's time.'

Then, without a word, she was whisked along a corridor to the chrome and linoleum delivery room. A metal bed, stirrups, a blazing lamp. Not a trace of rebellion could survive in here.

A young trainee nurse was in charge of Anna. The girl was excited. 'It's going to be my first delivery,' she announced. 'Don't worry. Sister will be in the next room. She'll keep an eye on things.'

Another spasm of pain, and she felt herself pushing. She tried to breathe but the pain tore her breath away. She rode the wild train all through the night. She tottered at the edge, then hurtled into the abyss, over and over, every time a new spasm arrived.

When the pain became too much, she heard a voice screaming, 'Shit! Oh God! Help me!' She realised it was her own voice, though the sound seemed to be coming from far away.

The sister came in and told her she was giving her an injection of pethidine. The pain melted away in a haze.

The trainee nurse had to cut her. The sister showed her how to do it. Anna didn't feel the cut. Her baby was born at 8.48 in the morning of the 5th of February. He was a big baby. All she saw was the top of his head, thick fair hair. She begged the nurse, 'Please, can I hold him?'

'No. He's marked for adoption. It's kinder this way,' said the sister.

She had seen her file in Matron's office. But Anna had not signed those papers. She had a right to hold her baby.

'Kinder? What the hell do you mean?'

'It's kinder for you. Don't argue. I know what I'm talking about. I've seen this hundreds of times.'

When the sister had left the room, the nurse let her hold him for a moment. Anna drew in great draughts of breath. 'He's beautiful,' she kept saying, marvelling at his perfect, tiny fingers, which locked around her own forefinger. His grip was so strong already! He belonged to her. Of course she had to keep him now. There could be no question about it. Surely they could see that?

The nurse took him from her as the nursing sister came back through the door. They held him on a table, the sister with a clipboard in her hands, weighing him, counting fingers and toes.

'Nine pounds, seven ounces.'

'Ten fingers.'

'Ten toes.'

'Eyes open.'

'Penis? Yes, one of those.'

'Testicles? Two.'

Anna was still drowsy from the pethidine. 'Please, can't I hold him?'

'I've already told you. It's not allowed. The baby is BFA.'

'There's been a mistake. I'm keeping my son. It's all been worked out with Matron.'

'We'll see about that,' the nursing sister said, as she picked up the baby.

'Where are you taking him?'

The sister did not reply. She carried the baby into the next room.

Later that morning, she went to the nursery. The duty nurse told Anna she did not have permission to enter. The woman looked directly at her, challenging Anna to defy her: *I'll show you who's boss around here, girl.*

Anna went back to bed in the maternity ward, but after lunch she returned to the nursery. This time, she strode through the open doorway and straight over to her baby, the only newborn in there. But just as she was reaching over to him, two nurses took her by the arms and marched her back to the maternity ward, while another one locked the nursery door and called the social worker.

'Don't try to make any trouble,' the social worker said, when she came and stood by Anna's bed. 'It's best that you don't see the baby again. It's kinder when the mother isn't allowed to bond with the baby.'

Kinder. There was that word again. 'You can't be talking about *my* baby!' Anna said. 'There has been a mistake!' She was agitated. Why did she have to explain all this to them? How could they be so *stupid*?

The social worker was a plain woman of thirty or so, dressed entirely in brown, though it wasn't a uniform. Anna decided that the woman did not belong to the Salvation Army. She smiled at Anna and tried to reassure her. 'I'm on your side, you know. I'm only trying to do what's best for you.'

That afternoon Anna went back to the nursery. This time there was a different nurse, a girl named Di, who let Anna pick up her baby and hold him on her knee. Was Di considerate, or unaware of Matron's orders?

Anna opened the front of her nightgown and put him to the breast. His face and eyes were still puffy. He stared up at her with his dark blue eyes, curious, alert. He held up his minia-ture swollen blue fists—he was going to be a sportsman, like his father. She uncurled the tiny fingers, marvelling at his delicate fingernails.

How Anna loved that precious little boy already! No one had the right to take him away. She called him Kim, because she had loved the novel by Rudyard Kipling.

She tried to time her visits to the nursery when Di was on duty. Anna talked to her baby and sang songs to him and patted him. She whispered to him, her plans for their future together. Anna would find another job with a crèche, they would find a place of their own, and he would go to school. She would always make sure his clothes were new and of the best quality. He would go to university and make a good life for himself.

Two days later Matron caught her in the nursery. 'What are you doing? Who told you to breastfeed him?' Then, turning to Di, 'What is this girl doing? Who gave her permission to be in here?'

Di looked alarmed; her mouth was open but no words came

out. Perhaps she really hadn't known that Anna was not allowed in here.

'I don't need permission to feed my baby,' Anna said to Matron.

'The BFAs have to be bottle fed.' Matron was frowning at Di.

Anna felt the dread spreading through her belly. 'BFA? But my baby's not BFA.'

Matron turned and smiled at her, and Anna didn't know where that smile was coming from.

'Mum knows I'm keeping him. Remember, I told you that?'

'I have been informed of nothing of the kind.'

It was all such a terrible mix-up. Anna wanted to cry with frustration. Instead, Kim's little mouth unlatched from the nipple and he began wailing. The sound of his crying filled the room. She lifted him onto her shoulder, facing away from Matron, and rocked him quiet.

Matron said patiently, as if she were explaining something to a child, 'This institution has a policy. It is not for me to change the policy. You can't just march in here, when you know full well it is against the rules—'

Anna turned to her in fury now, her baby still over her shoulder. 'Oh, to hell with your fucking rules.'

Matron's face froze.

The rage that coursed through Anna's body was like elation. If Kim hadn't been in her arms, she would have been afraid of losing her temper completely and assaulting the woman.

Matron seemed to lose her nerve. 'Well, I don't suppose a quarter of an hour can hurt,' she said. 'A quarter of an hour. Not a minute more.'

She marched off past Di without looking at her.

'Ha! Well, isn't that astonishing!' said Di, when Matron was out of sight. Anna felt sorry for her. She knew that Matron would make Di pay for her kindness.

Anna had her fifteen minutes with her baby. But that night, despite her resistance, she was given an injection to sedate her and, when she woke, she was back in her old dormitory room.

The next morning was Sunday and Mum and Dad came to see her. She took them to the maternity wing. They walked down the corridor to the nursery window and looked through the glass. Visitors were not allowed in the nursery.

'His name's Kim,' Anna said, hardly able to contain her pride.

Mum said he was 'just gorgeous' and Dad stood there with his mouth drawn tight, looking at his grandson and nodding. Anna wasn't sure if he was about to cry. Just then she felt sorry for him.

It must have been a hundred degrees in the courtyard as they headed back to the sitting room in the blazing sun. A fierce northerly was blowing and kept everyone indoors, the curtains drawn. The place had a dismal, abandoned feeling. Anna felt weak as they crossed the courtyard: she was still in pain from the birth. Mum said she was looking a bit peaky, and that she should put her feet up and rest.

At that moment, Matron came out from her green door with a bundle of papers under her arm. She seemed taken aback to see them. She gave them an embarrassed little smile, kept walking to the deep shade of the porch over the back door, and disappeared inside. Even though the courtyard was like a cauldron, Anna felt a chill of unease.

She stopped dead and told Mum and Dad she was going back to the nursery. They did not move. Dad was sweating in his suit, ribbons of perspiration running down his face from under his hat.

'If we were able to find a good family,' Mum began, then fell silent.

'Have you forgotten what you promised?' Anna said, her voice shrill, echoing in the empty space. A tide of panic slowly rose through her limbs and she felt dizzy.

'Listen, love. Before we came to see you, we had to go to Matron's office. She said she's got a form for you to sign.' Mum's voice was full of pity, almost a whisper. Dad had found something interesting to look at up near the roof.

'I *will* be coming home with my baby, with Kim,' Anna said, just to make sure she had things clear.

'Yes, love. I know I promised,' Mum said. They muttered their goodbyes, and left her to go back to the nursery by herself.

For the next few days Anna was left alone. Neither Matron nor the social worker crossed her path. No one stopped her visiting Kim and breastfeeding him whenever she liked. There was no more talk of BFAs or signing a form.

Anna couldn't understand why things seemed so easy. She was in a state of grace. And yet she couldn't quite believe that she had won the battle.

A week after her baby was born, the pressure to sign papers began. Anna was changing Kim's nappy when a woman walked into the nursery. She wore a cream suit and the heels of her tan shoes clicked across the floor. She was tall and slim, with dark hair pulled back in a bun.

'Anna?' she asked.

A stab of anxiety in her stomach. This visitor knew her name.

'My name is Miss Coutts. I'm not with the government, or the Welfare. I'm on the Ladies' Auxiliary. My title is Official Visitor. I always come to have a chat with the girls.'

Anna could see the bulge of her rings through the fabric of her ivory-coloured gloves. She carried a tan handbag, like a satchel.

Anna kept changing the nappy, doing up the safety pin securely, as if this visit might have been some trick to see if she were competent in the duties of motherhood. Kim chortled happily.

The woman's body seemed to sway ever so slightly in Anna's direction. Her mouth looked sensual, vulnerable. Her eyes didn't leave Anna for a second. Far from putting her at ease, the woman's friendly tone filled her with alarm. Why did Miss Coutts feel the need to be *nice* to her? If Anna didn't know better, she might have thought Miss Coutts was flirting with her.

Miss Coutts, it was. Not Major. Not Brigadier, like Matron. That suit of hers was more frightening than any uniform. And Anna knew without having to be told that this was the woman she had heard about from the other girls, the one they called the Consent Taker. She guessed that Miss Coutts had papers for her to sign in that handbag.

She picked up Kim from the changing table and held him close to her.

Anna preferred an open enemy like Matron, not the nice

ones who wanted to be liked. Miss Coutts had a smile that radiated warmth and understanding. It was kindly, but it also meant something like, 'We're not finished yet, young lady.'

The following day Miss Coutts was back, wearing a turquoise chiffon dress this time. Her manner was more brisk and businesslike. 'I don't have to tell you how hard life would be as an unmarried mother. You would feel people judging you every day of your life. Deep down you must know what's *really* best for your baby and yourself,' Miss Coutts told her.

Anna gazed out the window; the Edinburgh Gardens were tired in the February sun. Miss Coutts's voice was pleasant, not accusing. 'If you gave it some more thought, you would realise that you are being very selfish. Your son would go through life bearing the stigma of illegitimacy.'

Anna felt suddenly very tired, and she understood that it wasn't Miss Coutts who was doing this to her, but the future. It was the weight of the life that lay ahead.

'Don't think of yourself. Think of your baby.'

It was as though she had been drugged, and in that state everything Miss Coutts said sounded reasonable. Anna tried to fight the hypnotic pull of fatigue, but she was feeling more feeble every second. She managed to say, 'But I can't see what is wrong with wanting to keep my baby.'

'If you listen very hard, I am certain you will hear a little voice in the corner of your brain telling you otherwise. And that voice is the voice of your conscience.' She added quietly, 'God wants babies to go to good homes.'

How dull and slow Anna felt! If she didn't lie down, she would keel over! And still she heard Miss Coutts's words, but they came as if from a long way away and Anna could not make any sense of them. The sounds flowed by her, then suddenly the woman's voice was very near. 'Anna, I have come here this afternoon to ask you to give him up for adoption. You may not be aware that there is a legal requirement that consent papers cannot be signed during the first five days after the birth of a child. That five-day period has now elapsed.'

Anna felt the blood rushing to her face. And to think she had believed her victory already won! Only now did she realise why she had been given her period of grace. She felt such a fool.

'The question is not whether you love him too much to do it,' Miss Coutts was saying. 'It is whether you love your baby enough.'

Anna did not have the strength to answer. She hadn't changed her mind, of course. But Miss Coutts had somehow prised open a gate for doubt to creep in. She had to conserve her strength. She must not allow that supernatural power of Miss Coutts to steal her will.

'Look, if you don't sign,' Miss Coutts said, 'your baby will be taken from you. He will be made a ward of the state, since you can't support him. The choice is yours—an orphanage or a deserving couple.'

'But I *can* support him. I'm going to get a job.'

'And who will look after him while you're at work?'

'My parents are sticking by me.'

'We'll see about that.'

At visiting time on Sunday, Anna carried Kim down to the sitting room for Mum and Dad to see him. There were several pregnant girls sitting in the wood-panelled room, talking with their visitors. A couple of the older women stared rudely at Anna and her baby. They might have felt she was setting a bad example for the other girls.

Dad hung around the doorway, then made himself scarce, as usual.

'I want to go home, Mum,' Anna said.

'They won't let you go home until you sign the papers.'

'They can't keep me here like a prisoner!'

'They won't let you go home with the baby. Look, love. It's for the best. Life's hard for an unmarried mother. A married couple will be able to give him opportunities in life that you can't. Don't think of yourself. Think of your baby.'

Mum reached out to hold Kim, but Anna wouldn't hand over her baby. 'You promised, Mum!'

Mum started to cry. 'It's your father who's put his foot down. I've begged and pleaded with him, but it doesn't do any good. You know your father. Once he's made up his mind, there's nothing we can do to change it. We just have to go along with him. He won't let you bring the baby home.'

'But I have nowhere else to go,' Anna moaned.

'I'm sorry,' Mum said.

So Dad was the one betraying her! She wondered how many Sundays he had been slinking off and plotting all this with Matron.

Anna had to work in the laundry again during the day, but she was able to sneak up to the nursery on the pretext of changing Kim's nappy. She whispered to him, all the schemes she had come up with during the morning. They would escape. Where would they go? She would take him to the shack at Cockatoo. Hang on. That wouldn't be any good. There were the neighbours to think of. The Glass family could see right into their front garden. They would know that someone was staying at the shack and come to investigate.

She would think of something else. She would come up with another, better plan. The grease-streaked face of Charlie Allnut appeared to her again. *I don't blame you for being scared, Miss, not one little bit.*

One day when she was in the nursery, a doctor called in to enquire how she was going—not Doctor Jericho, one of the others. He closed the door and told her he had come to have a talk. She already knew what he was going to say.

Over the next few days, others tried, too. The nursing sisters. They were stubborn; they never gave up. *If you really love your baby you will give him away to a proper decent family with a mother and a father to support him.*

Still Anna refused to sign the consent papers.

Anna had heard about girls who gave consent while they were still under the effects of anaesthetic, even though Matron was supposed to wait the five days after birth. Others revoked their consent but were not given back their babies. She had heard about babies being taken away even though the mother had not given her consent at all.

'I have no intention of giving him up for adoption,' Anna repeated, every time they spoke to her about it. The only weapon she had at her disposal was her own stubbornness. She kept telling them of her plans to take him home to live with Mum and Dad, to find a job, to find a house to rent—she had to keep repeating it, otherwise all was desolation.

And so six weeks passed, and still Anna was in the Haven, and still she refused to sign. From the moment she had seen that BFA on her file on Matron's desk, Anna had known this test would come.

Miss Coutts came to see her in the laundry nearly every day, usually late in the morning. Always the same conversation. One day, Miss Coutts lost her patience. 'You are under twenty-one. We are legally entitled to get your father or mother to sign the papers in your place.'

Anna knew it was a trick. If this were really so, they would already have asked Mum or Dad to sign them, weeks ago. Anyway, it would be her twenty-first birthday in a few weeks and they'd no longer have any power over her. If only she could stay the course...

'You are not married, Anna,' Miss Coutts said. 'You would only be a bad mother and your baby would never forgive you.'

'I will *not* be a bad mother! And I *will* find a way to support him!'

'We shall see what the Child Welfare has to say about that.' Miss Coutts smiled. She must have used this threat many times in the past. 'How on earth do you think you could look after a baby?'

'I will find a way,' Anna said.

'You are a silly girl!' Miss Coutts finally lost her temper. 'If you really love your baby you will give him up for adoption.'

Just then, Matron charged into the laundry. She was angry that Miss Coutts had had no success. 'Look here,' she railed at Anna, 'you just sign the papers right now, girl! Do what's best for your baby! What decent man would ever want to marry a woman with a bastard child? Is that the kind of start in life you want to give your son—to be a bastard?'

She was marched across the courtyard to Matron's office. Matron had the relinquishment form all typed up and ready. Or maybe she kept a pile of forms by the Roneo machine.

CONSENT TO ADOPTION ORDER

I, *Anna Louise Ross,* the undersigned of *36 Hope Street, West Brunswick* in the State of *Victoria*, being the *Mother* of *Kim Ross* who was born at *The Haven Hospital* in the State of *Victoria* on the *5th* day of *February*, 1953, hereby state that I understand the nature and effect of an adoption order for which application may be made, and in particular I understand that the effect of such an order will be permanently to deprive me of my parental rights. And I hereby consent to the making of an adoption order in respect of the said infant.

In witness whereof I have signed this consent on the *25th* day of *March*, 1953, at *North Fitzroy* in the State of *Victoria*.

(Signature) *A. Ross*

Signed in the presence of—(Signature) *Matilda Mummery*

(Address) *75 Alfred Crescent, Nth Fitzroy*

(Occupation) *Salvation Army Officer, Matron*

A dull comfort was creeping through her body; her thoughts were lost in a fog. Matron took the papers and the fountain pen from her hand, and it was only then that Anna realised the enormity of what she had done.

As if in a trance, she went upstairs to her dormitory, empty at this hour. She lay on the bed; her head sank into the pillow and sleep overcame her, rich and deep, a release from the agonies of these past weeks, but also a kind of death.

They had defeated her in the end. Anna could never say, as she had heard other girls say, that there was coercion or duress. It was her own fault. There was no one else she could blame.

She told herself stories. It had been another girl who had signed the papers. Even though it was her own hand that held the pen, a ghostly power had traced her name, the name of her baby. 'It will be for the best,' they had all said. But she had felt removed from those actions, and wondered now if in fact she had been drugged.

Anna got out of bed and went to find Matron. She came across her in the foyer.

'I've changed my mind,' Anna told her. 'I'm going to keep my baby, after all.'

'It's too late. I have a lovely couple lined up for the baby. I've just come from speaking to them on the phone.'

'But you can't do that!'

'You've signed,' Matron said, and turned on her heel.

Anna went to the nursery. For a little while, at least, she still had her baby to love and attend to. She spent every moment she could with Kim now, his tiny hand locked around her finger. It was as if she were in another world, as she stared into his face stamped indelibly with her own features, and those of Neil. She would always be wondering about this child.

◆◇◆

It was going to be another hot day. Melbourne in March—there was something in the heat so early in the morning that made the day ahead seem endless. How could she ever get through such a day? She had Kim in her dormitory room. She had been told to get him ready.

Go to the window. See if they're here yet.

Nothing. Just the trees in the Edinburgh Gardens, tossing their heads and laughing. Maybe that was all God was—the will behind things that made the trees nod and laugh at her?

Eleven o'clock passed and still they hadn't come to take him. Anna had desperate thoughts. The impossible seemed true. *They've changed their minds. They're not coming for him, after all.* She would get to keep him.

But then one of the Salvation Army trainees, a girl named Bronte, appeared at the door, and Anna could tell by the compassionate look on her face that the moment had arrived. Bronte was carrying a parcel wrapped in brown paper and tied with new string, which she placed gently on the bedspread, her face solemn.

Suddenly Anna couldn't breathe. Tears filled her eyes and the world blurred. The truth had been there all along, hiding at the back of things. It didn't laugh at her or flaunt its cruelty. The truth was standing there, solid as a house. She had thought it had gone away when she had looked out the window. She had thought that everything was going to be all right, after all.

But here was the brown paper parcel. Here was Bronte still standing by the side of her bed.

To make her dress him in other people's clothes—this, too, was part of the ritual, and Anna couldn't work out if it was designed as a further punishment for her, or something that simply happened, without her feelings being taken into consideration.

With a sheepish smile, Bronte turned and left the room. Anna sat on the chair for a long time with Kim in her arms. She looked at the brown-paper parcel but she wasn't able to touch it.

A minute passed, or a year.

Bronte came back. She jollied Anna along, untying the string, unfolding the brown paper. 'What beautiful clothes they are,' she sang.

And it was true. They were beautiful baby clothes, and that made Anna feel better. The cream woollen jacket had been hand-knitted in pearl, with blue embroidery across the front.

Anna took over from Bronte. As her fingers touched her baby's soft skin for the last time, as she pulled the miniature singlet over his head, put on the embroidered jacket, the knitted booties, she knew that he was going to a good home.

Bronte folded the brown paper around the old clothes, the ones that Mum had brought in, and quickly looped the string around it without tying a knot. And then it was just Anna, in a chair, alone. Bronte was gone. Kim was gone. She hadn't seen them leave the room. In her mind, he was still there on the bed in front of her, dressed in those beautiful new clothes. She wanted to remember him like that, always.

She didn't know how much time had passed. The angle of the sunlight looked different through the window. So. He was gone.

The other girls stayed away from the dormitory. They were respecting her privacy, or maybe they were just busy at their jobs, because it was Saturday and they had to work. It was Anna's day, not theirs.

But then she realised that he would probably still be downstairs with Matron. The couple would have to sign papers and the rest of it. There was still time. She could charge downstairs, burst in and tell them she had changed her mind.

But it was hopeless.

For a moment Kim materialised again on her knee, his precious warm weight, the smell of his skin and his hair, a living spirit in this cold carbolic world. And then his smell went away too, and she knew then for certain that he was really gone, that he wasn't coming back.

She went across to the window, opened it and stepped over the low sill onto the upstairs balcony, looking down into the street, hoping for a last glimpse of him.

There was only one car parked in Alfred Crescent that Saturday. She could see it had yellow number plates, not black. So, they must have come from New South Wales, she thought. They'll be taking him to Sydney with them.

Part Three

Molly

ESSENDON, 1958

MOLLY BROUGHT HER face close to the dressing-table mirror and applied her lipstick. 'If you're a good boy, we'll go to Hearns Hobbies afterwards,' she said.

'Will I get a present?'

She turned away from the mirror, wound down her lipstick, and smiled at him. 'Maybe.'

'An Airfix model?'

'We'll have to wait and see.'

Two months after her fortieth birthday, Molly still had her slim figure. Her blonde hair was cut short and curled in a soft, stylish wave. She made her own fashionable dresses from printed Butterick patterns, run up on her Singer sewing machine. Other women often admired her clothes and told her she looked young for her age. Even when she was just going to the bank or the grocer, she put on high heels and make-up. Molly wanted to be the perfect wife.

David was home from school, already dressed in his brown suit with short pants, clean white shirt, tie. His brown, wavy hair was glossy with Brylcreem. Molly could see he was nervous about going to the doctor.

She put on her overcoat, hat, gloves, looked around for her handbag, checked inside to see that she had her purse. They travelled by bus from Essendon to Moonee Ponds Station, then took the train to Flinders Street. As they rattled past the loading yards and sidings of North Melbourne, she pointed out the coal wagons lined up.

They walked up Collins Street, past rows of sombre stone edifices with brass plates beside the entrances. They came to the building, waited in the foyer for the lift with its open wire cage to shudder to a halt, then stepped inside.

'Can I press the button?' David asked. Molly smiled and nodded.

'Second floor.'

There were leather armchairs in the waiting room, heavy damask curtains, oil paintings in gilt frames. From somewhere came the faint aroma of tobacco. Molly found these rooms comforting, the city below the windows hushed.

Doctor Frantz wore a three-piece suit and spoke with a slight European accent. He had a neat grey moustache and sat behind his desk, smoking a cigarette. A child psychiatrist, he had been recommended by her local doctor.

Molly explained that the boy had frequent bad dreams. He woke in the night and couldn't get back to sleep. Sometimes he was too anxious to go to school. The rocking back and forth, the banging his head against the wall, the screaming. What was he screaming about?

'Do you think he might be worried about something?'

'There's nothing I can think of.'

'Well, we can ask the young man himself.' Doctor Frantz smiled, showing part of a gold tooth. 'Well, David. What do *you* think is the matter?'

David looked down at his shoes, blushed, and when finally he began to speak, he stuttered slightly. 'I-I-I wake up because I have bad dreams.'

'Bad dreams? Would you like to tell me about them?'

Again, David seemed reluctant to speak. Doctor Frantz asked Molly to wait in the other room.

When he called her back, Doctor Frantz was standing behind David, who was sitting back in the doctor's chair on the other side of the desk, completely at home. He smiled brightly at Molly as she came in.

'David is an unusually anxious little boy,' Doctor Frantz told her. 'But you shouldn't worry too much.'

Molly nodded. 'But he has everything he needs. He has his own room with a bed and a desk, a mother and father who love him.'

Doctor Frantz prescribed phenobarbital and asked them to come back in a week.

On the way home, they went to Hearns Hobbies, down a few steps in Flinders Street, next to the station. David chose a model aeroplane kit. He would sit for hours with these, assembling the models with rapt concentration.

That night, while they were doing the dishes, Percy asked, 'What did Doctor Frantz say?'

'He said he's highly strung. These nervous illnesses are not well understood. He's given him a tonic.'

Percy was a practical man, a man of slide rules and design specifications. He had no experience of nervous illnesses. How could a boy of five break down like that, unable to leave his bed for days at a time?

'Maybe he'll grow out of it,' Percy said.

Molly went quiet. For a while, the only sound was the bumping of dishes in the soapy water. She put down the tea towel. 'I'm going to check on him.'

Percy gave her a reproachful look. She knew her husband thought she cosseted the boy.

David was sleeping soundly. The phenobarbital was doing its work. She stood there for a minute, looking down at him with love. She stared at his open mouth, his curly hair tousled on the pillow. He was such a good boy.

Molly pulled up the paisley eiderdown to his chin, adjusted the position of his teddy bear on the pillow, turned and went out, closing the door silently behind her.

Had his nervous disorder begun at the Haven? This was not something Molly was able to discuss with Doctor Frantz, or with her husband. She did not like to think at all about that place in North Fitzroy. There was something that had to be kept outside the frame of her thoughts: the anguish David's mother must have gone through when she had to give him up.

Molly had thought when they got married and bought their block in Essendon and Mr Harvey built their house, that everything would change. Life would be calm and stable, so different from her mother's early life in Footscray, and from her own disrupted childhood, moving house, going to live in the orphanage. And then, after trying so hard to conceive, and ending up adopting their little boy, she felt she had to be a perfect mother, as perfect as any plans on Percy's drafting board.

She sometimes felt as if an invisible authority were looking down from the sky into their house and judging whether she was fulfilling the responsibilities imposed upon them by the court when they had applied for adoption.

But, perfect mother that she was, when she thought about the woman who had given him up—well, she couldn't really think about it too much—she thought of that unknown woman or girl not as his '*real* mum' but as his '*good* mum'. No matter how good a mother Molly was, she could never 'deserve' David as much as the mother from whose body he had come into the world.

On the second visit, Doctor Frantz asked if the phenobarbital was helping. 'It's hard to say,' Molly said.

'I think he looks calmer,' Doctor Frantz suggested, nodding in encouragement. 'I think he's ready to go back to school.'

Molly accepted the doctor's verdict and agreed that David could return to school, but she was already planning for next week's illness.

At school, Aberfeldie Primary, the boy was especially shy. He told his mother he didn't want to play with the other children. Molly dressed David differently from the other boys. He wore a shirt and tie to school. She bought Paton's patterns, knitted jumpers for him in fair isle and cable knit, and tailored a belted jacket from a bolt of Donegal tweed she had hoarded through the war shortages.

His teacher, Miss Strange, wore a white laboratory coat over her frock. In her mind Molly called her Doctor Strange.

An old concrete building housed the school hall, the headmaster's office and some classrooms. The infant grades were in the newer building at the other end of the grounds. The third and fourth grades' rooms were in Nissen huts left over from the war, and next door were the boys and girls' toilets. The smell of cinders hung over the school. Every afternoon Mr Grant the cleaner went from room to room collecting the bins to empty into the incinerator. The boys played on the paddock, a sea of windswept onion grass.

Molly and Percy had bought David a leather schoolbag. He had been so proud of it, his initials embossed in gold. Molly filled his plastic drink bottle with orange cordial for playtime, and wrapped some biscuits and cake in waxed paper. She came to wait for him outside the infant classroom at lunchtime; they sat together while he ate his lunch. He had a cardboard folder with strings inside for the school readers, *John and Betty*, *Adventures*, with its purple and yellow cover.

After lunch, the children lay on the floor for their nap. Each child had to bring their own cushion to school. Miss Strange said there was to be absolutely no talking. David had the green vinyl cushion Molly had made for him. He lay down next to Gail Griffiths. He told Molly, in an innocent, touching way, that he liked Gail.

One afternoon when she went to pick up David, he said, 'Miss Strange brought some rope to school and tied up Mark Woodlock in a chair.'

'No! She didn't!'

'She did so. She put his chair up on the table and tied him

into the chair with rope. She said that was the only way to make him sit still.'

'When did this happen?'

'After lunch, before afternoon playtime.'

David was truthful. Percy joked he would grow up to be a minister in the church.

The idea that Miss Strange in her white coat had tied Mark Woodlock to the chair disturbed Molly. School did not seem to be a place where David might come to feel secure. It was not surprising that his nervous illness was getting worse, even with the phenobarbital.

In the mornings, after Molly had walked David to school, she stood with the other mothers, looking on as their little ones lined up for school assembly in front of a wooden rostrum with a flagpole, where the boys were taught to salute the flag and the whole school recited, 'I love God and my country, I will serve the Queen and cheerfully obey my parents, teachers and the laws.' The headmaster stood on the rostrum and addressed the children. Then two boys, one with a bass drum, another with a kettle drum, beat out the rhythm for the children to practise marching on the white line painted around the perimeter of the asphalt. Molly watched as David swung his arms enthusiastically, trying to fit in with the other children. The military beat was infectious.

She looked at the line of dark cypress trees, smelled the polish on the linoleum in the corridor of the infants' wing, caught the smell of cigarettes from the staff room and, for a moment, she was a little girl again arriving at the orphanage, adrift from everything that was familiar and safe.

She liked to think she understood David because she could see so much of her own experience in him.

The boy seemed less anxious when he was home from school and part of the domestic routine: Molly doing her housework, the familiar sights and sounds of the suburb, the rumble of the blue bus, the postman's whistle, the baker's horse and cart. Molly liked having him home with her, but it also made her feel guilty, and not only because he was missing schoolwork. It reminded her of that time when Alma had kept her home from school.

Molly and David listened to the radio together in the mornings, the winter sunshine dappling the pattern of the brown and orange carpet. Molly enjoyed helping him learn to read. 'This is a man. This is his hat. This is his house. This is his wife. This is his dog.' Although he loved the school readers, he was soon ready for more challenging books.

This was in the years before they bought a television.

In springtime, Molly taught the boy to name the daffodils, jonquils, the 'soldier flowers', Molly called them, because, she said, they stood to attention. The orderly garden was laid out in rockeries designed by Percy.

On stormy afternoons, the blue jets of the gas fire seemed brighter. Molly draped the washing over a wooden clothes horse. David was hiding among the sheets, rocking and crying. He was terrified of the thunder. 'There's nothing to be frightened of,' Molly told him. 'It's only God moving his furniture around.'

She gave him a dose of phenobarbital. It slowly took effect. He stopped screaming. He calmed down.

Molly had the knack of knowing when David was lying awake late at night, or in the hours before dawn. She went to his room to check on him, even though she promised Percy not to.

As the years of primary school passed, he asked to stay home more often. He said he was lonely at school, and had no friends. He complained that the other boys picked on him for his clothes and the way he spoke. At home, he wore pyjamas all day, the uniform of the invalid. There were weeks when David did not leave the house. There was something about the outside world he was afraid of. He passed the days in bed with his books—*Kidnapped*, *Treasure Island*, *The Count of Monte Cristo*, as well as the exercise books in which he was writing stories of his own.

Seeking her approval, when he finished a story, he leaped out of bed, rushed into the kitchen and insisted that Molly read it right away. They were typical tales of pirates and high adventure, though unusually detailed and descriptive for a child of his age, she thought. Afraid of denting his enthusiasm, she offered only praise. 'How marvellous!' she told him. 'You make me feel I am there!' But by keeping him home, she knew that she was allowing her son to sink deeper into an imaginary world divorced from everyday life, that the characters he invented were taking the place of real friends. Molly shared David's secret world, but kept it secret from Percy.

Most of the time, Molly played nurse. She made his bed, piled the pillows at his back. Although the thermometer never lied and his temperature was perfectly normal, she said, 'Your temp is a little on the high side. Better safe than sorry. We'll keep you home until Monday, and then we'll see.'

She knew that she was giving in to something in herself by

letting him stay home. There were times when the knot in her stomach came back, the feeling that something terrible was going to happen. It was the feeling she used to get about the man following her home from school, and afterwards, when she had found out about Alfred.

In the stillness of the suburban afternoon, doing her housework, or in Puckle Street at the butcher's or the grocer's, the fear suddenly came over her again that David's 'good' mother would come back and take him.

They had gone on a trip to Newcastle because of Percy's new job. He had recently become an industrial engineer with BP Australia and he was to determine the correct lubricants for the machinery at the steelworks. As he was to be there for a fortnight, they all drove up and stayed at a big hotel opposite the beach in Merewether.

Molly liked staying at the hotel, going to breakfast in the dining room downstairs, the tables with starched white tablecloths and napkins. It reminded her of their honeymoon in Lorne. But as the empty days passed, Molly had to find ways to fill in the time until Percy's return from the steelworks in the late afternoons. Bundled up in their overcoats against the cold wind, she and David went for long walks on the winter beach. She remembered the beach at Brighton, when she had been about the same age as David. They sat together on the seawall, waiting until it was time for lunch. In the afternoons, David had to take his nap on the fold-out sofa in their shared bedroom.

The desolate feeling she got in the mornings after breakfast when Percy drove off into the world of work—where did it come from? Molly tried to understand. Was it merely a matter of being away from home? The impersonal surroundings of the hotel?

It was not that she missed having a job. Her days at the knitting mill in Footscray seemed so long ago, now. She was content with her life as a housewife, keeping everything running for Percy and David. She had her routines, she was proud of her cooking, and enjoyed entertaining Percy's colleagues and their wives at home.

No, there was something else disturbing her.

There was a man in the breakfast room who tried to make conversation. About forty, dressed casually in a sports coat, he introduced himself as Max. He was handsome in an unusual way. For some reason, she got it into her mind that he was an actor. There was a shiny dent in one side of his forehead, which, oddly, made him seem more charismatic. The man always sat at the same table: he was a permanent guest at the hotel.

'And how is our young man this morning?' he asked.

Percy looked at David. 'Well? Go on, answer the gentleman. Say, "Very well, thank you".'

'Very well, thank you,' David stammered.

The man turned his attention to Molly. 'You should take him to the Ocean Baths. It's only a short bus ride away. I swim there every day, rain, hail or shine. I could make myself available, if you wish. It's healthy for a boy, learning to swim. It's something that will stand him in good stead in later life.'

Molly already knew that the prospect of being made to learn to swim in the cold water of the Ocean Baths would be unbearable to David. When they went upstairs to their room, he threw himself on the sofa bed and cried. He refused to leave the hotel all day.

That afternoon, she spoke to Percy. David was upstairs in their room. 'You know that man in the dining room? I really don't like him.'

'Why? What has he said to you?'

'No, it isn't that. There's just something about him that gives me a funny feeling.'

'The chap is only being sociable,' Percy said.

Next morning, David wouldn't go downstairs for breakfast. He was terrified the man would try to talk to him again, and perhaps even succeed in convincing his parents to take him to the Ocean Baths.

Percy took Molly aside. 'You can't teach the boy to be frightened of everyone who tries to strike up a conversation! And anyway, it wouldn't hurt for the boy to spend one afternoon at the Ocean Baths. The exercise would be good for him.'

'But Percy! It's the middle of winter! He'll catch his death of cold!'

She resented the strict line Percy wanted to take with their son. Molly, who was prepared to sacrifice everything in the interests of David's nerves, was surprised that her husband could not see the obvious risks.

Privately, Molly said to David, 'You must never talk to that man. You must be very careful never to go anywhere with him. Sometimes there are men who try to steal little boys.' Molly felt guilty when she said that, seeing the fear enter the boy's face. But she couldn't help herself.

The alien hotel, the incipient dread she could not shake, all made Molly realise again how much these feelings were connected with memories from her own childhood. During the first few days at the orphanage, when everything in that institution still seemed strange and threatening to her, she had felt that her mother had abandoned her. Despite everything else, the feeling of betrayal had never really left Molly.

Back home, Percy now complained more often that she overprotected the boy. They had been an outgoing and adventurous couple, he reminded her, adding that he missed their weekends with the motorcycle club. But now, for Molly, the world ended at the front gates. Molly kept those double iron gates closed all day until Percy came home in the car. She needed to guard her daytime domestic world, to protect David from whoever might be sent to try to take him.

Having David at home with her became an established part of Molly's routine. As he grew older, David liked to bring his mother cups of tea and help her with the housework. She taught him how to cook, supervised his baking of cakes. Molly gave him two shillings a week pocket money, which he put in his cashbox; she taught him how to divide his money and save for presents, the holidays, books.

Percy was busy with his new job. He often had to travel. BP sent him to Europe for three months on a study and research tour. Then he had to drive every week to the Riverina to test a new anti-bloating oil for cows. But Molly was proud that Percy was still a practical man who preferred to fix a problem or do a job himself. When the kitchen and living room needed painting, he spent his Christmas holidays on the ladder in his shorts and singlet with a paintbrush and roller. He painted the eaves and spouting, cleared blocked drains, built himself a workshop in the garage. When the car needed new paint, he did not think of paying a panel beater, he bought a compressor and sprayed the car himself.

He got up early. Molly woke to the sound of his electric razor in the bathroom. He dressed in his suit and tie, an overcoat and hat in the winter, picked up his briefcase and, at 8.15, no breakfast, no tea or coffee, he kissed Molly and David and left for work.

On Saturday mornings, Molly made sure that he took David in the car to Boon Spa in Footscray to pick up the weekly crate of soft drinks, before they drove to the nearby factory where they bought chocolates. Percy was a methodical man who approached everything in a logical manner. Once, Molly looked out the window to see her husband teaching David to mow the lawn 'in ever-decreasing circles'.

It was a mathematical world, to Percy. He wound the kitchen clock on Sunday nights. On Monday nights he dressed in his 'penguin suit' and went to the local Masonic lodge in Ascot Vale; most other nights he worked at the dining table with his slide rule and papers. He invested in blue-chip shares so that the family might improve itself financially. Percy was a solid, reliable husband. Molly trusted his judgment in all matters except one: she felt that he didn't understand how sensitive David was.

Percy was a perfectionist: every detail of his life had to be exactly right, every measurement precise. Molly stayed out of the way when he sat with the boy at the kitchen table to help him with arithmetic. Percy's frustration sometimes boiled over. There was a kind of mutual incomprehension between father and son. He couldn't understand how David could be so slow to understand even basic mathematical concepts.

Once, in a rage, Molly overheard him threaten to send David 'back to the orphanage'.

David sought out his mother. 'Why did Dad say that about the orphanage?' he asked, baffled.

Molly tried to smile reassuringly, but it turned into a grimace. 'Dad didn't mean it. Sometimes when we're angry we all say things we don't mean.'

'But he did mean it. He said he was going to send me back to the orphanage. What orphanage?'

'He got mixed up. He was thinking about another little boy.'

Later, Molly chided her husband. 'Please promise me you will never say anything like that again. You've really upset him. Besides, you know about me and the orphanage.'

Sheepishly, Percy agreed. But another evening, he threatened to sell the house and move the family to 'the slums of North Melbourne'. Molly knew Percy expected the boy to be grateful for what they had done for him, even though David had no idea what had happened. And Percy didn't mean to be nasty, she was sure. He probably wasn't even aware of it. Maybe he was resentful because of the problems they had had. He began to use the nickname 'Joe' for David, short for Joseph Puff—Joe Blow, a person without a real name. It was Percy's sense of humour, but it had an aggressive edge. 'Can you hand me that hammer, Joe?'

Molly felt tortured by the fact that David never could understand why his father called him Joe.

On Friday mornings, Molly drove Percy to the tram stop in Maribyrnong Road, so that she could have the car. Molly and

Olive picked up their mother from Eldridge Street on the way to do their shopping. They went to Forges to look for bargains. They called in to see Bill in his butcher's shop.

There were some weeks when Percy had a company car, so she was able to take David to see Olive in the afternoons, or earlier if he was home from school. Olive and Hoppy lived in Maidstone, in a street running off Gordon Street, near the ammunition factory. Their white-painted weatherboard house smelled of tobacco and the meat Olive boiled for the dogs. Inside the back door, David said hello to Cocky. The cockatoo said, 'Cocky wants a cup of tea' and drank from the spout of the teapot.

Olive was still an early riser, energetic, the way Molly remembered her as a child. She ran their sand and screenings business from the end of the kitchen bench, where the telephone was. There were piles of accounts and receipts in alligator clips. Molly was worried about Olive's hiatus hernia, and she sat for hours while Olive recounted her visits to various specialists. Hoppy was still the same. He walked with a slow gait. His smile was gentle and defeated. He drove a white FJ ute. There was only the two of them; they were a ghostly shadow of how Molly and Percy might have ended up.

At four o'clock, Hoppy swung his legs down from the cabin of his truck. He walked as if with every step those quarry boots were heavier. He wore old suit pants from the Depression years, a shapeless hat pushed back on his head, indoors and out. He sat on the back porch, rolling his Champion cigarettes, waiting for the sports edition of the *Herald* to arrive at the corner shop.

Every time she went to Eldridge Street, during these years, Molly remembered the day she was taken there from the orphanage when she was ten. Everything was the same: the same kitchen table, the dark wooden dresser. In the room leading off the kitchen, the copper for washing. In the parlour there was a wooden telephone on the wall. The toilet was still outside, with cut squares of newspaper, just as it was when she was a little girl. The same skies, the smoking factory chimneys, the farmyard smells of her childhood Footscray, chooks in backyards and tethered sheep grazing in laneways. Molly remembered that, during the Depression, sometimes a mob of sheep would be driven along their lane on the way to the abattoirs, and that Bill would wait inside their back gate until the man and the dog had passed, then steal the last sheep in the mob.

When Alma fell ill with cancer, the family gathered. Her mother lay dying in the big bed in the front room, the blinds drawn. The house was quiet and dark. Molly and her sister went over every day to look after her. Alma was sixty-seven.

It affected Molly badly, losing her mother. Everything they had gone through together during Molly's childhood had kept them close. For a long time, it was difficult to accept that her mother, who had fought so hard to keep Molly safe, was no longer there.

Molly couldn't bring herself to tell David that his grandmother was dead. She didn't let him go to the funeral. She did not want to admit the brute presence of death into his sheltered childhood world.

She told David that his grandmother had gone for a holiday, gone on the boat to England.

◆◆◆

When David had to have his tonsils out, it was his first night away from her. There were other beds in the hospital ward, other children. Molly sat at his bedside, talking to him quietly. In the morning he would have his operation under general anaesthetic. David didn't want her to leave, of course. Now came the crying, the pleas for her to stay, his fear that she wouldn't come back. Molly was seven again, in the dormitory at the orphanage.

For Molly, walking away, there were traces of another feeling that distressed her, too: leaving him in the hospital room felt like taking him back to the place in Fitzroy.

Every few months David had another of his mysterious nervous episodes. For two or three weeks at a time he stayed home in his pyjamas. He could not leave the house, even to go to the letterbox. He told Molly that he could not stand for anyone to see him and that there was something frightening in the daylight. And of course Molly did not want her son to belong to the world out there, of football and Boy Scouts, the school of hard knocks, as Percy put it when he badgered her about toughening up David.

Home from school, David read and wrote stories at the dining room table. On their trips to the city, Molly bought him new books from Robertson and Mullens in Elizabeth Street. She went to the school every few days to collect home-work from the teachers.

Day after day, together they sank deeper into a comforting interior world that existed outside time. Molly knew he was not really sick. But why did they both need to pretend he was sick, to keep it up week after week? In the routines of their days, David mimicking the life of a sick person, there was something reassuring for them both. Molly felt ashamed of her complicity. But she was still afraid that one day David might be taken away from her. She often found herself at the window in her bedroom, peeking out from the edge of the venetian blinds. If there was a car she didn't recognise parked in the street, her heart started to race.

It was only by being at home, play-acting the patient in his dressing-gown, that David seemed to thrive. He was a boy who needed to be kept apart from ordinary life, a boy who lived through his imagination, Molly convinced herself.

As David grew older, Molly noticed that he was always falling in love with his female teachers. She was shocked to think that there might have been some neediness in his nature that attached itself to Miss Blackwood, who was forever rubbing lotion into her beautiful pale hands. It was the same even with the female teachers at high school. Where had Molly gone wrong?

At fourteen he began complaining of stomach pains. The doctor at the Margaret Street Clinic sent him for X-rays. David had to take barium meal and lie flat inside the big X-ray machine. When the results came back, the doctor clipped the X-rays to the screen and showed them where the barium was ballooning out. He said the boy had a duodenal ulcer. Molly was devastated. She felt that in the perfect world of mother-hood she had constructed for herself from books and women's magazines, something else had gone wrong. She had missed doing something essential in his emotional life. She had failed.

One day in 1967 there was a knock at the front door. Molly opened it to find a short old man in a suit and hat standing there. She quickly pulled the door closed behind her and stepped out onto the porch. David was in the living room, watching television.

It was Alfred. Somehow he had traced her. He wanted to re-establish contact. His wife had died the year before. Molly remembered her terror as a ten-year-old, outside Alfred and Gert's house. Now he lived alone in his weatherboard cottage in Richmond. He had a lawn-mowing business, a Morris Minor van. He mowed the lawns of rich people in Toorak, Hawthorn, mansions across the river.

The first time Molly and David visited Alfred, they went to a Chinese restaurant in Bridge Road. Afterwards, they sat in Alfred's tiny lounge room and watched Dean Martin on television.

Molly and Alfred resumed their relationship as father and daughter. David was curious about this little old man who wore a suit and hat and smoked Henri Wintermans small cigars. Molly said that David could call him 'Pop'. David accepted this, but Molly could tell that he thought it rather strange. She was surprised he did not ask more questions about Alfred. She thought that perhaps David sensed there were secrets better not delved into.

It wasn't until the following year, when David happened to read a card Alfred sent for her birthday inscribed 'to my darling daughter' that Molly finally had to tell David who Alfred was.

When Percy got sick in 1969, at first the doctors thought it was a nervous breakdown. It turned out to be the flu. He was in hospital, home, back in hospital again. Molly never imagined that her husband could be seriously ill. He was always so healthy and energetic. But the flu turned into pneumonia and they found a granuloma on his lung. Then it was spinal meningitis.

When he was in the Royal Melbourne, Molly spent all day at his bedside. After school, David took the tram along Mount Alexander Road to the hospital. It was a shared ward with metal beds, each with a pale green curtain that was drawn around the patient when the doctors came. Molly stayed until the end of visiting hours, until the very last minute. David studied for his fifth-form exams in the corridor. Finally, they drove home and had something to eat.

When Percy came home, the months passed and he still spent most days in bed. He couldn't eat his meals. The doctor prescribed a drink of orange juice, egg and milk mixed together in the Vitamizer. The bones sharpened in his face and his gums shrank; he couldn't wear his false teeth. His skin looked yellow. There were nights when he screamed with headaches.

Molly was always in the bedroom, nursing him. She was drained, frightened of the future. Her husband had become a creature of pyjamas, like her son. Only when there were visitors did Molly help him pull on a pair of trousers and button a shirt. He seemed confused, bewildered. He perched on the edge of the chair in the living room with his newly thin face and pretended to follow the conversation.

The next month, he needed a sheepskin rug for bedsores. Then he needed an inflatable rubber ring under his hips. His lungs were clogged and at night Molly pummelled his back to try to move the congestion.

One afternoon when she went into the bedroom, Percy was lying on his back, not moving. His eyes were open and his lips had a bluish tinge. Molly knelt by the bedside, clutching his hand. Her mind registered the information but she could not take it in. She called to David to come quickly. David had his Senior swimming certificate. He knew mouth-to-mouth. She watched him pinch Percy's nose between his thumb and fore-finger, the way he had been taught. He placed his mouth over his father's cold lips to blow. Molly knew it was useless, but they had to try.

After her husband's death, Molly was exhausted. She couldn't get out of bed in the mornings without taking Vincent's Powders, with their kick of caffeine and phenacetin. There were occasional visitors, but most of the time the house had taken on a sinister silence.

There was still a mortgage. She had to buy all the books for David's final year at high school. She sat with the chequebook and a pile of bills. She lined up at the State Savings Bank in Puckle Street. Percy's pension from BP wasn't enough.

David had found a part-time job as a waiter in the ban-queting department of the Hotel Australia in Collins Street. He usually worked on Friday and Saturday nights, starting at five o'clock and often getting home after midnight. Molly was relieved that, if he worked late like that, they paid for his taxi fare home.

Molly went to work at a factory, calibrating speedometers. Then she found a job making costumes in the wardrobe depart-ment of the ballet company in Flemington.

◇◇◇

Molly and David began the new year at Cowes, on Phillip Island, where Teddy and Rosie and their kids had a holiday shack. David slept in a one-man tent in the back garden. He spent his mornings alone, reading the texts for English that year. One of the books on the course was Lawrence's *Sons and Lovers*.

Teddy came to Molly one morning after breakfast. 'You shouldn't let the boy read that kind of filth.' Now sixty, he worked as a cleaner at Footscray Technical College. 'I've seen these teachers and the obscene books they get the kids to read.'

'But he's doing his Matric,' Molly tried to explain. 'That book is on his course. He has to read it for the exams.' Now Percy was gone, everyone was trying to give her advice.

She did understand Teddy's concern. Another of Lawrence's books, *Lady Chatterley's Lover*, had been banned in Australia for many years. The Literature Censorship Board had finally allowed it to be published only a few years earlier, in 1965, and there had been much controversy about it in the newspapers. Molly would never have dreamed of reading a book like that— she preferred magazines like the *Women's Weekly* and *New Idea*—but she hoped the teachers knew what they were doing.

After the argument about the novel, David went quiet. He went off by himself. That night, he took from her handbag his brown cylindrical bottle of Amytal with its label from the United Friendly Societies Dispensary and swallowed all the tablets. He disappeared and hid under a blanket on the back seat of Molly's EH Holden in the dark. It was Molly who found him. She pulled the blanket away. David didn't move. He might have just been asleep but he felt cold to her touch. Overcome with dread, she managed to bring him around and drive him to a doctor in Cowes.

They cut short the holiday and returned home the next day.

'He's very fragile,' Molly told Olive on the phone. But Molly was fragile, too.

School resumed, but David did not attend. For six weeks, he hardly left the house. He watched television twelve hours a day, in the living room with the blinds drawn. When Molly protested, he told her that he found it comforting to hear the mawkish theme music come on before the midday movie, that he didn't want to think, or see anyone. He fired his toy gun into the phone when his English teacher called to ask about his absence, and began to smoke Fiestas and to drink brandy and dry ginger. Molly looked on, powerless. Something dark crossed her mind: she had lost her husband and her mother and now she was losing her son.

He stayed home from school. He smoked his Fiestas. He fired his toy gun into the phone.

When David came out of his retreat and went back to school, he was a different person. Girls. Parties. Beer. These were his priorities now. He was not so different from other boys, after all, thought Molly, reassured.

David was more sociable but he was also more combative. His politics veered sharply to the left. Molly tried to talk him out of going to the first big Vietnam moratorium, but he went anyway. That night she watched it on the news, 100,000 people bringing the city to a standstill.

David seemed to have contempt for anyone who didn't share

his views. He was argumentative, challenging everything she said. 'Anyway, what would you know?' he asked her. 'You're uneducated. You never finished school. You don't read.'

His behaviour frightened Molly. It was as though there were two Davids now. A quivering anger affected his face, his speech, his gestures. The little boy who had been 'highly strung' now began to exhibit volcanic eruptions of feeling, when he lost his self-control entirely. Was there a crack in him, a faultline in his psychic structure? Rage burned in the soul of her son, driving him towards a destiny which his mother felt could only be tragic.

After the night David had swallowed the bottle of Amytal at Cowes, Molly had tried to avoid arguments. But, without Percy, she felt she had to try to be firm with David. Sometimes she put on an act, but she couldn't make it last. David simply ignored her, or worse, flew into another rage. When he abused her, she took it all with a kind of pained smile. 'I'm deaf in one ear and can't hear out the other,' Molly told him.

Then she went to the kitchen and took a couple of Vincent's Powders.

Molly had protected David through his childhood, hidden him away from the enemies who prowled the streets in cars searching for him, kept him safe from bullies at school, taught him to dress well and encouraged him always to be at the top of his class. But now, Molly felt defeated.

One day, soon after he turned seventeen, Molly asked David to sit down in the living room with her. She had something important to tell him. She had been getting her courage up for this all day. Even now she had made her decision, she found it difficult to speak. Finally, she blurted it out. 'I didn't want to tell you. But you have a right to know.'

In this way, David found out he was adopted.

There no longer seemed to be any rules.

'You going out again tonight?' Molly asked.

'Yes.'

'But it's a school night.'

'We're going to the library at Melbourne Uni to study, Mum.'

Molly knew that from the university they went to the Mayfair Hotel in Elizabeth Street, even though David was under age.

'You going with Jack?'

'Probably.' (She knew that meant: yes, certainly.)

Still at school, but a year older than David, Jack already had his licence. David said Jack had a girlfriend, Kiki. Artistic. Short hair. Trouble. She dumped him regularly, got drunk, cut up her face, so he said.

David borrowed Jack's records. Bob Dylan. Jimi Hendrix. John Mayall's *Bluesbreakers*. The sound of Eric Clapton's wailing guitar came from David's room. Once Molly found a matchbox of marijuana in his sock drawer. 'What's this?' she demanded, when she confronted him with it.

'Just some grass,' David said. 'No big deal.'

Molly looked at David with the hurt look that had come into her face. She felt weak and vulnerable and so very alone. Her tone of voice was harsher, as if steeling herself for some further disaster to come.

'What time will you be home?' she always asked.

A useless question. She knew she wouldn't be getting an answer, but she felt she had to ask.

A new ballet was due to open and Molly was working all hours. She sat up late at her Singer sewing machine, the TV on for company. There were costumes all over the living room, lengths of material marked with her flat blue square of chalk, ready to be pinned up on her dressmaker's mannequin. David was out there in the night somewhere, with people she didn't know, at a pub or a party. She waited up for her son to come home.

When the Matriculation results finally came out in December, David did better than they had expected. He won a scholarship to study Law at Melbourne University. Molly could not have been more proud. All her years of struggle and sacrifice, trying to be a good mother, had worked out, after all.

Her son was going to make a brilliant barrister.

After Percy's death, Molly had continued to visit Alfred. She was accustomed to the drive along Victoria Parade to Richmond, turning right at the Skipping Girl sign. Sometimes, David went with her. More often, he was busy with his study and his friends, and Molly visited her father alone.

Now in his late seventies, Alfred's eyesight was failing. He could no longer drive, and Molly took on the responsibility of doing his weekly shopping, taking his pension cheque to the bank and paying his bills. When Alfred had a stroke, he went to live in a bungalow behind his niece Lily's house in Brighton.

Lily's house was only half a mile from Dendy Street. There was nothing left of the orphanage now. It had been torn down and turned into a housing estate. Her old school at Brighton Beach was still there, though. Every time Molly drove to Brighton to visit Alfred, she was overcome by an almost mystical feeling. That day, half a century earlier, when her mother had taken her to live in Mr Butler's orphanage, reappeared before her like a vision. Those memories were no longer accompanied by the presentiment of trouble and gloom, but by a golden feeling of peace.

Alfred was not happy living with Lily. One morning when Molly arrived to visit, she found him sitting at the table in his bungalow mixing a cup of rat poison. He eventually died from another stroke.

Molly was executor of Alfred's will. Before the sale of his cottage in Richmond, she went to clear out his things. There was a drawer in his wardrobe where he kept his documents: the will, the house title, and the marriage certificate, which told her the things she had found out when she was a little girl, the year she had come home from the orphanage. She also found a brass plaque, mounted on cherry wood, commemorating the death of his younger brother Archie, paid for by his regiment.

Part Four

Cathy

FITZROY, 1975

THE LANDLORD WAS planting a passionfruit vine in the courtyard the morning they arrived. Planting it with an ox heart, he assured them, was the secret to a healthy vine. He asked if they were married, and glanced at their hands. Yes, married, David told him. Cathy wore a gold ring that passed as a wedding band. Her belly had not yet begun to show. They signed the lease, paid a month's rent in advance, and the following Saturday they moved into the house. It was around the corner from the Standard Hotel, in King William Street.

Cathy had no furniture of her own. After her two years in London, she had been sharing a poky terrace house in Victoria Parade with some nurses. Hers was the attic room. It was how she'd lived in London, everything improvised, everything temporary. All her clothes fitted into one suitcase. The day they moved into King William Street, she packed her cassette player, the Pentax SLR she'd bought duty-free in Singapore on her way home, and her favourite novel, *Tess of the d'Urbervilles*, bought as a souvenir on a driving holiday in Dorset.

Cathy was twenty-two, the same age as David. She was tall, slim, pretty. She wore her glossy, chestnut hair long, and her brown eyes, outlined with mascara, looked huge. People sometimes asked her if she was a model. At weekends she wore jeans, cowboy shirts, a suede jacket. On workdays she wore skirts, jumpers, and the trench coat she had bought in London.

That afternoon, while David was still unpacking, Cathy went for a walk to explore the streets. She took photos of the neglected terrace houses, the derelict pubs, the Gothic doorways of St Mark's. She'd met a famous fashion photographer in London, and gone to his studio in Notting Hill. She had dreams of doing a course and becoming a professional photographer in London. She didn't want to be a typist all her life.

Saturday afternoon drunks stared at her through the open windows of the Napier Hotel. Women weren't allowed in the public bar. She passed abandoned workshops in the backstreets, a rickety garage where a lone man was tinkering with an engine, a panel beater's shed scarcely big enough for a car to fit inside. On the corner of George Street there was a milk bar run by a family of Greeks. At one end of Napier Street, near Gertrude Street, were the grim blocks of flats. Across a front wall, someone had daubed in black paint: *Smash the Housing Commission*. Towards the other end of the street was the Perfect Cheese factory, with its faintly nauseous aroma of parmesan.

No one wants t'be trapped inside a fantasy. The graffiti was painted over an advertisement for Glen Iris bricks; on the other side of the hoarding was an advertisement for Crest beer. She stood there for a long time, staring at the sign. *Trapped inside a fantasy.*

They met in London, where David was researching his thesis on the General Strike of 1926. They made love in her bedroom in Swiss Cottage, with its smell of sandalwood candles, watched over by a never-used spinning wheel in the corner that was there when she moved in. When she came home to Australia, she phoned him. 'It's Cathy,' she said. 'Do you remember me?'

'I certainly do,' David said, and she could feel his smile through the phone. There had been something about David that had stayed with her: his curly hair, his intense gaze, his idealism. He wasn't like the other men she had met in London, couriers for bus tour companies, hustlers, sleazebags. She was attracted to his intellect, the excitement of student life.

In Melbourne, they went to a few parties together. They went to the Clapton concert at Festival Hall in April. By then, David was staying most nights in her attic room in Victoria Parade. The window open at night, they could smell the Carlton and United Brewery.

Cathy was on the pill in London, but not when she came home and spent Christmas at the farm. Months went by. She didn't have a prescription. She kept meaning to go to the doctor. One night Cathy told David, 'I'm late.'

They talked about what to do.

'People say you should trust your gut reaction,' David said. 'I know *my* gut reaction—I'm happy you're going to have a baby.'

From the very beginning, David was sure.

The next days passed in a haze. Cathy was so worried, she couldn't think straight. Nothing had been decided. They might move in together, they might not. And as for getting married—who could tell what was going to happen?

'Still, if he asks me,' Cathy said to herself, 'I'll say yes to him.'

They promised themselves to sit down and talk about it, but they kept putting off the conversation. David in particular seemed to be procrastinating.

'I'm going to need to decide something soon,' she told him.

'Listen. I've never told you this, but I was adopted. I don't even know who my real mother and father were. Can you understand how that makes a person feel?'

Cathy threw her arms around him and hugged him. 'It must feel odd, not knowing who your parents are. Not knowing where your roots are. Do you ever feel lost?'

'Lost? No. But all my life I've felt different from other people.'

She wanted to keep hugging him, to console him, but at that moment something stopped her and she moved away. There were her own problems to worry about. 'Well, we still have to talk about what we're going to do.'

'I couldn't stand the thought of you giving up the baby. It's ours now!'

'It might be easier if we got married.' Both of them were quiet for a long time. 'I'm not asking you to do anything you don't want to,' she went on. 'But this is a big thing. We have to talk about it. It wouldn't have to be in a church. We could just have a big party with lots of food and booze and dancing.'

'Look, no one gets married these days,' David said. 'You might be able to go on the Supporting Mother's Benefit.'

He was still a boy, really. She doubted he was ready for the responsibilities of being a father. 'Maybe we shouldn't say anything to people just yet. Not until everything is settled,' she said.

David came over and kissed her on the side of the head. 'Let's not talk about it any more. Things will work out.'

Next day, he was on the phone to all his university friends telling them the good news, and they went out every night that week to celebrate.

THEY SLEPT IN David's single bed, but when David's mother visited and saw how they were living, she offered them her own double bed. David fetched it on the roof of Molly's station wagon.

Cathy had been dreading meeting Molly. David said he had told her about the baby, and Cathy was afraid of being judged. But within minutes the three of them were laughing and joking around. His mum had bought them some curtains to brighten up the place. David fixed the brackets for the curtain rods with superglue. Miraculous molecular bonding, promised the advertisement on TV.

Cathy had worked for temp agencies in London; now she worked for an insurance company in Queen Street. On weekday mornings, she caught the tram to the office in the city, rows of girls with typewriters and piles of claim forms, all frightened of the manager. At five-thirty, David was waiting for her at the tram stop on the corner, outside the Perseverance Hotel.

It was June; it got dark early. On their way home, they passed a terrace house where the owners kept the curtains open. Cathy liked to look into the lamp-lit front room, the fire blazing, the walls of books, the bottle of wine uncorked. Why was it that the lives of other people always seemed more authentic than her own? One day, she promised herself, she and David would have a room like that. When they got home, they ate spaghetti bolognese in the bare living room, huddled in front of the kerosene heater.

In the evenings, David hammered on the keys of his heavy, old-fashioned, manual Royal typewriter. There were pages and pages full of typing mistakes, angry crossings-out. She offered to type up his thesis for him. She could type faster than he could. Anyway, Cathy wanted to be a part of that magical university world. She imagined sitting in seminars with fellow students, discussing ideas. She would read great books and write essays, as David did. She loved the warm, dry smell of the Baillieu Library, all those books waiting on the shelves like unborn souls. But Cathy knew she was not a word person. At the National Gallery, the paintings gave her feelings. Colours, brushstrokes, human figures—with these she felt at home. Whenever there was any kind of confrontation or argument, she froze.

David paced up and down. 'This is such shit,' he kept saying. She knew he didn't really want to be studying history. He spent his afternoons in the library, reading interviews with writers in the *Paris Review*.

Cathy stopped typing and took a cigarette from her packet of Benson and Hedges. 'I'm going to have to tell my dad soon. All right?'

She'd been putting off telling him. Her father would want to drive down to Melbourne and see her, and Cathy wasn't ready for that. She and David were going to have a baby, but they weren't going to get married. Her father simply would not understand.

Cathy was an only child, and her father always thought she needed looking after. Her mother had died of cancer when she was twelve. It was a time of Cathy's life she didn't like to think about—coming home from school to find all those cars parked in the drive: the doctor, the District Nurse and so many other visitors.

She had left school at seventeen with typing and Pitman's Shorthand and taken a job in an office to save money and go travelling. She couldn't wait to get away from Arcadia, with its stifling narrowness. Arcadia. The little town near the South Australian border where she had spent her childhood. Dad had only agreed to let her go to London because her cousin Justine was already there. Cathy had stayed with her for the first few months, before she made friends of her own. They went travelling together in Spain, Portugal, Morocco. When it was time for Justine to go home to Australia, Cathy had stayed on, found herself jobs through temp agencies, and it was only then—so it had felt to Cathy—that her life had really begun.

London had given Cathy her independence. She travelled in the Soviet Union by herself, and spent an entire summer driving through Yugoslavia, with her friend Connie, in a beat-up car. She'd fallen for a boy and followed him across

America, before they'd parted ways in LA. And through all that, she'd never once had to ask her father to send money.

When she got home, she was appalled by the way nothing seemed to have changed. Dad still spoke to her as he always had. She was still the little girl who needed protection from the pain of losing her mother so young. He assumed that Cathy would continue to do officework and find someone solid to marry.

And now? She couldn't bear to think about what Dad was going to say.

'Do you know when I was happiest?' she exclaimed abruptly, when David still hadn't responded to what she had said about telling her father. 'When I was all by myself, hitchhiking in Scotland. Never knowing from one day to the next where I was going to sleep.'

David looked up from his pile of papers. 'I bet you didn't tell your father about *that*.'

'Even when I was little, I wanted to leave Arcadia and see the world. My fourth-grade teacher, Mrs Hampson, had been to England. She encouraged us to broaden our horizons. She used to have a map on the classroom wall, and all the children had to choose a country to do a project on.'

'Which country did you choose?'

'Cuba.'

'Why Cuba?'

'It was in the news that year. The missile crisis and all that.'

'US imperialism! The Bay of Pigs invasion! That was a CIA operation, you know. Castro sent the invaders back to America. I would have had them all put against a wall and shot.'

Cathy hated it when David talked like that. These violent

thoughts he came out with frightened her, especially when he talked with his friends in George Street, Murray and Vanessa.

She'd had the time of her life in the house in Swiss Cottage with her friends. In the evenings, someone taking their turn at cooking in the kitchen, the stereo blaring, Cathy and the others would perform for each other, miming and dancing along to their tapes.

One Monday evening in the July of 1973, they'd all gone to a Bowie concert at the Hammersmith Odeon. One of her housemates had scored free tickets.

Crack, baby, crack, show me you're real.

She'd been amazed by the way David Bowie *became* Ziggy Stardust. People can do that too, she thought. We don't have to stay the same all our lives. We can become whoever we want. That week, one of her friends happened to call her Ziggy, and it had stuck.

And now this other David. Could he see the Cathy who wanted to transform her life, to become a photographer perhaps, or even to go to university?

Every Friday night, they went to meetings at Murray and Vanessa's house in George Street. David belonged to the same revolutionary group. They had a committee for everything and David was always writing articles for their newsletters and pamphlets. They all got up at six in the morning to sell their radical newspaper, *Liberation*, at factory gates—the meatworks, the Newport railway workshops, the Williamstown naval dockyards. Cathy woke when the alarm went off and felt him leave the bed.

She had never managed to unravel their particular political pedigree. David told her there were dozens of such groups on campus, all of them arguing about shades of interpretation. He had tried to explain it to her, but it was all so complicated that she decided it was not entirely her fault she had failed to follow. Marxists were like feuding families, their differences hardened into implacable hatred.

Still, she was accepted by the little clan in George Street. Vanessa with her flaming hair, her faded army shirts, and her boyfriend, Murray, with his Afghani sheepskin coat, along with a changing guard of hangers-on. Vanessa and Murray weren't married either. *Marriage is slavery! Marriage makes women property! Marriage is an outmoded bourgeois institution!* Yes, marriage was becoming unfashionable, although Cathy knew from old friends that the couples in country towns and the suburbs who were still getting married could not understand why the inhabitants of Carlton and Fitzroy looked down their noses at them.

According to David, if anyone had a sound class analysis, it was Murray. But when he pronounced his views, it seemed to Cathy that she was hearing ready-made phrases that had been repeated by others, and that, while undoubtedly conscientious in his reading, Murray was just the tiniest bit inauthentic. When he used words like 'hegemony', she noticed that his voice wavered, almost imperceptibly, as though he had not entirely overcome what had once been his fear. It would be impossible ever to have a real conversation with Murray; she was sure he brought out those big words to hide how small he felt.

At those Friday night meetings, Cathy sat listening to them argue for hours. Even though she was exhausted after work, and had morning sickness, she was determined to stick by David, to take an interest in his friends, and perhaps even to somehow pick up the education she had missed out on. She sat with a glass from the flagon of rough red wine they drank, taking a careful sip from time to time. Booze only fuelled their eagerness to point out the faults in one another's 'method'. There was a self-righteousness in the tone of voice they used, all of them; it seemed like a virus. Even though she usually tried not to judge, she knew in her heart that they were narrow-minded people, in spite of their clothes and long hair, their grand pronouncements about how a future socialist society might be. They talked about liberation, but she couldn't see anything free about them. They were just learning to be dictators. New students came to meetings; others left the group just as suddenly. And all the time Cathy felt dishonest not telling David what she really thought of these self-proclaimed radicals.

Cathy was reminded of a family who had moved to Arcadia when she was a child. Cathy and her father had always attended the small, rural Methodist church stuck by itself near the cross-roads, where local families met on Sundays to pray and socialise. But this particular family went about trying to impose their ideas; they were strict, intolerant. She remembered one Sunday when the husband, Mr Eltham, had given an explanation of a reading from the Book of Isaiah—the sacrifice on receipt of good news. Why did they want to make a sacrifice when they heard good news, Cathy had wondered, and she wondered still. And within a month or two, without any reason, everyone had begun to talk like the Elthams, that same hectoring tone of doctrinal purity. Even Dad had caught the evangelical illness.

Instead of her sunny Sunday mornings, there was this punishing seriousness. Families who had been friends fell out and abandoned their little wooden church to the newcomers, and started going instead to the big brick one in town. That had been Cathy's first experience of how new people can turn up and cast a shadow over something that had been hers.

Even in the merry-go-round of new faces in Swiss Cottage, there had been shadows. A bossy couple, Tom and Maureen, had stayed for a while, know-it-alls who were always trying to outdo the others with their self-aggrandising travellers' tales. They'd been on the road longer than everyone else, been to countries no one else had. Secretly, Cathy had laughed at them.

David told her that by getting married, they would be giving in to the class enemy. Cathy thought the enemy probably wouldn't mind much whether they were married or not. But she didn't want him to go against his principles. After all, she'd decided they were her principles, too.

She had earned her stripes in London and wasn't going to swallow the country town's conformist expectations. In Arcadia, girls got married and looked after the house while their husbands farmed. Cathy didn't care any longer about husbands and wives and weddings in white, but she did want to be by David's side so that together they could achieve their dreams: she with her photography, and David with the novel he was now talking about.

At one of those Friday nights in George Street, Vanessa came up to Cathy and casually asked, 'Why David?'

Cathy froze. 'What do you mean?'

'Well, you two are such a mismatch.'

'A mismatch?' Cathy smiled. Vanessa hadn't meant to be

hurtful. But she made Cathy feel that her life with David was provisional: it might end at any moment. What hurt her most was that Vanessa had given voice to Cathy's own deepest fears. *Were* they a mismatch? Why *had* David chosen her? Were she and David together only because she was pregnant?

Cathy let Vanessa's provocation go unanswered. She'd never liked confrontation. At university, as far as she could tell, the mind was a weapon of war, and words its arrows. And why should she want weapons? Vanessa and Murray were only happy when there was some kind of argument going on; they changed, their eyes were brighter when there was intellectual dispute in the air. Cathy, too, was drawn to these mysterious, dangerous energies and understood the importance of con-testing ideas, but when David yelled at her, she felt it go right down into the fibre of her being.

She wondered if David might have been better off with a headstrong girl like Vanessa. And whether she should have chosen someone more stable and mature than David. Anything could set him off. And when his mood did turn abrasive—this wasn't easy for her to admit to herself—was that, too, in some way *her* fault? They were incompatible. She was pretending, and so was he. That wasn't easy for Cathy to admit to herself, either.

David often talked about 'the emptiness of here'. He told her one day that it was a quote from his favourite book, *My Brother Jack*, and that he admired the way George Johnston and Charmian Clift had left the stifling boredom of Australia in the 1950s to live on Hydra. David gave her his well-worn copy and, as she read it, Cathy imagined herself and David living on a Greek island too, shutters on the windows, a grapevine growing over the courtyard. She told David that she could see them there already—and there was their child, standing in the doorway! But somehow she couldn't bring herself to point out to David that George and Charmian were husband and wife.

Her cousin, Justine, phoned. She and Ian wanted to come around and meet the new boyfriend. Justine, now married, lived in South Yarra and worked in her husband's travel agency in Toorak Road. They drove a Mercedes. Justine's accent had altered to match that of the rich people she now mixed with.

Cathy was nervous all day. David's desk in the front room would have to serve as a dining table. She moved his typewriter, threw a cloth over the desk and laid out knives and forks and glasses. Four unmatched, wobbly chairs. Over the meal, David lectured them on politics. Whitlam, he said, had achieved admirable things. He had delivered Australia from the stupidity of its own history. He had abolished conscription and got us out of Vietnam; he had given us free hospitals and universities. He had recognised Aboriginals' and women's rights. But Whitlam's limitations were the limitations of social democracy. 'What we need now,' he declaimed, 'is the nationalisation of the means of production, transport and exchange.'

Justine gave Cathy a strange look across the table. When she helped her carry the plates out to the kitchen, Justine asked, with a kind of terrified smile, 'You're not pregnant, are you?'

Cathy didn't know what to say. She hadn't begun to show yet. How had Justine guessed? As soon as they got home, Justine would ring her parents, who would, no doubt, in turn ring Cathy's father. He would then sit up late, anxious, in that farmhouse kitchen she knew so well.

Next morning, Dad was on the phone. 'Your aunt tells me you've got some news.' He said he was going to drive to Melbourne that afternoon to have a talk with her. He was keen to meet David, too.

Cathy showed him around. She was ashamed of how cheap everything looked—the wobbly camping table in the kitchen, the torn Leon Russell poster covering a crack in the wall, the fact that they couldn't afford a fridge. She led him up the steep staircase to their bedroom, no wardrobe, clothes strewn around. The sliding window above the bed was made of opaque glass like a shower screen.

'I wish you had a bit more comfort,' Dad said when they were back in the front room, standing together awkwardly.

'Lots of people have to put up with worse,' David replied.

Cathy would have liked to have a few more chairs, a dresser, some framed prints, a little table with a lamp in the hallway. It was only David who was proud of their frugality. One night, walking home from work, when she had plucked up the courage to point out their neighbours' lamp-lit room, the walls of books, the open fire, the wine, David had said, 'I didn't realise you were so petit-bourgeois.' Cathy didn't talk about furniture again.

'When are you getting married?' Dad asked when they were sitting down. His voice sounded reasonable, friendly, hopeful.

'Marriage is outdated,' David told him. 'It makes the woman a possession—it's hardly better than prostitution.'

Cathy was afraid she was going to vomit. The last thing she wanted was David picking a fight with her dad.

Dad had a fixed smile on his face. A gentle man, he was not used to harsh words. 'Do you really believe that? Prostitution?'

Cathy looked helplessly at her father. Her own feelings were so mixed up by now, embarrassed by David, feeling sorry for Dad, angry at herself, defiant in the face of other people's expectations, that she felt a choking sensation, the words refusing to come out.

She knew Dad did not understand David's intentions, or how to make his own position clear in all this. 'When you live in the country,' he finally said, 'the good opinion of your neighbours is important.'

Later, in the street as he was leaving, her father took David aside. She could hear them talking beside Dad's old Ford Falcon. 'What's this business about not getting married? You won't find a better girl than Cathy,' he told David. 'You're entitled to your opinions about the institution of marriage and all that. But when the baby arrives, it deserves to have a family. As far as I'm concerned, if you don't get married, then you'll always be just some bloke that Cathy's shacked up with.'

David dismissed him with a wave and went inside, leaving Cathy to cross the street to the car and kiss her father goodbye.

Dad must have been cursing his misfortune. Cathy knew how David must have seemed to him: a wild young hothead, a disturbing influence.

The next Sunday night at seven o'clock, the phone rang. Cathy knew it would be her father. The long-distance rates were cheaper on Sundays. Dad asked if she would come up to the farm by herself one weekend. She could catch the train from Spencer Street after work and Dad would pick her up at the station in Arcadia. Cathy agreed to go. She would call him back and tell him which weekend.

She loved her father; she did not want to disappoint him. But she knew, of course, what her father was going to say. And what, really, was she going to say in reply? Although Cathy had grown out of the bridal swindle—the wedding-in-white lies she heard other girls carry on with—actually, she did not object at all to the idea of being married. Still, she knew she would repeat the same lines: 'we don't believe in marriage' and 'times have changed, you know'—and her dad would go on thinking she was allowing herself to be duped by this boy in the city who was refusing to face up to his responsibilities.

It wasn't just David's politics, his abrasive manner, his need to shock people. Cathy understood—without being able to discuss it with him—that David was angry about politics because he was unhappy with himself. More and more, she felt there was something unstable about David, something unhinged, and sometimes she was terrified of him.

The question about getting married still filled her with anxiety. It was settled; then it reared its head again. David told her they had to stick to their guns. The one thing she felt certain of was that she had to persevere, to get through this confusing year. Whatever the limitations of her life now, Cathy was determined that she would become great in giving birth.

Cathy's boss at the insurance company called her into his office one afternoon and asked if she was pregnant. She couldn't deny it. He told her she would have to hand in her notice. She would leave her job in two weeks' time.

She was afraid to tell David. With his temper, he was just as likely to go in there and punch the manager in the mouth. Finally, she blurted it out.

'Right, that's it!' David shouted. 'I'm going to have it out with him first thing in the morning!'

'Please don't.'

'Tell me the cunt's name.'

'Mr Davidson.' She felt such a coward, but it was the only thing that would shut him up. Again, she wondered what she was heading into.

In the end, the fortnight elapsed and she left the insurance company without a scene. David's meagre scholarship had to cover the rent and living expenses. Her father sent her a cheque for a hundred dollars to buy some clothes. Cathy didn't want to cash it—she knew he wasn't well off, there were stacks of bills, embarrassing meetings with the bank manager. She went to Myer's and bought a blue velvet tent-dress and a gingham smock. They weren't really clothes: they were covering. To hide herself—that was what the world wanted from her now.

David persisted in getting up early to sell his newspaper at factory gates. Although he had handed in his thesis, he still walked down Grattan Street to the university most mornings for seminars. But he spent his afternoons and evenings writing short stories that Cathy typed up.

It was a mild July in Melbourne in 1975, day after day of clear blue days. After lunch, David and Cathy sat in the courtyard, faces tilted to the precious winter sunshine. It was a rare respite from the strain of their life this year. The passionfruit vine was beginning to grow.

Sandra and Connie, veterans with Cathy of the Hammersmith Odeon and of Olympia, arranged to meet her on Saturday in the city at the Hopetoun Tea Rooms. Sandra burst into tears when Cathy arrived. 'What's happened to us, Ziggy?' And, for a minute, two minutes, the three of them hugged and cried. In London, it had always been pubs and parties; now they were in Melbourne in an antiquated tea room for staid old ladies.

They still called her Ziggy, but that was as far as it went. Was there a trace of bemusement in their eyes at her condition? A touch of irony in the way they spoke to her? Cathy couldn't be sure. She felt—but she had no evidence—that her friends no longer liked her. She wasn't *really* Ziggy any more: no longer Cathy the dag who had horsed around and mimed Bowie songs in the house in Swiss Cottage. Now, she was just the first of the old London gang to go the family way.

They were nervous, the three of them. Cathy heard herself saying things she'd heard David say, unwittingly copying him. The capitalist press. US imperialism. Sandra and Connie stared at her, as though they no longer recognised her.

Sandra had been the natural leader in Swiss Cottage. Now Cathy felt some authority because soon she would be a mother. In that, there was something absolute. She was moving away from her old identity, but she missed it. She knew that, once out of her presence, they would talk about 'how Ziggy has changed'. In the currency of friendship, change was the black penny that should never turn up. They needed to keep pretending they were still the same, even when they were not.

Later, they went to the gallery in St Kilda Road and lay on their backs on the carpet. They looked up at the stained-glass ceiling in the Great Hall, the fragmented colours and shapes. Their talk was fragmented, too. 'So tell us about this bloke of yours.'

'Why have you been avoiding us, Ziggy?'

'We heard at a barbecue at Suzy's.'

'Your dad getting the shotgun out?'

'What a thing to happen, eh? So when's the big day?'

Cathy gazed up at the ceiling, like the huge window of a church that had been turned on its side. 'Got a smoke?' Cathy asked Sandra, at last. She had stopped buying them, as her dad had suggested.

Dad used to be a terrible smoker. He could roll a cigarette with one hand. He always had one going, even on the tractor. One day he had decided to quit and he had never gone near another cigarette again. 'Don't teach your baby to smoke,' Dad had told her. He was right, of course, but you have to have one sometimes.

Out on St Kilda Road, they sat on the side of the moat, smoking. They talked for another half an hour, then went their separate ways. She knew she wouldn't see Sandra and Connie again. She was no longer the skinny girl they used to have fun with in London. Cathy walked all the way home. Brunswick Street was quiet at six o'clock. A few early customers going into the Last Laugh. The wind had come up, ripping at the lapels of her trench coat.

David took her to meet his friend Henry, who had a room in a student house in Napier Street. Cathy felt nervous about meeting him. 'Henry is the most intelligent person I know,'

David had told her. For a couple of years now he had been showing Henry his short stories. David said the two of them talked for hours about the books they were going to write.

Henry showed them into his gloomy hallway, packed with boxes and books and bicycles, like a junk shop. He was a tall, handsome young man with tousled hair, dressed in flannel trousers and a wrinkled shirt. His calm gaze reminded her of a head of Apollo she had once seen in Rome: the embodiment of idealism and light.

Henry's room was even more disorderly than their own place. From what David had told her, Henry was so absorbed in his work that he could type all night. He seemed not to notice the peeling paint on the walls.

Cathy liked Henry immediately. He treated her with consideration, even chivalry. He seemed not to be aware of the curve of her belly, or perhaps he was too tactful to comment.

The affection between the two young men was touching. They argued—was that all university people did, just sit around arguing?—but their conversations lacked the spite of the household in George Street. For once, David did not need to be right all the time. She liked the natural way the two of them talked, David perched on the edge of his chair, his head tilted, gesticulating in that nervous way of his, or sitting back, passionately listening to his friend. They disagreed on everything, but she could see that Henry's ideas inspired David.

They were talking about Henry's thesis on Dante. Once again, Cathy felt her lack of education like a weight. 'So what if you haven't read Dante.' Henry smiled at her. 'There is still plenty to talk about. Books are important but the things they point to are more important, you know.'

Cathy felt, that first afternoon, that in Henry she had found an ally.

About five in the evening, the late winter sun briefly blazed and the golden light poured into the room. With the cigarette smoke hanging around their heads, the light seemed to give each of them a saturation of colour—David the deep ruby red of a glass of wine, Henry a pure burning cerulean blue. In that instant, she could see the two of them so clearly. The sunshine seemed to emanate from within them and she felt the mystery of their connection. The sensation was over in a second, but she was convinced that what she had witnessed was something of the spirit. It was as though the two young men had been sitting there for centuries.

Cathy felt her heart swelling with love—for her unborn baby, for David, for something she could not even give a name to. She felt a twinge of envy, too. If only she could have a friend like Henry, then perhaps she would find her way in life, and even find that career in photography which had so far eluded her.

She shivered: a breeze of intuition caressed her skin. She realised, even as she was opening her mouth to speak, that she was about to tell Henry the secret they had not dared to share with anyone—the house on the rocky hill above the wine-dark sea.

She knew why they had not told anyone at the George Street house. David would have felt ashamed. They would have been accused of petit-bourgeois individualism, and instructed to go away and practise self-criticism.

With her decision to reveal, Cathy felt suddenly embarrassed by their plans, but Henry understood everything in a moment.

'Good,' he nodded. He turned to David. 'We all want to write novels, but you, you bastard, you will really do it!'

Cathy knew just then that Henry would always be the true north by which she and David would navigate life together, for Henry had that quality she had found lacking in David's other friends—integrity.

After that evening, Cathy and David went to see Henry regularly. They strolled down Brunswick Street in the evenings, drawn by some need. It was as if they were thirsty and Henry was water.

When they got to the Perseverance Hotel and turned the corner into Moor Street, Cathy suffered a moment of panic, as if they might have been heading for the battleground of George Street instead of the sanctuary of Henry's room.

Cathy saw that there were two Davids. There was the hothead of George Street, burning for the revolution, and another, more thoughtful David, drawn to Henry's world of books and ideas—the David she hoped might indeed become a writer.

When David showed her his stories, she encouraged him. But his heroes were martyrs, obsessed with social justice: a mirror for David. The mirror failed to reveal anything of his interior world, his secret life. His stories lacked psychological insight. But how would Cathy ever find the right words to tell him all this?

The aura of solitude which seemed painful in David was in Henry something serene. Henry spoke little of his own work— he wrote poetry, as well as completing his thesis—but he said succinct and sensible things about the stories David showed him, not puffing him up with praise, but not tearing him down, either. Cathy admired how Henry gently guided David's attention to the passages where his prose ran purple, then beyond them, to possibility. David had told her that Henry was the most intelligent person he knew, but to Cathy he was the purest.

The silvery prescience of Henry's mind, the way he was able to see the good in her and David being together, gave her soul relief. She let her guard down with Henry and came to trust him.

Girls came to Henry with their poems in progress. He wasn't fierce or intimidating like David. The only time she saw a different Henry was when Daphne was there, a lovely pale girl with dark bewitching eyes. Love took away Henry's tranquil power of thought. His love was unrequited: it was this, Cathy realised, that made her and Henry allies.

SHE WAS DRIVING David's 1964 Volkswagen, Bahama blue, fickle six-volt battery, to Arcadia, the familiar earth and skies of her childhood. Here, once upon a time, simple delight in the world had been possible. Now Cathy was coming back for the weekend.

The blond paddocks spread out on either side. Ahead, she saw the wheat silos at the railway siding; here she slowed and turned off onto the dirt road to the right. In her mind, she automatically said the names of the owners of the properties she passed—the Bunyans, the Glicks, the Griersons. When she came to the last main crossroad before the farm, it was the beginning of her family's land.

From a break in the gum trees along the side of the road, she saw the hill that rose in the distance, the only hill for miles in the plain; from her bedroom window as a girl she had watched the sun rise behind it.

Her father had recently ploughed these paddocks but the tractor was nowhere to be seen. Perhaps he was making repairs in the machinery shed. It was a sunny Friday afternoon; perhaps he was already in town, in the bar at the golf club.

The redbrick farmhouse came into view, same as ever, surrounded by fifteen hundred acres of wheat. The sheep had been taken to graze in the paddocks at the back of the property where the land sloped down to the Yerri-yerri, broad and still and brown, with the bleached trunks of dead gum trees poking up through the water, their smooth branches jagged at the ends, like arms without hands.

She pulled into the dirt drive, felt the slipping and bucking of the car's wheels in the fissures and runnels after rain. On either side of the drive were rows of sugar gums, mature now. Cathy remembered when the drive had been bare, and her father had planted the rows of saplings. They had been smaller than she was.

The weekend passed peacefully. After lunch on Saturday, Dad headed back to the paddocks in the ute. Cathy decided to visit Mrs McAlpine, who lived on the neighbouring farm, and who had often cared for Cathy in those difficult years after her mother had died.

She drove up to the house and called out at the back door. A voice within replied: 'Cathy, it's you!'

Mrs McAlpine was in the middle of washing up. Cathy went over and put her arm around her. She felt the older woman stiffen. Cathy picked up a tea towel. Mrs McAlpine had her head down, concentrating too intently. There was an eerie quiet in the kitchen, just the sound of the plates bumping in the sink under the soapy water.

At last, Mrs McAlpine asked her: 'What are you going to do? Are you going to get married?'

'I don't know. I mean—we haven't decided yet.'

'You must know that your father is worried,' Mrs McAlpine said, in a sympathetic tone.

There was no one around when Cathy returned to the farm. She sat in the August sunshine in the protected angle of the verandah. A rooster crowed. There wasn't a cloud in the sky. It was the quiet hour of the afternoon, the dreamy hour, suspended from time. Much of her childhood had been spent at just this spot. Waiting for dinner. Waiting for tea. Making up stories about how her life would be. The man she would marry. A house of their own, a bit of land. As a little girl, when her mother had still been alive, Cathy used to look at the clothes line, the clean washing dancing in the sunshine, and saw herself as a grown-up, hanging out the washing, the days of wind and sun, a husband to look after her.

A girl can only be happy with a husband. That's what everyone believed, didn't they? And those uni girls who said they didn't—weren't they just kidding themselves? You could end up a single mother because the man was not tied down. How to tie him down? Would a ring do that?

She used to play the part here in the garden. On the lawn next to the roses, a boy doll and a girl doll. A wedding dress from scraps of sheet. She would spread the rug on the lawn and perform her miniature wedding ceremonies with her dolls and tea set. 'Do you take this woman to be your lawful wedded wife?'

The world had changed, but now Cathy was back, staring at these worn verandah boards. She folded her hands over her belly. David said he was looking forward to being a father. He meant it. He was idealistic. He believed everything he said. But they were twenty-two years old. She knew he had not really understood all the responsibilities becoming a father entailed. And she had no idea, really, about what being a mother meant.

She went for a long walk. Through the gate, past the chook shed, along the dirt track towards the sandhills. Clear burning blue sky, red earth. The ghost gums showed the muscles in their round white arms.

If she could be a child again. Standing there, completely alone, unobserved, not being judged, for once. She looked at the lone hill, purple and brown in the distance. She had climbed its slopes often as a child, setting off with her friend Marion on their bikes with a cut lunch. The lives of the people in Arcadia had grown stagnant, perhaps, but at least there was stability here, while in Fitzroy there was only change and prickly, irritable people. In the city, people spoke their thoughts even before they had time to form them. When they laughed, the inside of their mouths was black. Instead of merriment there was sarcasm; instead of conversation, the exchange of political positions. The only time Cathy really liked to be in Fitzroy was walking by herself in the half-hour after rain. Now she understood, here, how miserable she was there.

She came to an eroded gully near the Yerri-yerri, full of rabbit burrows, where she always came as a child when there was something wrong. She had spent long days alone here when the evangelicals were causing trouble at the little church.

It was five o'clock on a Saturday night. David would be lifting his first pot of beer to his lips. Vanessa and Murray would be with him at the pub. David, caught up in the demands of that friendship, without a thought for Cathy. It wasn't like her to think the worst of people. They were just idealists, too, who wanted to change the world. Nevertheless, she resented the influence they had on David.

On Sunday morning, Cathy drove with her dad to the old Pierce place, a few miles away on the far side of the Yerri-yerri. The farmhouse was now owned by a couple of schoolteachers, away in Europe for a term. Her dad had promised to keep an eye on the place. The house was for sale; the teachers were moving next year.

Inside, everything was shabby, she thought, but also stylish in a bohemian sort of way. There were leather armchairs, a dining table for twelve, books in every room, paintings on the walls. There was even a ballroom. Her dad told her that a house like this could be bought cheaply: the surrounding land no longer belonged to the dwelling, and it was the land that was valuable. 'School teaching's not a bad job,' her dad added.

She walked from room to room. The house was miles from the nearest neighbour, dreamy in its quietness—a house where a novel might be written.

When Cathy got back to Fitzroy on Monday afternoon, she told David that she definitely wanted to get married. David went quiet. There was something going on in his head. His eyes were dull, as if a measure of their light had been drained off.

He was moody all that week. Was it her fault? Had the talk of marriage frightened him? Was he thinking of walking out? As the time approached, was there something in David that resisted fatherhood? Once more, she was filled with terror.

David must have felt he belonged in George Street, not with her. He was at home in the chaos of Vanessa's kitchen, with the burnt toast, the flagons of cheap wine, the sink full of dirty dishes, spaghetti sauce splashed around the tiles like excrement. It wasn't just the meetings. Their household seemed to contain some thrill for him, which their own lacked.

One evening, after a meal of scrambled eggs, David sat smoking at their wobbly kitchen table. Cathy reached across. 'Can I have a drag?'

She inhaled, blew out the smoke with a sigh of satisfaction, and handed back the cigarette. 'I know I shouldn't.' Then she asked, 'Do you think I'll make a good mum?'

'You're going to be a great mother.'

'But I don't know the first thing about babies. Neither do you.'

'Maybe it's one of those things you can only learn by doing it?'

'Maybe.' Cathy smiled.

'We'll work together, like a good socialist couple.'

'Like a good socialist couple.'

He looked hard at her. She had been surprised by the bitterness that had crept into her voice. She liked to get on with people, to feel that other people liked her, and she was confused by the way David saw everyone as a potential enemy—he was always waiting for people to make some remark that would 'show the error in their method', some slip that would reveal

269

their underlying bourgeois thinking.

'What's wrong with being a socialist?' he asked.

'Oh, nothing!' She heard the disgust in her voice.

'What, then?'

'Not everything is about politics. There are other things that are important. Ordinary things. Family life.' In a whisper, Cathy added, 'I only wish I knew how to make you happy.' And a secret thought to herself: I wish you knew how to make *me* happy.

One Saturday afternoon, she found herself alone again. David had left in his VW without a word. She was sure she knew where he was. The sullenness in David lately, his baffling silences—he must have been saving up his thoughts for his friends in George Street. At this very moment, he would be talking to Vanessa in their kitchen that no one bothered to clean, the table stained and clotted with old food, the piles of newspapers, the old potatoes sprouting little limbs. Who knew if they ever swept the floor—or perhaps that was bourgeois, too.

It was after four o'clock when Cathy finally went around to George Street. Vanessa was just out of the bath. She answered the door wearing a towelling robe, combing out that great spill of red hair. 'This is a nice surprise,' she said. Her eyes were untroubled. David was not there.

Vanessa invited her into the kitchen. As they sat at the table, her eyes lingered on Cathy's belly.

'When's it due?'

'January.'

'Not long.'

'No.'

'Are you ready?' Still Vanessa was watching her carefully.

'It's hard to know if I'm ready. I think so.'

'Good,' Vanessa nodded, but she didn't seem convinced.

Vanessa wore the same army shirts day in, day out. They made her look like a fearless guerrilla commander—perhaps it was her confidence that attracted David to her. Cathy knew he would not have been able to admit that it was sex. She now recognised how cleverly he tricked himself, so that his mind would put things to him in some other way.

In other parts of the double-fronted terrace, people were going about their afternoon. She heard a window shriek open upstairs, then a gust of wind rushed in and slammed the door and a faint shower of plaster fell in the corner of the kitchen. It was a bare, neglected house with forgotten food in the fridge. Cathy looked at the grubby place mats, the chipped teapot.

'I don't want to have kids,' Vanessa told her, after a while. 'I don't believe in biological destiny.'

'I see.' Cathy smiled. Right now she wanted to be seen as an equal.

'There are more important things for women to do in life than just being mothers. Women have fought long and hard for the right to work, to education.'

'I once thought of becoming a professional photographer.'

'But not any more?'

'I wouldn't know where to start.'

'Well, I suppose some women photographers have babies.' And both women laughed, though it was clear to Cathy that Vanessa hadn't intended to make a joke.

Vanessa and Murray shared a bed in the room at the top of the stairs, more storeroom than bedroom, with piles of pamphlets and old editions of *Liberation*. Was there enough fire and passion left over for bed? Or did they think of it as just some necessary bodily function in the time remaining before the next meeting?

Cathy went back to King William Street. The place was cold and empty. She put on the porch light for David. She expected the phone to ring at any moment, but it remained malevolently silent. Finally, when she was in bed, he returned. He had been studying at the university library, then he'd driven over to his mum's place. There were some jobs she'd wanted him to do. It wasn't much—moving the buffet and the dining table so the carpet layers could put down the new carpet on Monday. David said he was sorry—moving the furniture had taken him longer than he'd thought. Too humiliated to ask why he hadn't bothered to phone her, she swallowed her anger, but her mouth tasted like ashes.

The following week, things took a turn for the worse.

'They're having a rage around at George Street,' David told her. Rage. That was the word they all used. They're going to have a *rage* tonight. The party's going to be a real *rage*.

Everyone was drunk. Everything was loud. They were playing Lou Reed's *Transformer*.

There was something wrong with David tonight. He was mouthing the lyrics to her, a nasty expression on his face, as though he was trying to hurt her. *You're so vicious*, he sang.

In another moment, he erupted. On and on he went,

belittling her, telling her off. She was a liability, a dead weight, a burden.

Stunned, Cathy was unprepared for the force of his attack. She had angled herself into a corner and was staring at him, tears trickling down her face.

Later, in the kitchen, Vanessa asked her, 'What's wrong, Cathy?'

Before she could open her mouth. David snapped, 'She's just upset, that's all.'

Vanessa spun around to him. 'Why do you treat Cathy like that?'

'Like what?' he asked.

'Like shit.'

David went quiet.

'I'll tell you what,' Vanessa said. 'She's a fucking saint to put up with you. You're a dangerous cunt.'

'I'm not dangerous.'

'Yes. You *are* dangerous. Cathy would be better off without you. Some people say stupid things. But you're an extremist in the worst sense. You'll end up killing somebody.'

The question of marriage remained in the dark. Cathy woke sobbing in the mornings. She pretended she was just breathing deeply: she was too scared to let David see how upset she was. Now—she couldn't avoid it—she began to ask herself about the rightness of their connection. When she looked into the future, she saw them still locked painfully together. David took care of her, he paid the rent, he said he was going to stay with her. But surely, this perverse arrangement wasn't what love in a political age had come to mean? It didn't feel like love at all to her.

She sat in the house in King William Street, miserable, her smock covering her swollen belly, the little person growing inside her. It was the kind of destiny she'd read about in Thomas Hardy—from this locking together of lives, however cruel, from this ferocity, the feeling of family would somehow grow, at least Cathy hoped it would.

One afternoon, David used Cathy's camera while she posed naked on the bed. Her shape was changing, and they wanted to record it. When the photos came back from the chemist, she hardly recognised herself. The engorged, pear-like breasts, the dark pigment in her nipples, the hard belly that wouldn't let her get comfortable in bed at night, all seemed to belong to someone else. She looked frightened and alone.

THE NEXT SATURDAY, Cathy drove to Essendon to see David's mum, Molly. David said he wanted to stay home and write. He sent his stories to magazines, but he already had a collection of rejection slips. Although she had wanted to support the idea of his becoming a writer, it was only now she understood he was one of those people never satisfied with the reality of their own lives.

Molly was pleased to see her. She took Cathy from room to room, showing her the new carpet. Then they sat together in the kitchen while Molly made tea.

'I just want us to have some security about the future,' Cathy said. 'But when I talk about getting married, he starts yelling at me.'

'My mother and father were never married, so I understand

all too well. But David is just highly strung, that's all,' his mother said. 'He was always like that, even when he was a boy.'

'I've tried everything,' Cathy said. 'I can't see what more I can do!'

'It's not your fault, love.'

'But he always makes me *feel* it's my fault. I don't want him to be angry any more. I don't want him to be agitated and shouting.'

'Tell him to bloody well pull his horns in! That's what I used to do, when he got on his high horse. Has David told you he's adopted?'

'Yes, but he doesn't talk about it much.' In fact, he had mentioned it just that once.

'I'll have a talk with him, if that will do any good. He used to listen to me. We were very close, when he was little.'

After a while, Molly went into the dining room. Cathy could hear the buffet drawers being opened. When she came back, she was holding two photograph albums. She turned the pages, explaining to Cathy who was in each photo, where it was taken. Molly and Percy on motorbike rides, their house being built, the backyard bare, the rockeries not yet in place, no flower beds. There was David as an infant, standing on fat little legs, holding a stool for support, reaching for a tin of Johnson's Baby Powder. Cathy studied the pictures of David at all the stages of his childhood and youth.

'I can't tell you how happy I was when I heard your news,' Molly told her.

'Really?' Cathy said, relieved. This was the first time anyone had told her she was doing the right thing. It was so different from how her dad had reacted to the news.

'Yes, really. You're going to make a wonderful mum. And becoming a dad might turn out to be just the thing David needs!'

For a moment Cathy entertained the hope that Molly might be right about David changing. No, it seemed impossible. She put it out of her mind.

'I want to go to night school. They have courses for adults. I want to go to Swinburne and study photography.'

'I didn't go on at school, myself. None of us did, in those days.'

Cathy thought, 'No, it's no use me going back to school—what if I flunk? That will just make matters worse. Then he won't want to be with me at all.' Tears came. How was it that he had taken all her confidence from her?

Molly went over to the bench and picked up a box of Kleenex. 'Things will work out all right in the end.' She sat down again and put her arm around Cathy's shoulders and drew her in. 'I tried to talk David out of giving up his Law course, but he always gets his own way. I suppose it's my fault. I was overprotective.'

'If he always gets his own way, that's the end of me,' Cathy thought.

'Has he ever been curious about who his real parents are?' Cathy hesitated. *Real parents.* She wished she hadn't said that.

'He said he's not interested. He told me I'm his mum and that's all there is to it. Anyway, there's no way for him to find out who they were. When we brought him home, they gave him a new birth certificate with our names on it. The original birth certificates for all the adopted children are locked away in the government vaults somewhere. We chose the name

David, and that's the only name we've ever known him by.'

They sat on in silence. Molly reached across the table and held Cathy's hand. 'I'm happy you and David are going to have a baby. I'll help you learn to look after it. I had to learn everything myself, when he first came home. We'll love it and spoil it together! Just imagine—my first grandchild! It's going to be such a special baby!'

Molly told her about the morning they had driven to North Fitzroy and brought him home from the Haven.

'Then when David told me earlier this year that he was moving out and going to live in Fitzroy, you can imagine I wasn't exactly happy about it. Why *Fitzroy*, I wondered.'

Cathy realised that, for Molly, it must have felt like he was going back in time to find his birth mother.

'When he was little, we had to give him a sedative.'

'The doctors weren't able to tell you what was wrong with him?'

'It's just his temperament.'

Time disappeared miraculously that afternoon. Cathy sat at the table with her cheek resting in her palm, elbow on the table, tea gone cold in her cup.

Molly gave Cathy a hug as she went across to switch on the kettle again. 'You know something? You're lucky. Both of you are. Children give you real happiness. Of course, the buggers can also give you a lot of heartache.'

She sat down again and reached across to the plate of biscuits, then changed her mind. 'I'll take you to Footscray with me one day soon, and we'll start buying clothes for the little one. I had a cupboard full of clothes for David months before they told us we were going to get him. I made a lot of clothes for him myself, too. I always had some kind of knitting or sewing or fancy work in my hands.'

'I haven't bought any clothes yet.'

'Don't worry, love. Remember, you can come and visit me anytime. I want you to know that you can always come and talk to me, about anything.'

Molly accepted her. Molly did not want her to be someone else. Cathy now sensed that there was a great power to be found in believing in herself. Why had no one told her this before? Why had she never really believed in herself?

With Molly, more than with her friends, more than with her own father, she no longer felt that familiar constriction in her throat. It was something entirely new to her, this feeling of relaxed confidence.

It was getting dark outside. Molly hadn't yet switched on the lights. The kitchen was at the back of the house, the window darkened by an overgrown fuchsia. There was another window, of frosted glass, next to the sliding door into David's old bedroom. Cathy liked to go in there and see the traces of his childhood in that room, to feel the innocence that still reposed there.

Driving home to King William Street, Cathy felt light and free. Things were going to turn out well for her and David, after all. She imagined the house where they would live in Greece one day, the dark Mediterranean lapping softly against the rocks in the night.

She had come away from Molly's feeling safe, but when she got home, David was in dangerous high spirits. 'Come on,' he told her, 'we're going to Johnno's party.' There were a dozen bottles of Carlton Draught waiting on the kitchen table.

She put her coat back on, then changed her mind. 'I'm not going.'

'What else are you going to do?'

She went into the bathroom and stared at the mirror.

'There's a part of me that's still pretending,' she thought. 'Same for everyone, I suppose. Putting on an act.' Even with Dad, in a way, even though he was always understanding and tender. Cathy knew he loved her. Dad would always love her, even if everything did go wrong.

She wrenched herself away from the mirror and went into the bedroom to lie down. 'Maybe I should just go to the party, after all?' she thought. 'Why am I making such a fuss about it?'

Cathy had played the likeable clown for the gang in Swiss Cottage. She had then, too, briefly felt the unspoken fear leave her. It was the fear that had entered her when her mother died, and the light of the world suddenly changed. That's what she wanted to capture in her photographs: that change in the light. She wondered if something like that had happened to David, too, when his father died. Was this shared past what somehow bound them together?

Her friends from London were not the same now. It was impossible to return to those nights in Swiss Cottage. That time was gone. That Cathy was gone.

David came into the bedroom and sat next to her on the bed. His aura was penitential. 'Come on, let's go out,' he said. He had bought his carton of beer and was determined to go to the party.

'David, I'm not going out tonight.'

CATHY MANAGED TO persuade David to visit the farm in Arcadia during the September university holidays. They slept in Cathy's old bedroom, in the double bed with its brass bedstead. Each leg of the bed stood in a tin of water, because of the mouse plague of that year. She took David's hand and placed it on her round belly. 'Feel that?' she asked. She was five months pregnant. The baby was beginning to kick.

Cathy drove her dad's ute to show David around. The dusty cabin of the Valiant was littered with empty beer cans, the *Weekly Times*, girlie magazines. They bumped along the dirt tracks, Cathy stopping for him to get out and open the gates when they crossed from one paddock to another. It was a clear, blue spring day. They set themselves down on a blanket on the banks of the Yerri-yerri. There was no wind. The countryside spread around them, unnaturally quiet. They ate lamb and pickle sandwiches, wedges of sponge cake made from farm eggs with their deep yellow yolks. Cathy unscrewed the top of the thermos and poured their tea. David lay back with a cigarette and looked at the sky. Cathy had taken her father's advice and stopped smoking, but she still enjoyed the rich, dark smell of Turkish tobacco.

'Do you think you could ever live in the country?' Cathy asked.

'I don't know. It's not something I've ever thought about.'

'There's something I want to show you, later.'

'What?'

'I'm not saying. It's a surprise.'

'I hate surprises.'

'I know you do, but I'm showing you anyway.'

Later that afternoon, they drove to the old Pierce place, dreaming in its fields of wheat beside the lake.

'Well, what do you think?' she asked.

'Who lives here?'

'A couple of teachers. They're away in Europe. It's for sale.'

She showed him the ballroom which, she said, would make a wonderful library, the bay window where he could set his desk. 'Do you think you could write your novel here?' she asked.

'What about our Greek island?'

'It will still be there, waiting for us to find it.'

Time passed differently at the farm. Days seemed slow; then, suddenly, a week had passed. In the mornings after breakfast, Cathy went to feed the chooks the jug of kitchen scraps, just as she had when she was a girl.

Cathy set David up in the dining room. It was a large room, rarely used, with the piano and the organ and the oak table, where David clattered away on his typewriter, adding slowly to his store of pages. Morning sun streamed through the windows. He smoked, he typed. Cathy hoped he was happy.

In the afternoons, they helped with chores around the farm. While her dad drove the tractor in circles, ploughing fallow fields, David sat in the cabin of the old Bedford truck with his packet of Camels and *The Alexandria Quartet*.

David asked her dad to teach him to shoot.

'Why do you want to learn to shoot? You won't find much to shoot at. All the rabbits are myx-y up here.'

'I'd just like to have a go. I've never used a rifle before.'

The rifle was kept in the pantry as it had always been, the boxes of bullets on a shelf next to jars of homemade jam and tomato relish. It was a Sterling .22. Cathy helped him set up beer cans on a fence post to practise.

One day they watched her dad slit two lambs' throats. He hung them upside down on hooks in the corner of the machinery shed. That night in bed, Cathy was amused when David told her how he had been fascinated by the solemn way her dad performed the task, the moment when death came, the blood on the earth, the soft blue insides spilling out. Cathy had seen it often enough during her childhood; to her, it seemed unremarkable. The next day, the freezer was full of plastic bags of meat.

In the late afternoons, her dad lit the fire and he and David drank beer and played cribbage. Sometimes Cathy kept them company. They listened to Dad's stories from his days in the RAAF.

David said, 'I took a great deal of pleasure in seeing the

Americans getting their arses kicked in April, all those heli-copters evacuating the US embassy compound in Saigon.'

Cathy nudged his leg with her foot under the table, and gave him a pleading look.

'Of course,' David went on quickly, 'your war against fascism was completely different from the Americans in Vietnam.'

Dad looked dismayed. David's relentless critical stance was wearing him down. David seemed to find pleasure only in seeking division.

'When are you going to lose that chip on your shoulder?' Dad asked David, at last.

'What chip?'

'Your anger. The way you're negative about everything.'

Dad smiled at Cathy with his friendly blue eyes. 'The thing is—I'd really like you two to get married. I'd like to accept David as part of the family.'

Neither she nor David said anything. What her father said about family sounded so right, just then.

'School teaching is not such a bad job. Good pay, lots of holidays.' Dad caught Cathy's eye again. 'The old Pierce place is a good buy. I could speak to the bank manager, if you like. I know him only too well! And I might be able to find a way to help you with the deposit.'

'I appreciate the offer,' David said, 'but all I'm thinking about right now is finishing uni and writing my novel.'

'Well, you'd better hurry up and finish your book,' her dad said. 'In the meantime, the offer's there. Life usually works out different from the way we expect. When I was in the RAAF during the war, flying those Hudsons over New Guinea, if any bugger had told me that I was going to end up a wheat cocky, I would have told him he was mad.'

On Sunday David had to move his typewriter and papers. Dad had invited a couple from town, Maggie and Barry, for lunch. He explained to Cathy that he thought David might get on with them. They might even get him interested in a teaching career.

Cathy did the cooking, and by late morning the aroma of roasting lamb filled the house. Questions about the future hovered over the table. Barry, a bearded science teacher, asked what David was going to do when he finished his degree. David said he wanted to write.

'That's a vocation where many are called and few are chosen,' Barry said. It was not, he added, the kind of steady job required of a family man.

Barry's talk grated on Cathy's nerves. He was so smug! He could not imagine that others might aspire to a life different from his own. Cathy looked over at David and saw instantly that something in him had snapped. Without a word, he stood and left the room. A few minutes later, the peace of the wheat fields was broken by the sound of rifle fire. David had set up the cans on the fence post.

That spring they spent nearly every weekend at the farm. They drove up in the clapped-out VW on Friday, returning for David's seminars on Monday or Tuesday.

One day in October, they found themselves saying to each other, well, even though marriage was an idiotic, bourgeois institution, wouldn't it be nice to be married by the time their baby was born? David conceded that, after all, a wedding didn't have to be one of those ghastly spectacles with the white dress and a veil and bridesmaids and hired tuxedos. Their wedding would be fun. Cathy was thrilled. Things were going to work out. They planned a big party at the farm on a weekend in mid-December. They wouldn't be surprised if the party kicked on for several days. 'Bring your own sleeping bag,' they would tell people. They sat all day in the front room at King William Street, taking turns to type out the invitations.

When David's friend Jack came home from London, they gave him a party. He moved into the front room. David was pleased to have Jack living with them. The two of them spent every evening drinking beer and telling stories.

Cathy tried to respect David's freedom, but where was the novel he had begun? Petered out after few chapters, Cathy suspected. She was thinking ahead to the time when the baby would arrive. Where would they live then? Would they still be living in a shared house?

Jack's girlfriend from London, Julie, had arrived back in Melbourne earlier. Cathy felt awkward when they visited Julie's parents' place in Brighton. David argued with them about politics—Julie's parents were Liberals, of course. Julie told Cathy that her mother, a flirtatious blonde of about fifty, liked nothing better than to sit all afternoon watching the soapies with a couple of bottles of sparkling wine. Her father, a real estate agent, had the shifty, contrite look of a secret whisky drinker. Cathy was bored there and she was disappointed that David wasted his breath. Jack sometimes had Julie to stay at

King William Street. But there was also a Polish girl Jack had recently started bringing back. One morning, Cathy happened to find a syringe in Jack's room.

Cathy thought herself a good judge of character, whereas David was easily influenced by people. She could tell Jack was devious, secretive—the opposite of David—and opportunistic, a thief who would steal a watch or a transistor just because he could. He was good at telling lies, good at getting women into bed even when they thought they didn't want to.

That afternoon, she took David aside to have it out. 'When do you think Jack might start looking for a place of his own?'

'No rush, is there? I like having him here. He's my friend.'

'I know. I've seen the mountain of beer bottles out the back.'

'So? What's it to you if we have a drink?'

'Since Jack has been here, I haven't seen you sit down to write, not even once. Giving up your room is one thing. But giving up on yourself is something else. I believe in you, David. You know that. I support you in your writing. But you can't keep running away from it. And there's something else—' Cathy broke off, not sure if she should go on.

'What?'

'I think Jack is using heroin.'

'Who told you that? It's the first I've heard of it.' David looked serious. She thought his surprise was genuine. 'I mean,' he continued, 'we roll a joint from time to time. But nothing else. Nothing harder.'

'I'd hate to think he's got you into it, too. I don't care about what Jack does. But you—you're better than that.'

'Why don't you lay off Jack, for a minute?'

'I want you to ask Jack to leave. I want you to stay away

from Vanessa. And I want you to get back to your novel. I want you to stick at it.'

'Sticking at things.'

'What's wrong with that?'

'I've stuck by *you*, haven't I?'

CATHY WAS THE first to hear it on the radio. The government dismissed. They couldn't do that, could they? She went through to the living room where David was reading. 'Guess what?' she said. 'They've sacked Gough.'

'Bullshit.'

'No, really. It's true.'

Someone had given them an old black and white TV with an indoor aerial and fuzzy reception. There were images of the Governor-General, Sir John Kerr, and Malcolm Fraser, who Kerr had installed as caretaker Prime Minister.

And there was Gough on the steps of Parliament House calling it a coup d'état, a putsch. 'Nothing will save the Governor-General,' he was saying.

She started to feel anxious as she stood watching David lean right into the screen. Once again, there was that dangerous excitement in him. 'Fraser will be shot for this! Kerr too! They're both traitors! They'll both be put against a wall!'

'David!' she implored.

'Oh, you're always so squeamish!'

David had once described the Springbok demonstration he attended at Olympic Park in 1971. He had seen a cop push a pregnant woman down the hill. It horrified Cathy when he told her. It still horrified her. She didn't know how that policeman could live with himself.

Cathy had never been to a demonstration. She had seen them on TV, the famous ones where there was police brutality or where people had been killed, like at Kent State in the US. She would have liked to have the fiery conviction of Vanessa but the truth was that kind of ferocity frightened her.

She knew that David wanted her to be more outspoken. She knew, too, that David was angry with her—he had been secretly angry with her since their first weeks together. She was afraid that he felt humiliated by what had happened and, because he couldn't admit it to himself, he acted it out through his angry behaviour. He was only with her because she was pregnant: when she put it to herself like that, she felt a great black hand close around her heart.

'Let's stay home. Just for today. Come on. Just do it for me. I never ask you for much.'

'It will be no use taking action when history has passed you by!' David said, gesticulating. He looked possessed.

'I'm not feeling well,' she lied, and as soon as she'd said it, she realised it wasn't such a lie after all. She felt heavy with dread about what was to come. 'It's not just me that I'm worried about.'

'Just because a woman is pregnant doesn't mean that she's politically useless.' He reached over and patted her head, but it didn't blunt his sharp tone. 'Anyway, our child would never forgive us, when he grows up, if he discovered we chickened out of demonstrating against the coup!'

She knew he was joking, but he didn't sound light-hearted.

Well, this is it, she thought: I don't want anyone to speak for me anymore. Not Vanessa, not David, not Karl Marx himself. Married or not, it didn't matter. She was going to be a mother. And, whether she went to the demonstration or not, the roundness of her belly was the shape of her rebellion. Others could wave their fists and shout slogans. The Vanessas of this world could go to demonstrations, not her.

They heard on the radio that a large crowd had already gathered at the top of Bourke Street. 'Come on!' David yelled at her. 'This is it!'

Cathy didn't say anything.

'Which side of history are you going to be on? With the people or against them?'

'David!' she said. 'I'm seven months pregnant. Don't you think the people could excuse me on this occasion?'

'What?'

'I won't come along with you this afternoon, if you don't mind,' she continued. 'But I will go to a demonstration another day.'

'Another day?' he choked. 'But the bastards have sacked the democratic government *today*!' He stopped for a moment, then added, 'Well, I'm going. I'll go by myself.'

She thought, is this really how he wants to live? Every day like some sort of rehearsal for the revolution? And I don't fit into his plans at all, let alone a child.

'The time has come for action.'

'What action? Demonstrations? Selling your newspaper to two dozen people?'

Her tone cut him. He sucked in his breath, making a hissing sound with the saliva. 'There will soon come a time for real action.'

She looked at him uneasily. 'Like what?'

'Fraser's got a sheep station in the Western District. Rides around on his horse like a squire.'

'And you intend to do what? Stand at his fence and wait until he rides by, and take pot shots at him? David,' she begged, 'explain your ideas in a book, if that's what you want. Books can change people's lives. Like Henry says, that's the way to change history for the better, not what you're talking about. It's completely crazy.'

'What's so crazy about it?' he snapped at her.

'It's just that I can't agree with hurting people.'

'You're a sensitive soul, aren't you?' David's eyes were narrowed. She felt that he must really despise her.

How had they ended up in such a mess? 'You are so convinced of everything, aren't you? You might be right about it, or you might be wrong, but I don't want to hear any more,' she said. As usual she let herself back away in the face of his rage.

'You have the future all laid out for me, don't you? A school teacher. Ha!'

'Why should you think that? I'm not pushing you into teaching.'

'Because it's what your father wants.'

'Leave my dad out of it. I want you to write your book. I want us to earn some money so we can live in Greece, the way we planned. I'll find a job and save the money, if it comes to that.'

David could not keep still. He sat down for a moment, jumped to his feet again, marched back and forth in the living room, muttering to himself.

'Look,' she told him. 'Our future involves a typewriter, not a rifle. I just want you to drop all this nonsense about killing Fraser.'

'*Is* it nonsense?' he challenged her. 'Well? *Is* it?'

Cathy recognised the signs. She would have to watch out.

There was a knock and Murray barged in. 'Have you heard the news?'

Murray, with his tired, careworn face. Why was it that revolutionaries had pale faces? As if they deliberately made themselves look like martyrs, eschewing the luxury of sleep... staying up studying the political situation...wrecking their health for the sake of the workers.

A few minutes later, Vanessa arrived. The three of them left to catch a tram into the city.

So had it come to this? Cathy alone. David didn't even like her, apparently. It was hopeless, then. Lately, when she tried to talk to him about her feelings, he left the house. Where did he go? To George Street, of course. He was always with Murray and Vanessa; they were like commissars in khaki.

Cathy now regretted she had not gone with them. Her boiling thoughts would give her no peace. In the end she put on her coat and set off for the tram stop in Brunswick Street. The people on the tram seemed oblivious to the import of the day. But instead of settling or reassuring her, this only added to the air of unreality.

It was a blustery afternoon. The wind blew the sun out of the cloud, then snatched it away again. There were not many cars in the city. The police must have blocked the traffic down at Elizabeth Street. The intersection in front of Parliament House was already crowded and Cathy felt oppressed by the ugly mood in the air. People holding signs with Fraser swastikas were marching down Bourke Street. People holding up more signs. *Hang Fraser! Hang Kerr!*

Groups in the crowd were chanting, 'Kill Fraser! Kill Fraser!' There was a lot of noise. She looked around, panicked, trying to find David. After a while, the chanting died down. Then another chorus of chanting started up: 'Hang Fraser! Hang Fraser!'

Somehow Cathy found herself in a group marching down St Kilda Road to the American Consulate. There were lines of police in place. The demonstrators pushed towards the building; the police pushed back. She was caught in a wave of movement. Suddenly, there were people at the back throwing rocks. Instinctively, she ducked. There was the sound of splintering glass from the consulate. A cheer went up.

The mood had turned irrational, more angry shouting and chanting, more cries to lynch Kerr and Fraser. The crowd surged again, and she felt herself pushed forward. She fell to her knees. She was entirely helpless: there was just the sensation of falling, the letting go, then the sudden surprising motionlessness of being on the ground, waiting for the pain to arrive.

She felt eerily relaxed. Nothing much had happened. She was all right, the baby was all right. She was on her knees, that's all. Her knees stung, but it was nothing. Except: she couldn't get up. She tried one way then another to shift her weight and to use her hands to climb back to her feet, but she was still kneeling there on the sharp little stones of the gravel.

A hand was helping her up. Dark blue trousers, blue shirt, dark tie—it was a policeman! He was a young man, younger than David. That hand, she thought, might have been going to strike her. That taste of blood in her mouth was a presentiment of the blow. But now, as in a dream, the protesters continued to move and yell around her, their faces loud, their voices unnaturally muted and soft, and the policeman was still helping her to her feet.

'Are you all right?' he asked.

'Thank you.' She smiled. Cathy wanted to be polite to this man. Her knees were stinging, but she was not in any real pain. Not the diabolical pains inside that she feared. She pulled her dress down to cover her bloody knees and moved away.

The crowd was thinner. She could see the US consulate again. Near the front, there was David! His right hand was turned back, concealing the half-brick he was carrying. It was only because she was standing behind him that she could see it.

The election was called for the 13th of December—the day of their wedding.

David told her that, for the month leading up to the election, he had to exclude all other thoughts from his mind: he was campaigning for the re-election of the Whitlam government. The CIA-backed coup had to be reversed at all costs. David wore a permanent scowl. She accused him of making it his civic duty not to smile; he seized on any suggestion of humour or levity from her. Their wedding, his writing, seemed no longer important to him. It was as if he had shut the door on her, too.

If David went out, the prospect of his arrival home gave rise to a feeling of foreboding. On those evenings when there were visitors in the house, not just Vanessa and Murray, whose company Cathy had come to loathe, but even Henry, or their other friends, she preferred to stay in the bedroom. Anyway, she told herself bitterly, she wouldn't be missed: her pregnancy was to them an impediment to the revolution. She refused to be part of this national anger, this madness that had broken out, the vicious arguments and fights at social gatherings, the insults, curses, people who would never speak to each other again.

Through all this, Cathy kept to her room and, finally, she allowed herself to grieve for her mother.

She remembered how, in the year after her death, she would wake and feel her mother's presence. Not the sick mother of the final year, but the younger, radiant woman she remembered from earliest memory, the blue silk dress Mum used to wear for Dad, with nice shoes, and red lipstick and her blonde hair done up, pruning her roses, waiting for Dad to come in from the paddocks, the scent of wartime romance in the afternoon among the ordinary farm days. Dad still drove the old red tractor then, not the newer, green John Deere.

Mum was too sick to eat at the table and Cathy remembered those woeful mealtimes, just twelve-year-old Cathy and Dad, the awful silence as each of them put food in their mouths and chewed.

That's when it had started, the choking sensation when she tried to speak. For what, really, was there to say? Only unbearable things. It was better to live euphemistically than to look truth in the face. That block in her, the difficulty she still had trying to express herself: it had all begun back there.

Her mother would sit on the verandah in the late afternoon, if she was well enough, and look at her roses. When Cathy came home from school she would go and sit, still in her uniform, on the verandah with her mum. Mum, already diminished by illness, would try to ask her questions about school. And Cathy, full of intense sadness and dread, could only respond with a word or two. 'Yes, Mum, everything's good. I'm at high school now, don't you remember?'

Cathy feared there wasn't much time left, so she put her energy into noticing everything about her mother, trying to fix her image in her mind for all time. These mental photographs of the frail, precious woman were different from the mother who would later return from death to sit in Cathy's room in silent vigil while she slept.

One afternoon, instead of the invalid's nightdress and woollen gown, Mum had put on that blue silk dress (with her old slippers), made an effort with her hair, and applied lipstick. Even at twelve, Cathy had understood what Mum was trying to do. It was like a charm, just for a moment to escape from the broken present back into unbroken time. But the effort it cost her to dress like that had taken its toll, and she couldn't sit on the verandah very long that afternoon.

It was during these days of November—after Gough had been sacked, when the whole country had gone mad, when David's temper flared and his behaviour was at its most volatile and unbearable, when she needed most the sanctuary of her mother on the verandah to console her—that Cathy realised something important.

She had kept her mental photographs of her mother inviolate all these years. Now she understood that a crucial part of her had remained weak, the part that choked and struggled to find words as she sat at the kitchen table with Dad. In less than two months, she would give birth to her own child. She needed to let those secret, hoarded moments go in order to stand up to the world and protect her child.

The spell was broken.

As the tide of uncertainty swept the nation, Cathy went back to the afternoon on the verandah overlooking the roses. One moment her mother was sitting there in her blue dress; the next moment she had evaporated like smoke.

If David noticed the change in Cathy, her new strength, he didn't say anything.

When she tried to get him to sit with her and go through the lists she had compiled for their wedding—who would be sleeping where, how much meat they would need for the barbecue, how many kegs of beer they should order from the pub in Arcadia—he ranted about the Liberals, the scum who had got us into Vietnam and brought in conscription. What if they *did* win the election?

David quoted Chairman Mao: political power grows from the barrel of a gun. Be that as it may, she maintained resolutely, she could play no part in it. They were moving further and further away from each other.

She wondered if a couple like them could last, David its mind, Cathy its heart. It wasn't that she didn't have a mind of her own. A mind can be trained to argue and write essays. But can a mind be trained to love?

Another night, another scene. It was an argument over fish and chips, of all things. Jack pinched a piece of David's fish and he turned suddenly murderous, chasing Jack into the kitchen and putting his fist through the back door. Everyone was terrified. The following day, Jack moved out.

'How did the back door get broken?' her dad asked, on one of his visits. Cathy had forgotten all about it. She knew she had to pretend that things were all right, for the sake of her baby.

'Some idiot at a party one night,' she said.

THE WEEK BEFORE the wedding, they drove up to the farm. They stopped to have a counter lunch at the Royal Hotel in town. At the next table was a group of men in suits, real estate agents by the look of them, Cathy thought. 'When the Libs win on Saturday, it'll be just the boost the business community needs,' said one of them loudly.

'Just you watch the stock market pick up on Monday,' said another.

The next moment, David was on his feet, shouting at them. 'What the fuck are you morons talking about? Fraser should be shot!'

The publican asked David to leave.

A nation divided.

On Saturday morning they drove into town early to vote

absentee. The booths were set up in the primary school hall. David was wearing his Labor T-shirt. Locals turned and stared at them. A farmer said, 'Gough's going to lose, you know.' David glared back at him; all Cathy wanted was for him to remain calm.

They called in at the motel to check on David's family. Molly had driven up the previous afternoon. She invited them into the characterless motel room for a cup of tea. They sat on the edge of the single beds.

'Have you voted?' David asked his mother.

'Not yet.'

'Don't forget.'

'I won't. I'll do it on the way to the farm.'

Cathy and David tried to reassure each other that the election wasn't yet lost. But their hearts weren't in it. Cathy felt that their future was being stolen from them. She had noticed that Molly always tried to avoid getting David started on politics. Now she turned to Cathy with a smile. 'All set?' she asked. 'Is there anything I can do?'

'Dad's got everything organised, thanks.'

'I've made a few sponges. They're in the car. I'm keeping the cream in the fridge here so it doesn't go off. I'll whip it when we get there. How's the little one? Been kicking much?'

'Kicking? Oh yes!' Cathy put both hands on her belly.

'I'm going to spoil him rotten!' Molly smiled. 'We'll buy him so many toys, won't we? We're going to love him, and watch him grow into a wonderful man. Or maybe woman!'

There was a knock at the door. It was David's Aunt Olive, who was staying with her husband in the room next door. She was dressed in her best clothes, but she looked haggard and thin. Olive was in her sixties, but looked much older. Cathy guessed it must have been the hiatus hernia Molly had told her about. The trembling old lady with her burnished complexion and her white woolly hair gave Cathy the impression of a photographic negative. Molly boiled the electric jug and made her sister a cup of tea. The cup rattled on its saucer in Olive's hand.

'How's Hoppy today?' Molly asked.

'Oh, you know him. He doesn't like anything out of his normal routine. I had to drag him into coming at all.' She turned to Cathy. 'Are you going away for your honeymoon?'

'We haven't had time to think about that,' David said.

Cathy said, 'We're planning a few days at the pub in Lorne.'

'I haven't been to Lorne in years,' Olive said. 'I suppose you've got your wedding dress ready?'

David said tersely, 'I'm wearing what I've got on.'

Olive looked at her sister. 'Molly, are you really going to let him get married in *jeans*?'

'I'll bloody well wear what I like!' David roared.

'Now, David,' said Olive. 'We've always got on well together, you and me. Let's not have words, today of all days!' Olive sighed and went back to her room.

'What a bore!' David said.

'Everything's a bore for you, isn't it?' Molly said harshly. 'Everything's a nuisance. Why can't you just let yourself enjoy your wedding day? Why do you have to spoil things for everyone else?'

'Like who?'

'Well, like Cathy here, for a start.'

'Oh, Jesus Christ! Stop bugging me!'

Molly sniffed. 'You really are a piece of work. If you don't behave yourself, I'll get in the car and go home!' Molly turned to Cathy. 'I don't know what we're going to do with him.'

Cathy remained silent: no one would be able to say that it was she who had provoked him into a fight today.

'Go on,' said David, 'keep talking about me as if I'm not here. I'm going to the bottle shop.'

'A fat lot of good that will do!' Molly shouted to his departing back.

The two women were left alone.

'As if I could ever get him to do anything.' Molly shook her head.

'I know life hasn't been easy for you,' Cathy said.

'I had to learn some hard lessons about people when I was a little girl.'

Cathy knew that Molly had grown up in humble circumstances, but Molly had only recently told her just how difficult and complicated her life had been.

Well, we might end up living a difficult life too, Cathy thought. David a psychiatric patient. Or worse, drinking himself to death. Theirs would be a lonely, difficult road. There might come a time when there was no longer any connection between them. David quarrelled with everyone these days. Except for Henry, the friends he chose had a bad effect on him. Jack was in Sydney with some girl and couldn't come to the wedding, even though David had insisted on inviting him.

Cathy usually tried to keep her friends at a distance. She made excuses to them about David. They misunderstood his blunt honesty as rudeness. But today they would all be there.

And the election, on top of everything. And David had already started drinking…

Molly was still sitting on the side of the bed, shaking her head and muttering to herself. 'Yes, life was hard when I was young.'

'When I think of you as a little girl in the orphanage—it makes me want to cry!'

'It really wasn't all that bad,' Molly assured her. 'The kids all got along with each other. My best friend was a girl called Bonnie. We were in the same dormitory. I remember how we used to talk and talk. I wonder what became of her?'

'Have you ever tried to look her up?'

'It was a long time ago,' Molly said. 'Fifty years.' She shook her head, as if she could hardly believe it. And from the look on her face, Cathy knew she didn't want to talk about it any more.

Henry would be arriving on the midday train: he didn't drive, and they had arranged to pick him up from the station. Cathy was worried about Henry: he had been depressed since recently breaking up with Daphne.

Henry stepped down onto the platform, spotted them and raised his hand. He was carrying a scuffed briefcase and a rectangular parcel wrapped in shiny paper. Cathy smiled. Of course Henry's wedding gift would be a book. David waved back with his open bottle of Carlton Draught.

'So!' Henry grinned. 'Today's the big day! Congratulations, you two!'

'Have you voted?' David asked.

'Oh, yes. I voted at the Town Hall before I left.'

In the car, Henry sat in the passenger seat, David in the back with his bottle, while Cathy drove.

Henry seemed cheerful enough, she thought. He was looking out with interest at the passing summer countryside.

'We're going to beat the Liberal scum,' David said.

'But what if the Liberal scum win?' Henry asked. 'What will you do if Gough loses?'

'You remember what Joyce says? Silence, exile and cunning.'

Henry laughed in appreciation. He turned to Cathy. 'So you're still planning to go and live in Greece?'

'We've got a baby to settle in first. Then we'll see.'

'I can't wait to get out of this fucking country,' David said from the back seat.

Cathy stood in her wedding dress, a loose caftan of tie-dyed cotton, looking out over the shimmering fields of wheat. It was one of those glorious, early summer days, anticipation in the air. None of the other guests had arrived yet.

Behind the trestle table at the end of the garden was the eighteen-gallon keg Dad had brought from town on the back of the ute. David was trying to get the gas pressure right; Henry, even more impractical, was trying to help him. Beer spurted from the pluto gun like something alive. David was drinking the beers as soon as they filled the glasses. He's going to spew, she thought.

Later, she followed David as he wandered off alone past the machinery shed. The open, corrugated shed smelled like gum trees and petrol. David was on his hands and knees on the hard, oily ground beside the header. 'What's wrong?' she asked from the doorway.

'Leave me alone,' he said.

'You've drunk too much.'

'A bit,' he said.

'You've been sick. Do you feel better now?'

'I feel like I don't want to be here.'

'Come on back to the house and sit with Henry. He's our friend. He wants to be here with us.'

'I love Henry,' David said.

He is *really* drunk, she thought. It was the first time she had heard David say that he loved anyone.

Next to the machinery shed was the barn, set high off the ground on pylons to protect the seed from mice. This was where their friends from Melbourne would set up their sleeping bags tonight, people at one end of the bare boards, bags of wheat leaning against one another at the other.

David climbed into the ute. Dad always kept the keys in the ignition. 'Maybe we can drive out to the Yerri-yerri and hide there until it's over?'

'But it's our wedding!' she said indignantly.

The Yerri-yerri. The old house with the ballroom on the other side of the water. It seemed so long ago already that she'd had the pipe dream of them living there.

Cathy had wanted to celebrate their union in the wheat fields she loved, with the lambs and the gums and the crows and the carrion, the cycle of farm life she knew so well. From behind the machinery shed now a crow cawed out its single derisory note. Down on the road, the first cars were arriving.

◇◇◇

They came from Bordertown, from Naracoorte, from as far away as Adelaide, from Warrnambool and Colac and Portland. Some of them arrived in utes; most came in family sedans, newly washed, like themselves. Red-faced farmers, friends of her father she hadn't seen in years, their wives in floral frocks, faces like those from the early days of television.

After the first few introductions, David hardly bothered. If a hand was offered, he shook. If he was congratulated, he thanked. He was going through the motions. It was Cathy who went back and forth, greeting this one and that.

She passed the kitchen window and glimpsed Molly in there, laying out plates with a posse of local ladies. She had mentioned a few sponges, but she must have been baking for a week. Her famous pavlovas were puffed up on the kitchen table, waiting for her to add the whipped cream. Crystal bowls of trifle were steeping in wine. Tiers of wedding cake looked as if they'd topple at any moment.

The afternoon was already hot. More and more people were arriving now. For an instant, they seemed to Cathy like aliens approaching over the uneven ground, bearing gifts. The afternoon slumber of the Saturday paddocks was broken by the thumps of car doors. 'Did you remember to vote?' they kept asking each other.

Their friends from Melbourne had WE WANT GOUGH and I'M A LABOR LOVER stickers on the rear windows of their cars and vans. They tumbled out with their long hair and flared jeans and bright T-shirts, peering around as if stunned to find themselves suddenly in these fields of high ripe wheat. Murray and Vanessa were already steeling themselves against the likely election results.

A tarp over the Hills Hoist provided some shade, and there were seats for the older guests. Family members took up their designated stations. Some city and country guests introduced themselves, while others sat apart. Cathy stood watching Henry, behind the trestle table, exuberantly pouring glass after glass of beer. As often as not, the beer spurted everywhere. She kept walking.

Olive was helping Molly and the other woman to bring out plates of sausage rolls and party pies. The plate in Olive's hand made her tremor more noticeable. David's Aunt Rosie was helping too, a large, happy woman, her eyes watering from laughing so much.

A thin, elderly man was sitting on a folding chair near the bay window. He had withdrawn into the shadow as if intent on making himself invisible. Uncle Hoppy was wearing an ancient double-breasted suit with wide lapels, his hat pushed back, a hand-rolled cigarette in the corner of his mouth, his usual long-suffering smile. Cathy felt an affinity with Uncle Hoppy, she couldn't explain why.

David's Uncle Teddy stood rigidly beside Hoppy, his brilliantined hair completely white, still a handsome man with his powerful frame. Cathy was reminded again how Molly's fair complexion was completely different from Teddy and Olive's swarthy skin and dark eyes. Hoppy and Teddy were talking together in their usual laconic way, the same few phrases endlessly repeated, as they must have been doing since the 1920s. She knew they all still lived in Footscray, within a couple of streets of each other.

Cathy looked around, continuing to put names to faces. She felt satisfied. For the moment, all was well: David's earlier chunder seemed to have taken all the aggression out of him; now the more beer he drank, the more his speech and movements slowed, as if in a masquerade of patience and tolerance.

Mr and Mrs Anthony, neighbours, wanted to be introduced to David.

'This gentleman must be the groom,' Mrs Anthony said. *Groom.* It was one of those words like *husband* that David disapproved of. 'People usually ask if you're on the bride's side or the groom's side, as if the war has already started, ha-ha!'

Their teenage son, Tony, had come straight from cricket, his face flushed above his white shirt. He had that liniment and rubber smell of the change rooms. Cathy nudged David to offer his hand, but when they had finished shaking, David's hand hung in the air, as if his mind had wandered. 'You're a lucky fella to bag yourself a nice lass like Cathy,' Mr Anthony said to David. His wife's frock, handbag and hat would not have been out of place at Flemington.

Mr and Mrs Anthony probably didn't see this as a proper wedding, Cathy thought. To them, a wedding is white, a veil, the bride being given away by her father. There should have been a church, there should have been bells ringing to spread the good news. But, white wedding or not, they were getting married, and Cathy was grateful. It meant a lot to her father that the baby would be born in wedlock, the good opinion of his neighbours vouchsafed.

As the late-afternoon sunshine streamed through the venetian blinds in the dining room, the civil celebrant, a local insurance salesman, quoted his bit of Kahlil Gibran. Cathy felt that the ceremony was over before it had really started. Kodak Instamatics flashed, bottles of Bodega popped and the toasts were made.

Molly was standing between her brother and sister, their faces solemn, bearing witness. Cathy could see there was something in the set of Olive's and Teddy's bodies that was still protecting Molly. Their faces were alert and watchful, as if they were still on the lookout for some predator who might at any moment come looking for her. Molly's face was filled with pride, pity, love, fear.

By six o'clock, the party had divided into two camps. The Melbourne people were in the living room, lamenting the election results on television; the rest of the guests were around the barbecue in the garden, celebrating the victory of the conservatives. David had been ducking inside to the television all evening to see the latest from the tally room. Cathy heard him saying, 'I'd shoot Fraser and Kerr, if I had half a chance. I'm not kidding.' But the bravado of those boozy Fitzroy nights sounded out of place here.

Cathy was fiddling with the wedding ring, sliding it on and off her finger. She was married, then not. Married, then not. Her wedding was not supposed to turn out like this.

Sometime after midnight, they got to bed. Finally things went quiet outside. David slept peacefully but Cathy was wakeful, thoughts racing. She tried to convince herself that everything was going to be all right. They would survive as a married couple. In a year or two they would go and live in Europe— David was convinced Australia had now lost its chance at greatness.

Next month: the baby, the three of them a family. No matter what time might do to them—disappointments, failure, lack of money—they would support each other. She was David's wife now. He was her husband. This was their baby on the way. That was all that mattered.

She reached over and took David's hand and placed it over her belly. She felt a fierce love for him just then, but also pity. She leaned across and kissed the side of his head. He seemed calmer, chastened in sleep. No rage, no struggle now.

She left the bed at dawn and went outside. Morning mist covered the paddocks. The sound of bagpipes. She saw Henry wandering down the dirt track. Suddenly, Henry looked up. He had heard the bagpipes, too. At that moment, the piper came into view through the mist. It was her dad, marching through the wheat field, bagpipes wailing out a skirl that sounded like a lament for something.

Part Five

Anna

COCKATOO, 1990

ANNA THOUGHT SHE heard the postman. She was whipping egg whites; the Red Cross luncheon was on Thursday. She turned off the Mixmaster, listened. Hearing nothing, she turned it back on again. When she went to the front gate later, there was just one letter in the mailbox, her name and address type-written on the envelope. The letter gave her an uneasy feeling.

She phoned Mum every night at six o'clock. On Monday, Mum was apologetic: someone had rung. An old friend, he'd said. He'd lost Anna's address. Forgotten her married name. Mum gave him Anna's address without thinking. When she asked who was speaking, he said it didn't matter and hung up.

She opened the letter, read it, put it back into the envelope and placed it against the fruit bowl on the kitchen table. David. David?

During the afternoon, she began crying uncontrollably. Waves of emotion broke through her body. She thought she must have been having a nervous breakdown.

When Eric came home from work and saw her like that, he wrapped his arms around her. She cried and cried. Anna didn't have to tell him what had happened; Eric already knew. 'May I?' he asked, and reached for the letter. He removed the single sheet and read in silence.

All Anna could think was how relieved she was that she'd told him before they were married. Imagine what they'd be going through right now, if she hadn't!

'We don't know anything about this man,' Eric said.

Anna whispered, 'It's him.'

Eric considered for a moment. 'He might be after money.'

'Oh, Eric. He's searching for his mother.'

'He'll probably want to meet you.'

'Yes.'

'It's just that—with a stranger—it's best to be careful. It might have a disruptive effect.'

'On the kids, you mean?' Anna inhaled deeply, trying to get the weeping under control. 'What are they going to think of me? All my life a paragon of virtue and then suddenly—this. They'll think me a terrible hypocrite. They're going to lose all respect for me.'

'Our children worship you, Anna.'

'I've let them put me on a pedestal. But I am not really the mother they know.'

'Of course you are. It's just that it might be wise to take things slowly.'

'You think I shouldn't reply! But I can't just ignore him. I can't just pretend the letter never came!'

'All I'm saying is that I don't want you to get hurt.'

'It's too late for that.'

'You see? It's hurting us already. Hurting our family. You've got four other children who *do* know you, and *do* love you.' Now Eric was angry. He held up the sheet of paper and read, his voice harsh, '*To whom it may concern*!'

'It must be what they told him to write.' She remembered all too well the day five or six years ago when she had read on the front page of the *Sun* that the Victorian government had changed the law to allow adopted people to have access to their real birth certificates, and to trace their natural parents. 'I can't just go on as before, Eric. This changes everything. Even if it might be uncomfortable for us.'

'We've both worked hard all our lives. Don't you think we *deserve* a bit of comfort?'

Eric turned and went out the back. Soon she heard him chopping firewood, even though there was already plenty in the wood bin in the lounge room.

By tea time, he had calmed down. 'Anna, you never think of yourself. And perhaps, just this once, you should. Don't you see? You're not obliged to acknowledge the letter, you know.'

'I've locked him away for thirty-seven years. I had to, so that no one could ever make me suffer like that again. I can't think of him as he must be now. To me, he's still Kim, the baby he was that day they took him away. Do you understand that, Eric? My mind wouldn't let him grow up. But perhaps now I have to.'

Eric looked down at the table.

◇◇◇

On Sunday morning at eleven o'clock, Eric went into the kitchen to make the call. Anna listened from the next room.

'Anna can't come to the phone right now. She's very upset. Too upset to talk. You must understand that your letter was a shock for her.'

She heard Eric talking to the stranger on the phone. She still couldn't think of him as Kim. 'Anna is a fine person,' Eric was telling him. 'She is a wonderful mother, and she does voluntary work for the Red Cross, she visits hospitals.'

Eric spoke about their other children; she was startled at the words 'half-brother', 'half-sisters'.

After a few minutes, Anna went into the kitchen. Eric looked at her, then handed her the phone.

'David?' she asked. Her own voice sounded very far away.

'Yes. This is David speaking.'

A calm, confident voice. How could this be the voice of her baby?

'I know this must be hard for you,' he said.

Despite her resolutions, she felt herself breaking down again. He didn't seem to mind her silence.

She asked him, 'You're married? You have children?'

'Married to Cathy. Two boys and a girl.'

'What are their names?' Her voice was still shaky.

He told her the names of his children, her natural grandchildren. She asked about their home, which she knew from the address in the letter was near the beach. How long had they lived there? How big was the garden?

A hint of impatience in his tone as he replied, 'We're not all that interested in material things.' What an odd thing to say, she thought. Perhaps he was some kind of hippy?

No one knew what it had been like to be forced to give up her own child. Because she had relinquished him, there would always be that tear in the tissue of the universe. Anna already felt the impossibility of ever knowing him. She could tell right away that there was a certain unhappiness in him. Behind his voice, so full of poise, yet on edge, she sensed a man who was lost—a man who would always be lost. Anna knew already she could never really be part of his life.

Eric watched her from the other side of the breakfast bar. He was one of those men who always feared the worst. She smiled and nodded, trying to reassure him that things were going well. Then she turned away to face the window.

The man on the phone said that he wanted Anna and her husband to come to a public reading he was giving in a few weeks' time. It was to be held at Mietta's, 'a posh place in the city,' he said. 'It will give us an opportunity to get to know each other.'

Her heart leapt in alarm. *Not so quickly. Not so soon.*

'I don't know. Perhaps in a little while,' she said. 'We *will* meet, I promise, but you have to give me more time. I must give *myself* time, too.' She took a deep breath, then caved in. 'Well, I suppose we *could* come to your reading. I am eager to meet you, don't think I'm not. Of course, I've always wondered. There's not a day that's gone by when I haven't thought of you.'

29th July, 1990
Dear David,
    This letter is difficult to write as I keep bursting into tears. My love for you has never changed. I have four other

children and, although I love them all dearly, my love for you and the torment I went through when I had to give you up have never left me. My thoughts were with you every birthday, even though I didn't know where you were or even that you were alive.

I am very grateful to your adopted parents for giving you all the good things in life which I never could. I knew you were going to a good home because the clothes your parents brought in for you were beautiful. I had to dress you in them, take you downstairs and sign the papers. It was very difficult to dress you because I was so upset about our parting.

I have been through bushfires and other crises without being reduced to tears. I am normally someone others lean on for strength. I have learned to cope with every other problem in my life, except for you. The Haven was an experience I never got over. The very thought of you would always bring tears to my eyes.

I do not know whether to tell my parents about you. Please don't get me wrong, my mother would throw her arms around you in welcome. It's their age (they're in their eighties) and Dad's health problems which hold me back. When my mother told me someone had rung I knew that you were trying to make contact.

The same day you went to your new life, I went home. After a couple of days I got a position in the pay office at Holeproof in Brunswick. My parents gave me a 21st birthday party in May that year. Mainly relatives came as I hadn't long left the Haven and had no friends—or, to be more precise, I had dodged my old friends. Anyhow, I made a reappearance, saying I had been in the country.

I met Eric in 1954 after I had picked up my life. It was at the Saturday night 50/50 dance at the Coburg Town Hall. Eric is a very good ballroom dancer. We were engaged in 1955 and married in December of that year. Eric is an actuary. He is very straight, he has his feet on the ground and he would never hurt me. I knew he would make a good father and husband. I have never regretted marrying Eric.

I kept working at Holeproof to pay off our house. It was meant to be for a short period only. I was devastated because I could not get pregnant. I went to see a specialist and, after treatment, I was able to have more children.

On our block here, we have a couple of cows, a flock of geese, a few chooks (the foxes depleted our stock), cockies, dogs, cats and fish. We have had sheep and a herd of goats.

I chose the name Kim because as a girl I loved Kipling. Also, the name was uncommon then and I was unlikely to hear someone else use the name. I wanted to avoid the agony of wondering if they were calling you. For years after I lost you, I would look into every pram on the faint chance it was you.

I would dearly love to know of your whole life, your wife and children. Eric agrees that at a later date (when I am more composed) you could meet our children as a friend, if you wanted to. If the children were married and leading their own lives it could be different. They're not yet. I'm their mum too, they have put me on a pedestal. I don't know if a couple of them could handle the shock.

I never dared hope that you would try and find me. The reason I had to give you up was not that I loved you so little, but that I was not wise or strong enough to know how to

keep you. I knew in my heart that it was the right decision,
but that knowledge didn't ease the pain.
    Eric will bring me to the reading.
    Until we meet,
    Your mother,
    Anna

She remembered those grey days after she had left the Haven. She was not the same girl. There was no beauty in life. She felt lifeless. The weeks passed, then months. She waited for something to happen. After losing Kim, nothing seemed important. There was only sadness. In the end she found a way to stop herself feeling even that. A way to forget. She dug a well. She placed her baby in the well, the lid screwed on tightly, and she rarely allowed herself to visit him. It was a sacred site, that place deep in her heart where her baby still existed. There, he had never grown older by a single day.

But a baby is not something that can be sealed up and forgotten. When she heard the voice on the phone, she knew she would have to make one more visit to the well. She would have to set her baby free. The moment they met, her most precious treasure, buried inside her all these years, would disappear and be replaced by—what? A real person. No matter how glowing a character, no matter how golden and accomplished his life— no real human being could ever match the memory she had kept protected inside her for thirty-seven years. She would have to get to know this other person—this David.

After his disapproving comment on the phone, she worried that David might not find her and Eric interesting. He might think her life boring and conventional. But Anna was old enough to accept that she could not be anything other than herself. Nevertheless, she couldn't bear the thought that David, with all his expectations, when he actually did meet her, would be disappointed. Even after they'd met, she realised, there would be a part of him that would remain incomplete.

Should she tell Mum and Dad what had happened? Like her, they had always known there was a possibility of him one day coming to look for her. But there were others, friends and family, who had not known of her disgrace. To her children—her other children—she was the perfect mum; the discovery of this secret in her past might pull their world apart.

She never heard about her friends from the old days now—it was another life. When it had happened, she had allowed them to drift away. Sometimes she saw a death notice of an old friend or acquaintance in the *Sun*. That's all. And sometimes she saw members of Neil's family around Cockatoo, but either they didn't see her or perhaps they sensed that Anna didn't want them to recognise her. She'd never seen Neil again.

She knew that, when Mum and Dad still had their week-ender, they used to see Neil's family from time to time. The Glass family were good, simple people: they didn't hold it against Mum and Dad that once upon a time their daughter had given Neil a close shave. They hadn't snubbed them, the way lots of people would. People of Mum and Dad's generation seemed to have an extra acre of feeling in their hearts. She supposed it came from living through the Depression, then the war. The mystery was why she and Eric, in deciding to quit the city, had come to live, as if by fate, here at Cockatoo. She was held by this place. Even when their house had burned down in the bushfires, they had rebuilt here.

David probably believed he was ready to love her, but what exactly was it that he was ready to love? An ideal, an image. Nothing to do with the real life of Anna Ruhlman, with her husband and grown-up family. It was she who loved *him*, had always loved him. But she loved the little baby in the well—not the voice on the phone.

Her love for her other children was simple, or as simple as love can be, with its fierce needs. The love she felt for Kim had been honed by sacrifice and great pain. Suddenly Anna felt a chill pass through her. She was back in the Haven, being judged, being found inadequate, not living up to the world's expectations. She was confident of her other children's regard. But how would David feel about her? Would there be resentment? That was not his motive for making contact with her, of course; but was there a resentment so deep that he wasn't aware of it? The prospect of meeting him terrified her.

Right up until the Thursday of the reading, Eric had continued to express doubts. He always resisted anything out of his usual routine. Still, he was trying for her sake. 'We might even end up in one of his books,' Eric had joked.

Anna didn't know what to wear. David had told her the place was sophisticated. Eric wore a tie and jumper. He had just one suit, weddings and funerals only. In the end, Anna decided on the loose green velvet dress. It was quite old now, but she still liked it. The dress didn't so much cover her shape as drape it, she liked to think.

They found a park in Exhibition Street and walked to Alfred Place, the Paris end of Collins Street. It was a stately nineteenth century building that had once housed the Naval and Military Club. They lingered on the footpath while Anna admired the facade. Inside, the decor was at once elegant and bohemian. They passed through the spacious hall into a large dining room, which was furnished in a way Anna imagined a grand mansion might have been, with red velvet sofas, marble tables, chandeliers. At the front, a microphone and lectern had already been set up.

A waitress in a white shirt and black bow tie appeared and showed them to their table. They were nearly an hour early and there were only a few others there. She asked if she could get them something to drink. Anna asked for a lemon squash. Eric looked uncomfortable, out of place. Anna felt that somehow, irrationally, Eric blamed her for David getting in contact. This business had disturbed Eric more than he let on. At last he decided on a beer.

The room slowly filled. The noise of conversation grew louder. There must have been more than a hundred people, Anna reckoned. All the tables were reserved.

Eventually, two men and a woman appeared and sat at a table on the low stage. The woman was dressed in black, with a short haircut. The older man wore a jacket without a tie, the younger man jeans and a striped blue T-shirt. The younger man, with his curly hair, his narrow blue eyes—Anna might have been looking at a version of herself. He seemed shy, self-consciously not scanning faces in the audience, even though he must have known she was there.

The three people on the stage poured each other glasses of water, chatting and smiling. They seemed determined to pretend that the audience did not exist.

After a few minutes, the woman introduced David and he rose to his feet. He was as tall as Neil, the same broad shoulders. He walked to the lectern with his papers. He looked briefly around the audience. His stern expression did not change; his tone of voice was serious. 'Tonight I have decided not to read from my novel, but instead to read to you an unpublished story.'

At the tables around her, people glanced at each other: this must have been something out of the usual.

That severe look of his—was it disapproval of the audience in general? Or did it come from a store of private emotion connected with Anna in particular? She had no way of knowing. But it seemed to her as if that clipped diction and excessive formality might have masked some underlying rage.

Anna knew from the moment David got up and walked to the microphone, before he'd even said a word, that she wasn't going to be spared.

The story was about a reclusive boy of fifteen who developed a duodenal ulcer. Anna understood that the boy was a version of David himself. Through the story she was given a glimpse of a devoted mother and father.

He was still reading in the same monotonous voice, devoid of emotion or warmth, as though with distaste for the events he was describing, as though the events had not the remotest connection with himself. She recognised that he was speaking a secret language. There were more than a hundred people in the elegant room, but his words were meant for Anna alone.

Behind this story about memory and loss, there were things which could not be spoken. The pain of separation was incurable. Of all the people looking up at him, listening to the story, only she knew what was really going on.

He had been given many advantages in life, but also, invisibly, unmistakably, something of the Haven had stayed with him and coloured his mind. The story took place in his safe childhood home, but she was convinced that it had its real origins in the dark corridors of the Haven. Without his even knowing it, David had carried with him all his life the oppressive atmosphere, the smell of those rooms, puzzling, as if he couldn't quite place it, couldn't quite remember; but he carried its stain around with him, an enigma, part of the mystery of himself.

Then it struck her: this wasn't blame or attack. It was his way of calling to her in this room full of strangers. He was making public his most private and intimate feelings about being lost in life. He had put on a mask, armour to do it. But he was calling to her. He was calling to his mother.

Over the years, Anna had been able to forget the green-painted corridors with their smell of boiled beef and cabbage. Now, listening to this man reading his story, she was back there again, unwrapping the brown paper and string, seeing the fine baby clothes they had brought in for him.

Anna heard the squishy beat of blood in her ears. The man on the stage grew blurry; the people around her grew blurry; her eyes filled with tears.

When the reading was over, David lingered at the front of the room for a long time. People kept going up to talk to him—his fans, Anna supposed. People congratulating him on his story, or wanting to talk to him about his novel. A woman joined him, tall, attractive, long hair, probably his wife. Their children were with them.

Finally, he came to find her. David walked straight up to her table, his family behind him. He must have known all the time where Anna was sitting. 'Hello,' he said, and no more. He had a penetrating gaze. He made no move to put her at her ease, no embrace, no handshake.

She kept waiting for the surge of emotion that refused to arrive. It was like waking from a dream, her real life empty, drained of meaning.

He introduced her in a matter-of-fact way to his wife and children. Anna smiled at Cathy, and at the children, those faces she was connected to by blood, her grandchildren. One of the boys was about fifteen, the other little boy and girl much younger. They looked at her politely, well behaved, curious. David must have told them about her.

'David, sit here next to me,' she said, taking his hand and holding it. Is that what he wanted? For her to make the first move? 'Eric, let David sit here next to me, please. He's the guest of honour, after all.'

But David remained standing, still holding her hand, and said gently, 'There's another guest of honour tonight—my mother, Molly.'

She had been standing there all the time at the back of the group, a diffident woman of about seventy, with dyed blonde hair, wearing a suit of shiny grey fabric. Molly smiled and nodded. She seemed lost for words. Perhaps she was overcome. But Anna also saw immediately that Molly feared her. That was to be expected, of course. Now that David had found his birth mother, Molly must have been terrified that the bond between her and David might be weakened. Anna now saw that the older woman was crying, like herself. David reached for her with his other hand.

Molly said, 'He was always such a good boy. I knew his mum must have been a good person.'

Anna stood, took a step towards Molly, and they embraced. The woman who had kept her son safe all these years.

They talked about where each of them had lived, where they had done their shopping. Molly was surprised that Anna and Eric had lived in the next suburb in the 1950s. 'Just fancy that,' Molly said. 'You shopped in Puckle Street, too!'

Anna told her how she used to look into every pram in Puckle Street, hoping.

'When he was little, he used to refuse to let me dress him, or even to tie up his shoelaces,' Molly said. 'He always had an independent way about him. David was always different from other children.'

Anna envied Molly. When Anna had been spending her days in the drowsy pay office at Holeproof, Molly had had him all to herself. It was she who had been with him on his first day at school, on every birthday.

'They grow up too fast, don't they?' Molly said.

'Oh, yes, they sure do!' Anna told her about her own grown-up children—allowing Molly to retain full possession of David, for the moment.

Molly told her about David's childhood, his achievements,

what his father had been like. Percy's illness and death, how ghastly it had been. Anna could see that, for the last twenty years, Molly had never been able to get over losing her husband. She was still stuck back in 1969, where the solid road of her family life had come to a sudden end. How can anyone ever get over something like that, she thought, as she hugged Molly again.

'There's something I want to ask,' Anna said to Molly.

Molly tensed, as though expecting bad news. 'What is it?'

'It's just a little thing. But it's something that's been puzzling me these last few weeks.'

'All right.' Molly nodded encouragement.

'The morning you and your husband arrived at the Haven to collect David, there was only one car parked outside. I remember it had yellow number plates, from New South Wales. Was that your car?'

'New South Wales? No, that wasn't ours. We had a little Renault at the time. The matron asked us to park in the lane at the back. She said it was normal procedure for the babies to be picked up out the back.'

Anna nodded. So that's what had happened.

She waited for David to say something more, to give her a signal about what their relation in the future might be. But perhaps that was something he could not give her—something he could not give to anyone?

Once upon a time, he had grown inside her belly. Now they were just ordinary people sitting in a room talking. In time, each of them would have to learn a new language. Anna would learn his language, and he would have to learn hers. For the moment, they could only converse as strangers.

The children sat at the next table with their glasses of Coca-Cola. From time to time, David directed a remark to Eric, who listened carefully, as though he were being asked trick questions. Eric was looking for the fault in David that would justify the caution he had urged on Anna. She realised that, for Eric, the day the letter had arrived, it would have been as though Neil himself had suddenly walked through the door.

'You used to be a teacher, David. Why did you stop?' Anna asked.

'I liked the kids, and I enjoyed being away from the city. I got the best results in the state for my Year 12 history class. It was the other teachers who were the problem. They sat around the staff room with their magazines and their knitting, gossiping about their colleagues. It was impossible to have an intelligent conversation with them. I spent recess and lunchtimes out in the yard with the kids. Well, three of those meddling mediocrities made a complaint about me for swearing. But what can you expect? In my experience, the majority of teachers are morons.'

Anna was taken aback. Where on earth had this contemptuous tone come from? Temper flaring up out of nowhere. Such wildness seemed at odds with the sad, rather gentle man who had given the reading earlier.

'David had to leave teaching when he punched the principal.' Cathy smiled ruefully.

Oh. Then he really was a wild man, both fierce *and* reserved. 'Poor principal!' Anna said. 'What did he do to deserve that?'

'He deserved it, all right,' David said, but it was clear he wasn't going to go into details.

'So—you were sacked?' Eric asked.

'I suppose you could say that.'

'He wasn't suited to teaching,' Molly said.

'But you have your writing, at least,' Anna said. She gave Cathy a sympathetic smile. Did his wife find him a difficult man to live with? she wondered.

Anna had been expecting to encounter a man who took after her own nature—docile, dutiful, devoted to others. But meeting him tonight had thrown down a challenge to her. She did not share David's ferocity. But what had happened to the spirited, adventurous girl who had fallen in love with Neil?

The dreams for herself she'd had at sixteen! When she left school and got her job at Victorian Railways, she used to promise herself that she would save up the fare and take the boat to London, get a job overseas and see the world. On Sundays, she sometimes took the tram to watch the ocean liners leaving Station Pier. Now, she suddenly asked David, 'What was it like, living in Greece?'

David described how they'd found a house in a village for a year; the rent was ten dollars a week. They scratched together a few sticks of furniture. Their son had attended Greek school. Every morning, David had sat at a rickety wooden table and struggled with a borrowed typewriter that had a German key-board. Molly had flown over and stayed with them for a month in the summer.

Anna could tell that living on the island, writing his first novel, Molly's visit, was already part of the family's mythology. Anna would never be part of that. But she couldn't stop herself from feeling, just then, as well as envy, a measure of pride in the things David had achieved.

The mystery of his birth—he said that's what he had gone

to Greece to discover. 'For me, it was the right place to write a novel. Something to do with having all that time, the natural beauty, the light. It makes you think about what's important in your life. The things you really want to do with your time on earth.'

'Why can't you do all that in Australia?' Eric asked.

'It was just so depressing here at the end of the seventies. Gough gone and the country going backwards. Everyone was moving to Europe.'

Since she'd received David's letter, all the forgotten pain from Anna's past had surged back—the part of herself she had had to forget. Now, it was as though the girl who had gone to sleep just to get through those experiences at the Haven—did she remain half-asleep all those years?—had suddenly opened her eyes.

Yes, her life had been settled before that letter had arrived. But now she felt hungry for new experiences. That was David, she supposed. Yet in another way, it had nothing to do with David.

She remembered the silent agitation of the tree in the Edinburgh Gardens, its leaves trembling, even in the absence of a breeze. Anna had thought she had seen God in that tree. What had He been trying to tell her, back then? To keep her baby? To give him up? Not to betray all her dreams?

Anna was fifty-eight, a wife and mother, a stalwart of the community. She had built a solid life. But that wasn't all of her. I'm not one person, Anna thought, none of us is. All the secret feelings I've kept inside—they are all the different people I am.

Already she was planning her trip. She would go to the travel agent next morning. Eric would have something to say

333

about that, of course. Eric would not want to go to Europe. But, with him or without him, she was going to travel.

She was going to London! After all, stranger things had happened. She had been stuck in her life for too long. Ever since what had happened to her at the Haven, something had always held her back, kept her from taking risks, kept her locked into an exaggerated sense of her obligations to others. Now she was coming back to life, or at least coming to a different life. She felt she had the right to want things for herself again.

The room had slowly emptied. The tables around them had been cleared. Near the door, the hostess hovered—a pale elegant woman in a black dress.

Outside, on the footpath, they said goodbye. David promised further meetings, a lunch one Sunday at Cockatoo, when they would come and meet the rest of the family, Anna's parents, her other children. Molly said she would like that.

Anna watched them walk away.

Well, that's who we are, she thought. If I hadn't had him, there wouldn't be this complicated man with his nice wife and his beautiful children and his book. She would look out for his next novel in the shops. And anyway, they'd keep in touch, wouldn't they?

ACKNOWLEDGMENTS

I would like to thank Michael Heyward and Penny Hueston at Text Publishing for their faith in me and in the project. I'd like to thank Penny in particular for her wise guidance and enthusiastic editorial work on the manuscript.

I am grateful to Maria Jones for her careful reading and suggestions, and for all her support during the writing of this book.